NIGHT STOP

BOOKS BY ELLESTON TREVOR

CHORUS OF ECHOES
TIGER STREET
REDFERN'S MIRACLE
A BLAZE OF ROSES
THE PASSION AND THE PITY
THE BIG PICK-UP
SQUADRON AIRBORNE
THE KILLING-GROUND
GALE FORCE
THE PILLARS OF MIDNIGHT
THE V.I.P
THE BILLBOARD MADONNA
THE PASANG RUN
(IN ENGLAND: THE BURNING SHORE)
THE FLIGHT OF THE PHOENIX
THE SHOOT
THE FREEBOOTERS
A PLACE FOR THE WICKED
BURY HIM AMONG KINGS
NIGHT STOP

NIGHT STOP

Elleston Trevor

DOUBLEDAY & COMPANY, INC.
GARDEN CITY, NEW YORK
1975

All of the characters in this book are fictitious, and any resemblance to actual persons, living or dead, is purely coincidental.

Library of Congress Cataloging in Publication Data
TREVOR, ELLESTON.
Night Stop.
I. Title.
PZ3.T7285Ni3 [PR6039.R518] 823'.9'14
ISBN 0-385-07472-7
Library of Congress Catalog Card Number 74–12859

Printed in the United States of America
BOOK DESIGN BY BENTE HAMANN
First Edition

TO HERMAN BOXER

CHAPTER ONE

THE ONLY PERSON who saw the car go into the ravine that night was Berlatsky.

Coming off Interstate 15 onto the side road he began hitting sand before he'd gone a mile. The wind was whipping it out of the desert flats and sending it across the road in gusts and he tried using the windshield wipers but it wasn't any good: they couldn't sweep the stuff away like they did with rainwater.

Soon after leaving Las Vegas he'd picked up weather warnings on the radio: there was a full-scale Santa Ana condition building up and northwest winds were scouring the mountain and desert areas, and fifty-mph gusts were being encountered. Not long ago the southbound lanes of Interstate 15 had been blocked for twenty minutes and Berlatsky had sat there with a couple of hundred other drivers while the highway patrols and a wrecker had cleared a house trailer off the road: coming through Mountain Pass, it had been overturned by the wind.

He switched on the radio again and got another National Weather Service advisory for motorists on most freeways from the Mojave Desert to the Colorado River, but he changed the station and got some music instead, because the motel was only another mile or two along the road at Indian Rock and he was going to dig in there and forget the whole thing till the morning.

The sand was blowing in dull yellow waves and he put

the headlights on full beam but had to dip them again right away because of the back glare. The stuff was like fog, except for the way it came hissing against the side of the car: another few miles of this and he'd need a repaint job. The wind kept buffeting and he slowed to less than thirty, hunched forward in the seat and trying to see where the hell he was going.

The red lamps were there suddenly, right ahead of him, and he hit the brake and felt the tires sliding across the loose sand. The lamps grew smaller, drawing farther away, and then another gust came and he could see what looked like headlight beams swinging at right angles to the road and he braked again and watched them as they dipped and vanished and there was only the dark again, and the blowing sand.

"Oh shit!" Berlatsky said, because it looked as if the other car had gone into the ravine and he'd have to go and do something about it. It'd been a lousy day, even for a Sunday, and he'd made himself exactly seventeen bucks and instead of getting to the motel and catching the Early Show he was going to have to pull people out of that car, all bloodied-up and yelling their heads off, while his new summer-weight pinstripe suit got mussed and his Chevy stood here at the roadside being systematically sandblasted by the wind.

There wasn't anything more to see of the other car so he judged the distance as best he could and pulled onto the shoulder and cut the motor and got out and felt the warmth of a gust hit him, the sand stinging his face. In Vegas today the noon high had been ninety-seven and even here in the desert the air hadn't cooled down much because the night was only just beginning. He stood shielding his eyes with his straw hat clamped low across his face but still couldn't see anything in the ravine. When the gusts came he just had to shut his eyes, then betweentimes when the sand wasn't rising he caught glimpses of the moonlit terrain, the silvered surfaces of rocks and their black shadows, and the softer shapes of low scrub. There wasn't too much of a drop here:

this was a gully rather than a ravine and much less steep than he'd imagined when he'd seen those headlights dip and plunge out of sight.

He screwed his eyes shut again as the next gust came and the sand rose, stinging his face. Above him the telephone cables whined in the wind and somewhere on the road a beer can was bowling along and making flat musical notes like a Chinese gong, eerie because he was alone. When the gust died away he cupped his hands and hollered out, "*Where are you?*" and stood listening, calling again and getting no answer. He was going to have to get down there and that would rip his white calfskin shoes, with all those rocks and cactus, and he was also beginning to worry about what he'd find, because nobody was answering when he called.

Christ, if he'd only had the luck to blink at the right time when that car had gone off the road he wouldn't ever have seen it, and he'd be at the motel by now. This was going to finish up a rotten goddamn day, he could see that already.

"*Where are you?*" he yelled again.

He began going down, using the intervals of calm between the gusts, then finding it easier the lower he went because this was the lee side of the road and he couldn't hear the beer can anymore. It was almost full moonlight now and he looked around at the shapes of the rocks and the scrub and the tall saguaros, the sweat starting to creep on him because the rocks had the look of scattered tombstones and the saguaros were taller than he was, standing darkly with their arms raised from their sides.

"*You here anywhere?*"

Maybe he'd been mistaken. Maybe his own headlights had picked out a stream of flying sand that had looked like headlights too, at right angles to the road; and the red lamps had just been an illusion because he'd been straining his eyes. That would be really great, if he'd imagined the whole damn thing. The trouble was, he knew he hadn't.

"*Where are you, for Christ sake?*"

There were boulders waist-high in the gully and he had to climb over them and take a look and go down and climb again, losing his balance once and grazing a shin and stopping and standing still and feeling sick with the pain, going on again when he was ready, calling again and getting no answer. That car could be anywhere, lost forever between these boulders, or buried deep in the scrub and the low thorn trees, and he was beginning to panic because if there were people hurt bad or even maybe dying somewhere here in the wreckage he'd need to get to them as fast as he could and there just wasn't anything he could see that had the shine of paintwork on it.

He'd forgotten about getting his clothes mussed and his white shoes ripped, because he knew the car had gone down somewhere in this area and there must have been people inside it and they weren't answering. It sounded so quiet now, with the wind far away, high up where the road was, and he didn't like it, any part of it.

"*Can you hear me?*"

He listened and went on, stumbling from rock to rock and calling again, until suddenly there was the smell of gasoline and a dark shape came lurching against him and he let out a kind of yelp, scared to hell, and caught it and held it before it could fall, so that for a while they both stood swaying in a weird kind of dance while he let the fright go out of him.

"You hurt bad?"

The guy was a deadweight for a minute, then got some of his strength back and stood upright, so Berlatsky began helping him up the slope between the boulders, talking to him but not getting an answer, not caring too much, because at least the man was alive and not even hurt too bad.

"Take it easy now."

Sometimes they had to stop when the man reached up and tried to hold the back of his neck, throwing his head up and just standing there for a whole minute with his face to the sky while Berlatsky held on to him, waiting, watching the pain in his face, the eyes screwed shut and the mouth drawn back and the light gleaming on his teeth as the spasm went through him and slowly passed away.

"You want me to get an ambulance, get a stretcher down here?"

All the man could say was something about his back, hurt his back, be all right in a while, and Berlatsky dragged him up the slope as fast as he could, worrying now about the stories he'd heard: the police didn't like you to pull people out of wrecks or do anything to help them except just throw a blanket or something over them, or sometimes they'd just drop dead on you while you were doing your best to help, and then you'd be in serious trouble. You could kill people like this, because their neck was broken or something.

Berlatsky was wishing he'd never started this. The wind was whining again through the cables up there, and sand was already drifting down from the roadway, peppering his face. They had to stop half a dozen times before they finally made it, the man holding his neck and squeezing his face against the sky, a dark gray trickle coagulating across one cheek, the moonlight taking the color out of it. It was quite a distinguished-looking face, Berlatsky thought, even screwed up in pain this way, a good straight nose and a mane of thick hair, and heavy gray eyebrows, perfect teeth under the drawn-back lips. But he was past middle age and bulky, and that made it hard to get him up the slope because Berlatsky was a thin man, tall but with no weight to him, no muscle.

"Guess we're almost there. You okay?"

It sounded like 'yes,' and Berlatsky dragged him onto the roadway, the sand half-blinding him as they met the full force of the wind. The Chevy was rocking on its springs as they reached it, and he got the passenger door open and shifted the five black jewel cases onto the rear seat with the rest of the stuff. The big man stood clutching the open door, one hand reaching across his shoulder again like he was trying to tear some kind of devil off his back, his face drawn in pain.

"Listen," Berlatsky said, "I'm going to get you to a doctor."

The man didn't say anything, couldn't talk.

"You gotta get in the car," Berlatsky told him. "Then you'll be okay."

The man held on to the door another half minute, swaying as the wind came; then he bent his legs and lowered himself onto the passenger seat, keeping his back straight; and Berlatsky shut the door and kicked against the beer can as he went round the other side and got in and started the motor, his eyes streaming tears because of the sand that had got into them. He sat letting them water till the scratching had gone from under his lids.

"I'll drive slow," he said.

The man answered him this time, speaking heavily on his breath, as if he'd been saving himself for the effort. "No doctor. Understand?"

Even in these few words Berlatsky heard a tone of authority, but the guy wasn't making any sense.

"Listen, I'm going to get you to a doctor or a hospital or an ambulance station—for all I know you could've bust your neck and I'm not qualified to handle things like that."

He put the stick into drive and got moving, and heard the top case slide off the others in the back of the car, hitting the floor and breaking open, the best place for it, on the goddamn floor, seventeen bucks the whole of the day, a solid heart pendant he'd sold to a kid who didn't look like he could afford the thirty-five dollars retail, must have been in love.

"No doctor," the heavy man said. "I just need to rest."

"Listen, guys like you can keel over when people are trying to help them, and I don't intend—" but he broke off because he'd snatched a look at the man and saw he'd passed right out, oh Jesus Christ he shouldn't ever have stopped to do anything, he should've gone right on past and phoned the police from the motel, must've been crazy.

He began sweating again as he strained to keep sight of the road through the flying yellow sand, crouched forward over the wheel and thinking the best thing was to get this dude to the motel and call up an ambulance and hope it'd come before the guy died on him and fixed him with a manslaughter rap. For forty-three years Berlatsky had made a point of keeping out of trouble and now look at this.

Between the wind gusts he kept taking a look at his passenger, hoping to see him come to, but the heavy head lolled against the back of the seat and the hooded eyes stayed closed. It was a noble-looking face, Berlatsky thought, a strong mouth and a strong nose, the mane of graying hair making him look like a lion asleep, the gash across his temple adding to his strength in an odd kind of way, a lion wounded. The blood had soaked into the lapel of his expensive sport coat and the heavy silk necktie was pulled around, and Berlatsky noted these things because all his life he had noted things, like a sparrow picks at crumbs. You could miss a lot of chances by not using your eyes.

Berlatsky was using his eyes and he could see this guy was someone important, a top banker or the president of a company, and that would be great, absolutely great, when he finally fell down dead on the motel floor in a few minutes from now. How much could you get sued for, by a classy set of relatives? A million? Five million? Well come to think of it they wouldn't do themselves too much good because all he possessed was this six-year-old Chevy and a few cases of crap reproduction jewelry that'd make any top banker's wife throw up just to look at.

Every time there was a break in the wind gusts he took a quick look at the man beside him to see what color he was, because if he died right here in the car Berlatsky was going to stop and drag him off the edge of the road and leave him there and get back in the Chevy and keep on driving till he hit the Mexican border.

He was peering through the windshield again at the blinding sand when the man said clearly:

"I need to rest."

Berlatsky jerked a glance at him, scared at the sudden way he'd come back to life but glad as hell that he had.

"You bet you do."

A minute went by. The man watched him, sizing him up.

"Get me to the nearest motel."

"We're on our way right now, don't worry."

There was another silence. The man was having to kind of gather his strength for the effort, every time he wanted to say something.

"No doctor. No ambulance. It was just a small accident, and I need some rest. Do what I tell you."

Again Berlatsky noticed the authority in the man's voice. He wasn't having to shout or anything: it was just there, in the way he said it. The way he said it, you could tell he wasn't fooling around.

"But for Christ sake . . . ," Berlatsky said.

The man had shut his eyes again but this time Berlatsky saw he hadn't passed out: his head wasn't lolling and his mouth hadn't come open. Color was coming back to his face, under the blotchy tan.

Lights came again ahead of them, a whole string of them swinging in the wind, and Berlatsky slowed and saw the sign at the end of the long frame building—*Desert Winds*—with some of the colored bulbs missing and the sign itself at an angle, like it was having a hard job staying up there at all. He'd never pulled in here before but he'd gone past it plenty of times, and tonight he'd made a beeline for it on account of the weather advisories he'd heard when he was coming out of Vegas. It was a cinch that all the fancier motels on Interstate 15 would be jam-packed with people running for shelter, but nobody would want to pick a dump like this if they had more than two cents to rub together, even on a night like this.

He drove the Chevy into the auto court on the other side of the gas pump and cut the motor and said:

"You stay right here, okay?"

The big man's eyes came open, a little glazed-looking.

"Is this a motel?"

"Right."

"Get me a room."

"Listen, you're going to stay right here while I get you some help. If you start moving around you'll–"

"Get me a room."

Berlatsky doused the lights and said, "Okay, anything you say," because he could walk across the auto court a lot faster than this guy and just as soon as he got a telephone in his hand he was going to pass the buck before it got too hot to handle. "Stay here and take it easy, okay? While I line you up the room."

He got out and clamped his straw hat down against the wind and went past a dirty window full of rock-hounder's trash–*Gems of the Desert,* the notice said–and looked back once before he went into the building, to make sure his friend in the Chevy was staying put.

Suddenly there was no more wind or stinging sand, but the smell of cooking instead, and he stood in the reception lobby looking around for the phone. A truck driver was hunched in a makeshift booth across where the sign said "Café," so that was where the phone must be. Berlatsky went over and pushed at the swinging door of the café and saw a group of guys laughing their ass off around one of the tables, cards fanned out in their fists. A girl in sweater and jeans was taking them beer on a tin tray and one of them put an arm round her waist and she jerked a foot sideways and caught him on the shin and he yelped and the rest of them burst out laughing again.

"Hey!" Berlatsky called, "is there another phone?"

She looked at him, holding the empty tray. "Is there what?"

"Another phone!"

"Just how many can you use at the same time?"

He guessed she was trying to get another laugh, but the men were busy slapping their cards down.

"Some guy's using this one!"

"So what's the rush?"

She was coming across to him, heavy in the hips but making them work for her, the jeans down low and showing her navel, some navy-blue fluff in it from the sweater. Berlatsky would have laughed at the act but he was too uptight about that guy out there half-dying in his Chevy, and went back into the lobby to wait for this character to get the hell off the horn.

"You want something to eat?" the girl asked, swinging the tray. She'd followed him out.

"Huh? Nope."

"You checking in?"

"Listen, for now all I need is that phone."

She put the tray down on the stack of newspapers by the desk, hooking her thumbs through her belt loops and watching him with her head on one side.

"If it's an emergency," she said, "I'll get him off the phone, you just have to tell me."

Her stone-blue eyes watched him seriously and it occurred to him that he must be looking pretty upset, exactly the way he was feeling.

"Okay," he said, "will you do—"

The door opened behind him and he heard the rush of the wind outside. The girl was looking past him, kind of shocked, and he swung round and saw the man, blood still on his face, his eyes red from the sand. He let the door slam shut behind him and stood there stiffly looking at Berlatsky.

"Did you get me a room?"

Berlatsky didn't say anything. There were things he needed to think about and he had to do it very fast: there was a decision he had to make and he sensed it could be important and he could feel his own instinct kind of working in him, trying to guide him. It was a feeling he knew quite well, and he let it take charge, giving it time.

"Hey, Sammy," he heard the girl say, "get off the phone, will you? We have an emergency."

The big man looked quickly from Berlatsky to the girl, only his eyes moving, his neck held stiff.

"No," he said.

The girl and the truck driver looked at him, hearing the way he'd said it, quietly but like he really meant it. Berlatsky let his instinct run free, trusting it, saying nothing.

"Did you have an accident?" the girl asked, worrying.

Berlatsky watched the man as he answered her, noting the pain in his face and the way he was fighting it, the effort he was having to make to show them he meant what he said, because it was important to him, very important.

"It's nothing serious," the man said.

The girl looked at Berlatsky. "Didn't you want to call a doctor or someone?"

Berlatsky heard the big man taking slow deep breaths, like he was fighting to stay conscious, to keep control of things. Berlatsky noted the man's breathing, like he noted everything he could on his way through life, because if you didn't you could miss a lot of chances.

"No," he said, "he doesn't need a doctor. He just needs a rest. Do you have a couple of rooms for tonight?"

CHAPTER TWO

"This okay?" the girl asked.

"Sure."

"You're right next door."

"I'll see it later," Berlatsky said. "Just gimme the key."

She stopped in the doorway on her way out, taking another look at the big man, and another look at Berlatsky, trying to figure out what the score was.

"You better register," she said.

"I'll be right out."

She went out and shut the door and the big man said to Berlatsky, "You look after me and I'll look after you. Is that understood?" Then he went down with his knees jack-knifing and one hand going out as he tried to save himself and Berlatsky got to him just in time to stop him smashing his head on the corner of the dressing table.

"Oh Jesus Christ," Berlatsky said.

The guy was out cold. He'd kept up the effort to stay conscious all this time and now he knew everything was okay because he had a room set and there wasn't any doctor coming, so he just let the whole thing go.

"Oh Jesus," Berlatsky said.

The man was too heavy to lift onto the bed so he brought the pillow and eased it under the mane of graying hair and got the blanket and put it over him, then peeled it away again because the expensive sport coat was gaping open and showing the edge of a wallet, and he drew it out and took it under the lamp on the dressing table, hesitating a second and then going through it without any compunction because if he was going to look after this guy the first thing to do was find out who he was.

A hundred and ninety bucks in clean new bills, that was a lot of money to carry around. American Express, Bank-Americard, Cosmopolitan Hospital Plan, Reserve Insurance Company's certificate for one million dollars—Jesus! He read it over: *This is to certify that John K. Stevens is protected by excess personal liability insurance coverage of up to One Million Dollars per occurrence.* He could use this kind of policy himself, Berlatsky thought, if he was going to pick any more well-heeled busters out of wrecks. Two more credit cards, driver's license, and a police department pass. This was the one he went on looking at, holding it under the light and reading it over and then looking down at the guy who was lying on the floor at his feet.

Superior Court Judge John K. Stevens, Los Angeles County.

After a minute Berlatsky put everything back into the pigskin wallet and kneeled on the floor and slid the wallet back inside the sport coat and pulled the blanket up and got to his feet and stood against the door with his arms folded, looking down at Judge John K. Stevens while the sweat started creeping on him again. There wasn't any air conditioning in this crummy joint, or it had broken down, and the temperature on this September night must be around eighty after the day's heat, but Berlatsky didn't normally sweat, even when it was this hot—he was too thin and couldn't ever get his blood going around fast enough. He was sweating now all right.

He hadn't thought about this situation before, not with any kind of coherence. Driving through the yellow clouds of sand with this man beside him, standing in the lobby just now when he'd come through the door, he'd let his instinct guide him as to what he should do. Now he looked at this thing squarely for the first time and saw it was very simple, and very strange. When a person climbs out of a car wreck with his back hurt so bad he's in terrible pain, the first thing he wants is a doctor. And if he has the luck to find some stupid jerk who's prepared to fight his way through rocks and cactus and thorn trees in the hope of rescuing him, that's the first thing he'll ask that stupid jerk to do for him: take him to a doctor, fast. Get me an ambulance, will you? Or can you drive me to a doctor? And tell the police there's been an accident, a personal injury case. And hurry.

But it hadn't been that way.

Berlatsky pulled a Kent out of the pack and lit up and tipped his straw hat to the back of his head and sank slowly onto his haunches and looked at the face of the stranger he'd met tonight in the dark and the blowing sand, the man who had his reasons for choosing pain, a lot of pain, instead of a doctor who could have eased it just with a needle, the man who'd said to him a while ago: *You look after me and I'll look after you.*

Crouched on his haunches, watching the heavy features with their noble nose, the thick graying hair and the massive brow of Judge John K. Stevens, almost as if he hoped to stare right through this skull and into its thoughts, Berlatsky smoked the cigarette down to the filter before he got up and mashed it out in the cheap plastic ashtray on the table, seeing himself in the mirror and taking his handkerchief and wiping at the sweat on his narrow face, his eyes looking into his eyes as he forced himself to consider what he should do, and what he shouldn't do, and what he was going to do.

When he'd made up his mind he leaned over the Judge and listened to his breathing, pulling the blanket down a little and holding his palm to the moist silk shirt, feeling the slow beat of the heart, looking again at the closed hooded eyes and then drawing the blanket up again and getting on his feet and opening the door quietly and going out.

The truck driver was still on the phone in the corner of

the lobby: it could only be a girl friend. The wind was moaning through the auto court and the sign banged every time a gust came and Berlatsky made a detour in case the thing finally blew down and tried to brain him. There were three trucks, a pickup and two private sedans out here and he wondered how many there'd be if it wasn't for this sandstorm. He didn't think there'd be many.

The first trip he took his overnight bag and five of the jewelry display cases and put them in his room and the second trip he brought in the other seven cases, and when he came into the lobby the truck driver was off the phone and the girl was talking to him, saying "no way" about something and sounding very emphatic. She saw Berlatsky coming in.

"Hey! You better register!"

"Be right back."

"That's what you said the last time."

He went on to his room and stacked the jewel cases in two rows of six on the top shelf of the clothes closet and wound up the clockwork vibrator alarm and put it in place. This junk had cost him less than three hundred bucks but the total retail value was around seven hundred fifty if he could ever sell it all, and that was a lot of scratch in any language, even if there were people who thought it wasn't, like Dolores, blast her, went off with a guy who owned a racehorse, may she forever be covered in horseshit.

He walked quietly back past the room next door because the Judge had to get some sleep and rest his back and then they could talk and work out the score and then Berlatsky would finally decide what he should do, and what he shouldn't do, and what he was going to do.

The girl was waiting for him in the lobby, fixing her straw-colored hair in the mirror, had it in braids, kind of Norwegian, with her stone-blue eyes as she turned to him, the blue-gray color of seashore pebbles.

"How's your friend?" she asked him.

"Fine."

"What happened?"

"When?"

"I mean how did he get hurt?"

"He fell off his donkey."

"He *what?*"

"Where do I register?"

"Right here."

He felt her watching him, maybe wondering if he was some kind of nut. He'd been wondering about that himself, as a matter of fact, during the past hour, but very slowly he was beginning to think he might not be any kind of a nut at all, and that would make a nice change.

"I have to see your driver's license."

He got it for her and she filled in the line on the card, writing slowly and shaping the letters and figures carefully, as if she liked things to look nice when she did them. Then she read what he'd put.

"Charles M. Berlatsky. Hi, Charlie."

"Hi."

"What's the *M* for?"

"Mary."

"Huh?" She stared at him with her eyes kind of going round in circles, then she saw he was kidding. He thought it took her about five seconds, a shade slow for the course. But she had a nice smile.

"You're kidding!"

"How did you guess?"

She filed the card with the rest.

"I kinda like that name, you know? Charlie Berlatsky—it kinda goes with a kick."

"Maybe that explains it."

She'd never get it first time. He began counting.

"Explains what?"

"Why I get so many kicks." He took his driver's license back and suddenly thought maybe he shouldn't have told her anything, should have stalled her till he was more certain of things. But it was too late now and anyway the desk was deserted most of the time so he could always whip that one card out of the deck if he had to blow, and leave her to explain about the gap in the serial numbers.

"*Whaddid she have to go an' die for, with all this work to do?*" There was a sudden sizzling noise, like frying.

Berlatsky cocked an eyebrow at the girl.

"Who's that?"

"My pa."

"Who died?"

"My ma."

"Recent?"

"Six months."

"That's too bad."

"It's okay."

"He do the cooking?"

"Right."

"I guess if he cooks good, I'm about ready."

He made a move for the café door.

"He has to register too," she said. "Your friend."

She wasn't slow all of the time.

"He's asleep. Needs rest."

"Sure. But he has to register." She pulled out the next card. "What's his name?"

"He didn't say."

It was the only answer he could give her, the only safe one.

She was thrown again. She threw easy.

"I thought he was a friend of yours."

"Anybody can make a mistake."

"Well who is he?"

"I have no idea."

"But listen, Charlie, I mean we have to get him registered. You don't know the trouble there is if the police find out there's someone been staying here without—"

"Sure, okay, I understand. But right now he's asleep and

I don't want to wake the poor guy up just for putting his name on a card. He hurt his back pretty bad, you saw the way he looked."

She thought about this for a while, the blank card in her hand, the phony gemstone ring on her finger catching the light from the mirror.

"Well, okay," she said grudgingly, "but he has to register first thing in the morning, I'm just telling you. I mean it's nothing to do with us, Pa and me, but the police—"

"Sure, they make things tough for you. Where did you—"

"You'd never believe just how tough they can get! We're not too far from the state line, see, and there are some oddballs around. How come you brought him in here, if he isn't your friend?"

"He had a little accident, that's all. Where did you get that ring?"

"This one?" She tilted her pink raw-looking hand around in the light. "Guy gave it to me."

"You still see him?"

"Who? Him? No."

Charlie took her hand and looked at the thing again, like he was interested in it. "Then I guess it's okay for me to say that's about the crummiest piece of junk I've ever seen."

"Well, listen now—"

"You want me to show you something with a little class?"

Her eyes opened up a lot. She always showed what she was thinking, and he was beginning to enjoy watching her eyes as the thoughts came there. He always made a good sale with people like her: once you'd seen it in their eyes that they were ready to buy, you could talk them up from fifteen bucks to fifty without giving them any pain.

"*Hey, Rose!*"

It was the same voice as before.

"That your name?" Charlie asked.

"Huh? Yeah."

"It's my favorite name for a girl."

"You're kidding!"

"Not this time."

She stuck her thumbs through her belt loops again and he noted her face coloring a little. She wasn't used to compliments. She was used to having her ass pinched and her navel stared at but she wasn't used to being told there was something nice about her. He would remember this, and other things, because it was easy to learn about people, and then make them do things for you. You couldn't do anything in this life without people.

"I have to go," she said, not wanting to.

They could hear Pa yelling again from the kitchen.

"Okay," Charlie said, smiling.

"But will you show me, afterward?"

"Show you?"

She looked worried that he'd forgotten so soon.

"You know, Charlie, the something-with-some-class you were telling me about."

"Oh sure. Sure. There's plenty of time." He went across and opened the swinging door for her to go through and she wasn't too used to that either. "Make it a double burger, baby, and forget about the other guys in here."

"Holy Christ!" Pa hollered again.

Charlie could see him through the hatch, a leather-skinned old-timer with a white fuzz around his jowls, his eyes buried long ago in their puckered sockets, heavy purple tattooing in the V of his open shirt. There'd be sons and daughters, Charlie thought, all over the world, older than Rose.

It must be a TV hung up there above the hatch because Pa kept staring up at something while he cooked, then he'd burn his fingers and holler out again.

"He isn't my real father," she said, bringing some apple pie.

"Your real father must be a very nice man."

"What makes you think so?"

"You're a real nice girl."

He didn't normally use this pitch with a girl like Rose. Frankly he didn't go for braids and heavy hips and raw-looking hands and a navel full of fluff, but you had to make people do things for you and he had the feeling that tonight and tomorrow he was going to need a lot of help.

"He just lit out on us when I was so-high," she said. "I don't think he was a very nice man. I think he was a shit."

"*Hey, Rose!*"

"Okay, okay!"

After the hamburger and apple pie, Charlie felt less jumpy. Maybe it had been the wind or something, and all that sand blowing, like the place was under siege, with trailers overturning on the freeway and weather advisories on the radio the whole time. You'd expect to feel a little jumpy, a night like this.

He lit a cigarette, although he was trying to cut down. He knew goddamn well it wasn't the wind. If only that guy had been just a banker, or the vice-president of a small company, someone the size he could have handled. But Jesus—a judge!

"I'll be free after ten," she said when she brought more coffee. She smiled, meaning about the "something with class" deal. She had nice teeth.

"It's a date, Rosie."

"I hate being called that."

"Okay. Rose. It's my favorite name, remember?"

"Sure."

When he'd finished his cigarette he went and looked in at Room 7, inching open the door and not making any noise. Light from the passage fell slanting across the figure on the floor, but Charlie couldn't tell anything, and had to go in and squat on his haunches listening to the breathing. It sounded okay, deep and steady. Charlie had had a kid, once, a long time ago, a boy, with chest troubles, and he used to go in there every hour, all night, night after night, to listen over the crib and make sure he was still breathing, till the time came when he wasn't.

Listen, for Christ sake, the guy's hurt his back, that's all; he's not going to die on you. Relax.

He went out and put the key in the lock and took up the pressure of the spring so it didn't make a click, then he got the flashlight from his overnight case and slid it up his sleeve before he went out through the lobby and into the auto court and got into his Chevy.

It was worth a try and he'd give it an hour. Maybe the beer can was still there, caught in the roadside scrub; that'd be a big help. He had to try, because the Judge might have an overnight case in the car, or there could be other things that would tell Charlie more about him. He had to find out as much as he could, because when they had their little talk in Room 7 that buster was going to tell him exactly what he wanted him to know, and nothing else, not a word. So he'd have to find out for himself.

"Hello, Beauty," he said.

He backed up, easing out from between two of the trucks, turning and heading north. He always said that, when he got into his Chevy, especially first thing in the morning, because she was old and she was faithful. On a long haul he'd say other things, talk to her like you'd talk to a horse, because there wasn't ever anyone else he could talk to, or there hadn't been for the last five months. Cynthie had left him long ago, soon after the kid had died, and Marge had stayed just two months. Phyllis—that was Chicago, met her in a snowstorm, you ever get into a snowstorm in Chicago, get the hell out again quick before Phyllis finds you—then there was Boops and finally the only girl in the world, the real one, the true one, with her silky locks and thirty-inch waist and the lovely way she sang "Killing Me Softly," just for him, killing him softly. My lovely Dolores, may your beautiful shoes be forever covered in horseshit.

Charlie Berlatsky was a loner now, and talked to his Chevy

and Dolores and other people. They said it was the first sign you'd end up in the nut house but he didn't care. You had to talk to somebody, or you'd end up in the nut house.

The wind was less strong, or maybe it was because he was heading north now and it was blowing on the other side of the car. The yellow sand flew in it, making him slow, and he went almost three miles before he knew he must have missed the place and had to turn and come back, moving at a crawl, looking for the beer can, Jesus, it wasn't much of a landmark. He should have paid more attention when he'd got the Judge into the Chevy, looked for a shrub or something, but then he hadn't known he'd ever want to come here again.

In ten minutes the lights of the motel came up and he cursed and turned in the auto court and headed back north and missed the place again because it was only about a mile from the motel and he'd gone more than two, noting the figures on the mileage indicator now. The paintwork was getting sandblasted to hell, he could hear the stuff hissing against the doors every time there was a wind gust, and there wasn't any point calling her Beauty and then driving her up and down a lousy road like this with the sand flying as thick—*beer can.*

He saw the beer can.

Or he saw *a* beer can, one of the hundreds of goddamn beer cans there could be along this stretch of road tonight, blowing from Vegas to Los Angeles.

But when he got out of the car he saw there was a gully right here, with scrub and thorn trees growing in it because the winter rains were channeled here. There weren't many gullies between Interstate 15 and the Desert Winds: he'd driven this road pretty often in daylight.

He switched on the flashlight and went down and thought of something else he'd forgotten to do—change these fancy white calfskin shoes for the rough-weather boots he kept in the trunk, but to hell with it, he was more than halfway down to where that guy had come lurching out of the dark against him. Who knows, Charlie Berlatsky, if you play the cards right this time, play them right just this once in your life, you might not get yourself more than a new pair of fancy white shoes?

Lower in the gully there was no sound of the wind. The sand drifting down from the road had been thinning out gradually and now there wasn't any. In the clear moonlight he could see the shapes of the boulders and the scratches and dents in them, and the spines on the tall-standing saguaros. His eyes were getting used to the light and he found gaps between the rocks, crossing the gully from one bank to the other and back, sometimes having to clamber over a boulder, twice brushing his leg against a cholla and feeling the spines go in, pulling them out through the leg of his pants and feeling the sting already; it'd be months before the blisters went, goddamn it.

He'd noted the time, getting smarter, at least one thing he hadn't forgotten to do, and it was fifty minutes since he'd left the Chevy and his leg was throbbing because of the cholla and the flashlight was getting dim because maybe fifty times he'd stood on a rock and switched on the light and swept the beam around, wasting his time, wasting the batteries.

"I guess that's about it," he said. "Just as soon as that buster wakes up he's going to talk and I'm going to make him tell me everything I need to know, the whole bit, so I don't have to kill myself looking for his crummy car, it can go screw itself."

The air was quiet down here, and because of the way his own voice sounded, talking to nobody, his scalp had begun creeping as he stood here among the tall saguaros with their arms raised pointing to the sky, one of them fingering the moon itself, towering, the silver from the moon flowing into its blackness, making him feel alone, because they were touching. He could hear the wind again, crying softly up there through the telephone cables, and had to talk again, shivering just once and unexpectedly in the warm air.

"Okay, come on, we'll get the hell out of here."

Soon after he began climbing, the wind sent some kind of an eddy and he smelled gasoline, the way he'd smelled it before, when the guy had come at him out of the night. So the damn thing wasn't far away and he'd go find it.

It took another half hour and when he got there he saw how he'd kept on missing it: for one thing it was buried quite deep among the thorn trees and for another thing it had finished wheels uppermost, and instead of the shiny paint-work he'd been looking for there was only dried mud and rust. The gasoline was really stinking now, maybe still dripping out of the filler cap, so the judge must have moved quite a distance from the wreck by the time they met.

There was something pale on the ground, sticking halfway through one of the windows, and he flicked the flashlight on and looked at it.

"*Oh Christ!*"

He jerked backward and tripped and caught his foot and wrenched it free and scrambled away and after a while sat down with his head between his knees, trying not to pass out.

CHAPTER THREE

No way," she said. "Like I told you, no way."

"But Rosie–"

"Don't call me that. How long have you known me?"

"Rose, listen," he told her, "they could go along with us! I just talked them into it on the phone!"

"That's fine, Sammy," she said, watching some headlights swing across the windows. "The thing is, you don't have to look after things here, but I do."

"But listen–"

"Who's going to look after things here if I go to Florida for three whole days?"

"Your pa," he said, "and Mabel!"

She laughed, imagining it, just imagining it, Pa with his eyes glued on the TV there while the burgers went black in the pan and the sunny-sides turned as hard as oyster shells while Mabel was in here bringing the wrong orders and giving the wrong change; three whole days of glorious abandon and losing half the regulars just for the sake of feeding the alligators in the Everglades.

"No way," she said, laughing, turning away and going back to the hatch. She didn't like Florida anyhow, the place was a steamy swamp, and what did she want to go to Florida for when there was Las Vegas and Palm Springs and Hollywood right here, with all the stars and millionaires you could ever dream of? Too, she'd have to fight Sammy off every night and he'd get loaded and she'd have to double-lock her door. Sammy was okay but just because a guy was okay it didn't mean she was going to sleep with him. And he wouldn't want to go to Florida anyway if he hadn't won the TV show prize vacation trip—he hated the place.

"*Hey, Pa!*"

She had to wave her hand in front of him to make him look down, and he pushed the pan off the gas, the onion rings almost black. Three days . . . you couldn't leave Pa on his own for three minutes!

"You got some coffee?" someone was calling.

"Sure!"

At the back of her mind she was aware that the door hadn't opened, but they'd certainly been headlights crossing the windows a minute ago. When she'd taken the percolator to the man at the corner table she went out to the lobby to see if anyone had come in but there was no one. Maybe somebody had been turning in the auto court, losing their way. The gas-pump bell hadn't rung.

Going back through the swinging door she thought of Charlie Berlatsky, the way he'd pushed it open for her, and how he'd said he was going to show her "something with some class." He meant some kind of ring, or jewelry, because they'd been looking at the ring that guy had given her. She could believe that Charlie could show her something more classy because he was a kind of quiet man and he dressed nice and had nice manners: he was the sort of person you could easily imagine being a famous film producer or a millionaire, but kind of secret about it, like Howard Hughes. Just think, if it was the windstorm that had made him turn into the motel here, sort of looking for shelter, and—

"Holy cow!"

There was a sizzling from the other side of the hatch and she went and cussed her pa, who wasn't really her pa, for letting the hash browns burn, and her heart sank, like it did often, because she didn't know what was going to happen to this place, Desert Winds, now Ma wasn't here. Up to when Ma had gone into the hospital they'd been easy times, and Pete had wanted to marry her and buy into the business, do the place up; but a couple of months after Ma had gone he'd stopped coming so often and then said he'd got a job in New Orleans; they never saw him again.

"Pa!" she said through the hatch. "Will you turn that damn thing off and try and concentrate?" But he wasn't looking at her, which meant he couldn't hear, so she waved her hand through the hatch and he looked down, but as soon as he read her lips he looked at the TV again so she'd know he wasn't going to listen to the rest.

She didn't know what was going to happen to this place.

"Rose!"

"Yeah?"

"Whadda ya doin', ten o'clock?"

"Busy!"

He tried to pinch her ass as she went past. She'd like to tell Bob Dawson to get the hell out of here and don't come again but they had just fifteen regular customers and he was one of them.

When the card game was over and three of the truckers had gone and no one else had come in, she went into the lobby and buzzed Room 6 from the desk, but there wasn't any answer. She tried a few times because Charlie wouldn't be in bed yet and she hadn't seen him go out. Maybe he was talking to his friend in 7. She didn't buzz 7 because that poor guy was wanting to rest.

Sammy went at a quarter after nine, earlier than usual to show he was sore at her.

"I'll tell 'em you'll think about it, Rose."

"Okay, you tell them that."

"You mean you'll think about it?"

"No, I just said you tell them that if you want."

The last trucker and the repair man from Indian Rock left

soon after, and she went into the kitchen and stacked the first heap into the dishwasher, wondering where Charlie was.

She buzzed 6 again but it didn't answer, so she went along the passage and stood listening outside 7, but couldn't hear them talking. There wasn't any light under the door either.

It was kind of funny.

She stood listening again but couldn't hear voices. The whole thing was kind of funny, when you thought about it, the way the man had come in quite a few minutes after Charlie, although Charlie had said he was helping him. Why didn't they come in together? And Charlie wanting to use the phone so bad, at first, and then changing his mind so fast when his friend said he didn't want a doctor. Charlie looking so uptight, and the blood on the man's face.

She got the passkey and knocked on 6 first, going in when she didn't get an answer. Charlie's bag was on the bed, so he hadn't just lit out for some reason. It was a relief, but still and all, where was he?

She didn't knock at 7 before she went in, not to wake the man if he was sleeping. If he wanted to know what she was doing, coming in here without knocking, she'd say she was getting worried about him, which was God's truth, with Charlie nowhere and the silence and everything. The floor was dark, but the light from the passage was sweeping across it and the next thing she saw was the man's face and she caught her breath and didn't move the door any more, her chest kind of empty and shaking as she stared down at the white face with the blood on it and the closed eyes and the way he looked so still on the floor, not on the bed, but on the *floor.*

The wind hit her as she ran out to the auto court and saw the two cars and the pickup truck, knowing who they belonged to and knowing Charlie's car had gone, but where would he go? Where would he go, not telling her, leaving his bag, leaving the man in there in 7 lying on the floor? Running back to the building she thought it's no use telling

Pa, he'll only say throw some water over the guy or get a hearse or sump'n, just don't bother me, will you now.

You'd think you could tell Pa a thing like this, there's a man dying in 7, dead or dying on the floor in there all alone, and Charlie's gone off and left it for us to deal with, you'd think you could tell *anyone* and maybe you could, too, anyone except Pa, thinking all this, the thoughts tumbling through her as she ran, hitting the door open and going straight to the phone and dialing for Dr. Adams.

He sat there a long time with his head resting on his knees, or it seemed like a long time but it was probably only a couple of minutes. Far away he could hear the whine of the wind through the cables up there, but down here it was very quiet. He sat listening to how quiet it was.

Okay, Berlatsky, do something.

He'd only seen three dead people before, except for his kid when he'd stopped breathing. One of them they'd pulled out of the ocean at Malibu when he'd been halfway through an ice cream cone, and he'd got sick right off. The other two had been in a car wreck, and it was strange because the minute he saw them he thought of an ice cream cone. He'd thought of one just now.

"Berlatsky," he said, "do something."

He got up and climbed the gully, because there wasn't any question now about what he should do: He should go back to the motel and call the police and an ambulance and get Judge John K. Stevens out of his life, the hell out of it. He was almost at the top of the gully when he turned and began coming back down, because of what he'd been thinking. There was still no question about what he should do, and there was still time to do it; but he'd come here to find out everything he could about the judge, and he hadn't done that yet.

When he came to the wreck again he took three deep

breaths like he'd read somewhere about doing when you need to steady yourself, then he switched on the flashlight and moved the yellowing beam across the woman's body. She was young and was dressed in a flashy Las Vegas way, and she had been killed when the car overturned. The Judge must have seen that, when he climbed out of the mess.

Charlie worked as fast as he could because the flashlight batteries were almost shot. Scattered around the inside of the roof was a fistful of semiprecious stones, unpolished and with dirt still sticking to them; they looked like they had spilled out of the canvas bag that was near them, among the fallen maps. The passenger seat belt was still clipped against the roof but the driver's was hanging loose, and this was maybe how the Judge had come out of it and the girl hadn't.

He had to stop work and go a short way from the wreck and take deep breaths again because of the stink of the gasoline and the way the girl looked, with her eyes like that. After a time he came slowly back and switched the lamp on and took the keys out of the ignition and opened the trunk, and a heavy leather case dropped and hit the ground, with a small rock pick and a chrome-plated hammer and a few other things. He opened the case.

Halfway through looking at the things in it he stopped and spoke out loud, because here in this place he felt alone and scared. "Hey listen, you shouldn't go looking through other people's things!" But he thought about it and remembered he was doing it because of what the Judge had said: *You look after me and I'll look after you.* If he was going to look after the Judge he had to know something about him, and this was why he'd come here. So did it make any sense finding a suitcase and not even looking inside? "You'll have to quit fooling around this way, Berlatsky."

There were only clothes, and a copy of *Serpico*, and a set of muscle-developers, and the briefcase. The things in the briefcase were interesting, a batch of papers and magazines and notebooks and stuff like that. Two of the magazines—*Los Angeles Consumers' Journal* and *California Horizons*—showed a photograph of Judge Stevens on the cover, and some of the pictures inside showed him with Mrs. Stevens and their dog. Also there were a lot of reports and memorandums about initiating a campaign: John K. Stevens for governor. A couple of press clippings said he was to resign his office in jurisprudence early next year and enter his gubernatorial nomination, and most of the listed news items referred to the Judge as "the leading Republican gubernatorial contender."

Charlie didn't want to use up the last of the batteries on the rest of the stuff: he'd already got the picture. He shut the suitcase and left it ready to take away, and then went to breathe some fresh air again, squatting against a rock and listening to the faint cry of the wind up there, wanting to go, wanting all the time to go back up there to his Chevy and drive to the motel and call the police and then forget it, wanting to go and not going.

When he was ready to face it he went across to the wreck and bent down and took a breath and moved her leg so as to get at the handbag that had fallen under it, surprised how fast his stomach was acting up because of how it felt, her leg, heavy and stiff and cold as he slid both hands around it and pulled, thinking that only yesterday—only a couple of hours ago!—he would have given a lot for a girl like her to let him touch her as intimately as this, thinking how terrible it was, the little time it took for death to turn a pretty girl into something so disgusting.

There was an object near her foot and he pried it free and saw it was a flashlight, smaller than his own but brighter when he switched it on. This was how the judge had known, hitting the seat belt release and calling to her—*are you all right?*—trying to get an answer and then finding the flashlight and switching it on and seeing her like this and switching it off and dropping it as he squeezed his way out of the mess and went away from it, and from her, just in any direction, knowing there wasn't anything he could do.

The light was bright from the smaller flashlight and he looked at everything in the handbag, reading the little notebook and the Nevada driver's license and the other things, finding out more about Judge Stevens the more he looked, much more than he'd learned when he'd actually been with the man, right alongside him in the Chevy, much more than the man would ever tell him when finally they got to talking. He already knew from the magazine photographs that this wasn't Mrs. Stevens, and now he knew her name: Theodora Creaturo.

"That's a hell of a beautiful name," he said, "Theo—" but he stopped, his scalp creeping suddenly as he thought of saying her name aloud, and her not answering, or worse, here among the tall dark saguaros with their fingers touching the moon, answering. The sweat was coming on him although he felt cold, the chill moving across the desert as the night grew late, and he began hurrying, putting her handbag inside the car, letting it lie with the other things, the canvas container and the colored stones and the spilled maps, taking only her driver's license as she watched him, the sound of the scream still in her eyes, making him hurry.

He'd been wanting to light a cigarette for a long time but if he lit one here he'd blow himself up, so he waited till he was halfway up the gully with the leather case and then lit one, stopping to drag the smoke in deep again and again while he thought about the Judge.

At the top of the slope the wind hit him, needling his face with blowing sand.

"Hello, Beauty. That's a mess down there."

He drove slow, his eyes narrowed against the back glare as the sand streamed past, till the lights of the motel came up and he turned into the auto court and parked and cut the motor and sat thinking again for maybe five minutes. Then he got out and took the leather case from the trunk and clamped his straw hat down and headed for the entrance. There wasn't anybody in the lobby but he heard her voice.

"Charlie!"

She'd had the swinging door bolted open so she could watch the lobby and now she came through and kicked the bolt out of its hole in the door and let the door swing shut behind her as she stared at him with her stone-blue eyes, relieved to see him but wanting to know things, looking at the heavy leather case.

"I didn't know where you'd gone!" she said, half sore at him.

"You didn't?"

It was all he could think of to say, because he hadn't been ready for this, for her worrying, and there was the other thing on his mind.

"I called the doctor," she said.

"*You what?*"

"I couldn't find you and I went in there and he–"

"When? When did you make the call?"

She looked too scared to answer, just went on staring at him, and he knew he must keep this whole thing cool, play it slow, kid her along till he knew what he was going to do.

"Rose, when did you call?"

"Ten minutes ago, maybe fifteen. Charlie, I–"

"Okay. It's okay, don't worry."

"I went in there and he looked–he looked kind of bad, Charlie." Her voice grew sharp suddenly. "Where did you go? Is this his?" She meant the suitcase.

"Sure. I left it in my car." He was at the phone now, with a dime in his fingers. "What's the number, Rose? The doc's."

"It's there on the–"

"Oh sure."

A list of emergency numbers, their black print showing through a whole web of other numbers people had written here.

"Charlie–"

"This one? Dr. Adams?"

"Yes, but–"

"Everything's okay, don't worry." He began dialing and thought suddenly he could be wrong about this, the Judge could actually be feeling bad like she said. But if he went to take a look he'd risk having the doc start out, if he hadn't started out already. He went on dialing.

He could hear someone calling her from the café or the kitchen but she didn't answer. There was a throbbing noise, maybe the dishwasher.

"Dr. Adams' residence."

"Yeah, I–this is the Desert Winds Motel. We called you just a few minutes ago. Has the doc left there yet?"

"Yes he has."

"Are you sure?"

"Why, yes, at least his bag's gone from the–"

"See if his car's gone, will you?"

"Why, I–"

"Stop him if you can. I'm trying to save him the trip."

"Oh."

He waited, not looking at Rose, pulling out a cigarette, though he was trying to cut down, lighting it. He could hear a door slamming in the wind, on the line.

"*Hey Rose!*"

"For God's sake!" she called out, going through the swinging door. Guns were firing somewhere, a TV show. Horses screamed.

"This is Dr. Adams."

"Hello there, Doc. Listen, the young lady called you up about a friend of mine here because she thought he was taken bad, but–"

"Who're you?"

"The Desert Winds Motel–"

"Oh yes, now I got it."

"The thing is, he's not too bad, Doc–he strained his back,

and there's a bruise, but we don't have to call you out on a night like this, understand?"

"Well if you'll just make up your minds."

"It's too bad we troubled you, Doc, really. You stay right home and catch the ball game, huh?"

"Hell, no trouble. Listen, if you want me there, call me."

"Okay, Doc. I really appreciate that."

He leaned on the side of the makeshift booth for a minute after he'd hung up, letting it all go slow again, taking his time, drawing the smoke in, figuring what he would tell Rose. Then he lifted the suitcase and went along to Room 7, putting the key in quietly, inching the door open, looking down at him as the light fanned across the floor. He could see how Rose had felt, expecting to find the man on the bed instead of stretched out like this right at her feet.

He brought the suitcase in and then kneeled down, looking at the man's face in the light coming through the doorway, putting his hand inside his coat, listening to his breathing. He was alive, all right, and Charlie got onto his feet as he heard someone coming through the lobby, light footsteps, the squeak of sneakers on the linoleum. Then she was in the doorway, looking in, her face in shadow from the light behind.

"Charlie?" she whispered.

"Okay."

He was going to step over the man on the floor, but stopped, feeling you shouldn't step over people who were alive, and went around past his feet, bumping into the dressing table and hearing the drawer handles swinging.

"Do you have any codeine?"

Sudden heat flushed Charlie's skin as he heard the voice and it worried him to know how jumpy he was. He bent down quickly.

"Did you say codeine?"

"Yes."

"I'll go see. How're you feeling?"

"A lot of pain."

"I get a doctor?"

"No. Tomorrow"—he rolled his heavy head across the pillow, squeezing his eyes shut—"tomorrow I'll be okay. Don't do anything until tomorrow, is—is that understood?"

"Sure. I'll be right back, okay?"

Charlie stood up and went into the corridor, whispering to the girl, did she have any codeine? She'd go ask Pa. He pulled out his key and went into his own room, switching the light on, going to wash his hands, the touch of her leg on them, the cold stiff leg of Theodora Creaturo, the disgusting thing out there where the cactus stood against the sky.

"Charlie?"

He started again, and took a breath, going to the doorway. She didn't have any codeine, only some aspirin, and some stuff in a tube. He went back into Room 7, getting water and bending down.

"Aspirin any good?"

In a few seconds, "Yes."

"How many?"

"Four."

Rose came through the doorway and knelt down, holding the man's head forward; but he couldn't drink.

"Can you turn your—"

A spasm shot through him and they waited.

"Oh Charlie, we ought to—"

"Don't worry. He's okay."

She didn't say any more and after a time the Judge moved his head on one side, across the end of the pillow, and Charlie held the glass and he drank, some of the water dribbling away and puddling on the linoleum, shining in the light from the corridor. When he rolled his head back, Rose got some Kleenex, wiping his face and neck and putting some of the stuff in the tube onto the wound, the smell of antiseptic coming into the air as Charlie watched her. We'll look after you, she was saying quietly, you'll be okay, not knowing who she was talking to, Charlie thought, just talking to a man who'd dribbled the water down on the floor, not to the leading Republican gubernatorial candidate—what would she say, if she knew?

Charlie straightened up and put the glass on the dressing table, and they went together into the corridor.

"Charlie," she said, worried, "he needs—"

"He's okay. Listen, is there some place we can talk?"

"There's just the café, I guess."

"Who's in there?"

"They all went. Listen, Charlie," she whispered, "I want to know what's going on, okay? I mean it—I want to know why we can't get a doctor, with him on the floor like that and—"

"I'm going to tell you, Rose, but we have to talk somewhere. Does your pa keep any liquor?"

"Sure, but—"

"Listen, I need a drink, so be there in the café. I'll be a couple of minutes—and don't tell him anything."

"Pa?"

"Right."

"He wouldn't ever listen to anything I told him."

"Be there." He patted her arm.

When she'd gone he ducked into his own room and reached up and hit the button on the top of the vibrator alarm to deactivate it before he slid out the third case down on the right-hand side, the best one, the Casino Royal Collection with the twelve Simustone rings, nothing but the finest for Rose tonight, a lot could depend on her.

He reset the alarm and pulled the door shut after him, going along the passage and hearing the wind banging the sign out there and the throb of the dishwasher or whatever it was, working out what he'd say to her, and the way he'd say it.

She was there with a bottle of Old Crow and two glasses and some ice.

"When you do a thing," he said, the case under his arm, "you do it right." He couldn't see Pa in the hatch or anywhere.

She liked what he'd just said, and the anxiety went out of her eyes. He put the black simulated leather case on the table, sliding his fingertips across it and squaring it up the way he'd learned all those years ago when they said he could make a fortune in just ten lessons.

"Is that what you were going to show me?" she asked, trying not to sound too interested.

"This," he said quietly, "is what I was going to show you."

He let his long fingers play across the case a little before he flipped the catch and slowly raised the lid, watching her eyes as the light from the neon tubes in the ceiling began sparking on the rings. She was maybe twenty-four, twenty-five, but he could see her now as she'd been when she was very young, with her blue eyes coming wide like this, seeing the very first snowflake.

Softly she said, "Oh Charlie . . ."

They looked pretty good and if he'd wanted to make a sale he could have pitched for fifty bucks just for the Princess Grace alone and got it without any pain.

"I invest in them," he said.

"You mean you"–she looked up at his face–"I don't understand."

"World currencies are on the skids, see. The dollar, the pound sterling, the French franc, even–" but she wasn't listening, her eyes going down to the dazzle of stones against the black velvet. "I just mean with gems like these you don't have to worry about the future."

In a while she looked up again.

"Are they real?"

He looked puzzled. "How's that again?"

Uncertainly she said, "Are they real?"

He looked disappointed in her, maybe wondering if he'd been right in deciding to show her this collection at all.

"Rose, haven't you ever heard of Simustones?"

She shook her head, feeling a little stupid.

He shrugged philosophically. "You probably think that when famous celebrities, people like Elizabeth Taylor and Jackie Onassis, wear jewels at those fabulous parties, they're wearing the real thing? I guess a lot of people do–I don't blame you, Rose. But if you think about it you'll realize that the insurance companies wouldn't allow it, because–"

"But it always says in the papers–"

"Oh sure." He gave a knowing smile. "It's good publicity, and people like to read things like that. But the truth is that these Simustone gems have been created to protect their owners from the risk of huge financial loss, understand? They look so much like the original stones that only an experienced jeweler could detect the difference, yet their cost is only a fraction–though of course they're still quite expensive." He looked around, lowering his tone. "What you are looking at, Rose, is the Casino Royal Collection. It's from collections of this quality that movie stars choose the jewelry they intend wearing in public. As a matter of fact, connoisseurs like myself, who know this, refer to them as 'the stones of the stars,' but only in private of course–the expression is too vulgar for use by the wrong people."

She was only half listening, but he'd said it so many times that it kind of ran on by itself while he watched her, thinking again that she was maybe of Scandinavian stock, with her straw-yellow hair and honey-colored skin, the long fair lashes half hiding her eyes, the reflection of the rings throwing spangles of light against her face. He watched her without feeling the contempt he usually had for the women who stared at this kind of junk like it was the crown jewels while he pitched them the spiel and screwed the last buck out of their handbag. Maybe it was because he wasn't trying to sell anything to this baby.

"You mean," she said, looking up, "that people like Elizabeth Taylor wear rings like these?"

"Exactly like these."

She blew out a breath, laughing. "It's just too much!"

"They have this effect on people," he told her quietly, "as I know from experience, when I've shown them to exclusive friends. Simustones are handcrafted, artistically created, high-fidelity reproductions of the most priceless minerals ever to be artifacted by man." He leaned forward, lowering his voice again. "Rose, I'm going to ask you to do something for me. I'm going to ask you to choose any one of these rings and wear it on your finger, for your very own."

As she stared up at him he could see it all there in her eyes: Was he hoping to lay her? It couldn't be that—he hadn't even made a pass at her tonight. Did he go around giving away fabulous jewelry to every girl he met? He didn't look that crazy. Maybe she'd gotten it wrong.

"Will you please say that again?"

"I want you to pick one of these rings, as a present from me."

"But I—I couldn't do that, Charlie!"

"There aren't any strings. Believe me."

"But I don't understand. I mean they're so—"

"Okay, I know it's difficult for you, with these stones the value they are. Let's say it's by way of apology."

"What did you do?"

"I'll tell you later." He leaned forward a little more. "Right now I want the pleasure of seeing you make your choice."

She laughed again, and said again, "It's too much!"

"Not for a girl like you."

He squeaked the cork out of the bottle of Old Crow and poured a double shot for each of them over the rocks but she wasn't aware of what he was doing because she'd suddenly settled for this whole crazy thing—a guy walks in out of the night and offers her a fabulous ring just like in a fairy story and dammit she was going to take it!

He began on the whiskey, needing it, this girl reminding him of the other one out there, the one who'd been a much better looker till she was turned into a disgusting thing on the ground it made you sick to touch, the wind whining through the phone cables and her all alone and not hearing, Theodora Creaturo, the dead end of a car ride. He watched Rose, thinking how alive she looked, and wondering *what is it that the other one doesn't have anymore, what have we got inside of us that we can lose just as easy as that, is it some kind of a flame, some kind of a vibration?*

She was looking at the left side of the case most, up and down with her eyes, up and down, her raw pink hands clenched together on the edge of the table, finger-size seven or eight, be okay if she chose the Raja Ruby or the White Marquise or the Florentine Cluster, save the hassle of having to alter it for her, what would she do with that bit of crud she had on her finger right now, throw it away? He bet she'd throw it away, better than even money, sixty-forty.

The ice was chilling the palm of his hand through the glass and he listened for sounds as he waited, wanting to know everything he could about this place. He couldn't hear a TV on anywhere, so Pa must have his room at the other end of the building; he knew Pa spent his life with his eyes glued to the thing. The dishwasher was churning in the kitchen out there through the hatch, and apart from that there was only the wind banging the sign, every bang another bang nearer the day when the whole damn thing came down and brained some bastard. It wasn't going to be him: he had the distinct feeling he'd be a long way from here, a hell of a long way, and very soon.

"Charlie?" she said, her voice soft and kind of humble.

"Yes?"

"Are you sure you mean it?"

"Dead sure, baby."

Looking very solemn, she pointed with one finger. "I'd like this one, then."

Charlie smiled.

"A ruby for a Rose. You know something? That's the one I guessed you'd choose."

"It is?" She laughed delightedly.

"Sure it is. It goes the best with your fair coloring—that's always important, and obviously you have instinctive good taste."

"Well, I don't know—"

"Go ahead and take it. What're you going to do with that old one?"

"This thing?" She tugged it off, leaving a ring of verdigris on her finger. "Throw it out with the garbage, I guess." She put it on the tin tray and looked at him again and hesitated and said, "I don't like kind of—"

"Okay." He picked out the Raja Ruby and took her left hand, slipping it onto her second finger, turning it until it was perfectly straight and then spreading her hand flat on his own and tilting it to catch the light; it was always the older ones, the widows, who liked this best, the younger ones thought you were trying to get fresh. "Looks beautiful, doesn't it?"

"Beautiful," she nodded, looking nowhere else, only at the ring. "But I just don't know how I can thank you." Then she heard what she'd just said, and thought about it. "I—I mean you said there weren't any strings."

"That's absolutely right."

She took her hand away from his, still keeping it flat and tilting it in the light, watching the glow of the stone.

"You said it was a sort of apology." She looked at him with sudden directness. "Will you tell me now what you did?"

The first step, he thought, had been when he'd given in to the Judge about calling a doctor. The second step had been when he'd got back here and hadn't called the police to tell them about Theodora Creaturo. The third step would be when he told Rose what he was going to tell her, deliberately involving her in this thing that didn't have any real shape yet, except in his mind. Of course there'd still be time to pull out, this side of the morning, time to cut and run. But as he took this third step he found himself lighting a cigarette without even thinking about it first, because of the uneasy feeling that with each step he was going in deeper, and a little too fast.

"Sure," he said, "I'll tell you."

CHAPTER FOUR

THE MAN ON THE FLOOR was moving, though nobody saw, because he was alone. Even here in the desert the night was still warm as the Santa Ana wind scoured the valleys, and the man felt the heavy air come blowing under the door and against his face.

He was moving his hand, bringing it out of the blanket and covering his eyes, as if there were light in here. He lay like that for a long time, with his thoughts drifting through the ebb and flow of consciousness as the shock-aftermath and the aspirin combined to keep him in twilight sleep, and his fears dragged him, time after time, awake. Often he saw Evelyn, looking at him as if for the first time in her life and this time seeing him for what he was. And because she had never looked at him like this, her own face was strange and he didn't easily recognize it, and he wondered how they could have lived so long together as companionable strangers. These were the images, drifting through the coming and going of consciousness, that he couldn't take, and this was why he had drawn his hand across his eyes in an unreasoning attempt to shut out sight.

Sometimes he saw Barnes Morgan, his short strong figure moving energetically onto the platform, the suddenly flashing grin as the applause began, his lifted hand bringing immediate silence: *You've heard John K. Stevens and now you're going to hear me, and the first thing I want to tell you is that he's a friend of mine and that's the biggest compliment*

I can pay any man, getting the laughter, cutting it short, *but the second thing I want to tell you is that I would make a damned-sight better governor.*

Sudden pain needling into his skull and a blue-white flash of light behind his eyes, then dreams again, with Ashley's pale and watchful face floating close to him, *and always remember, John, he'll never say a word against you, right through this campaign, but don't you ever turn your back on him or you'll feel the knife go in.*

John? Other faces, other voices, coming and going through the numbing half-world of his waking sleep, *John darling, where are you?* The heavy warmth of the wind below the door, brushing past his face, *Kenny, I want you, oh Kenny,* her eyes staring like that as she screamed, and the choking smell of the gasoline, one of the wheels still spinning, *don't leave me for dead,* coming away, the draft on his face from under the door, a noise somewhere, of banging, a door in the wind, the sweat cold on him as he lay with his head on fire.

Moments of extreme lucidity, more terrible than all the nightmares, as he realized that it was all over suddenly and there wasn't anything he could do to bring it back. He knew it was getting late because he had looked at his watch a few minutes ago when it had said five before ten, so Evelyn would be worried by now because he never returned later than eight on a Sunday evening when the court was in session, so that he'd rise early on Monday morning, fresh in his mind. At a few minutes after eight she would have started worrying, knowing his rigid habit of joining her for Sunday dinner, no matter what.

Pain again, and then restlessness, difficult to breathe, the strong dark face of Barnes Morgan as he listened at the telephone, *Indian Rock? Where the hell is that?* The thick brows gathering as he concentrated, at first disbelieving, *he was with who?* and finally exulting as his aide on the other end of the line gave him the whole story, *okay listen, get Stein and get Lombardi and tell Mike to handle the press, shock and dismay, he'll know the line. Whatever the initial police inquiry brings to light we'll crucify Stevens and leave him hanging there in front of the electorate. And Nicky, not a word against him, understand? Just a note of righteous consternation, you get the message. Boy, what a break!*

A period of calm and the sense of time passing; perhaps he had slept a little, his mind clearer for it and dwelling on a certain case, sordid and banal but a perfect example for his theme in the second chapter of his book *Dilemma in Jurisprudence*. "I should like here to exemplify my contention that events are essentially occasioned by circumstance. In the case just quoted we have a man and his wife in their kitchen, the woman cutting the bread for their meal. As their argument becomes impassioned she seizes the knife, scarcely knowing what she is doing, and wounds her spouse mortally. Now I am saying no more, and no less, than this: Had there been no argument, or had the argument taken place in the bedroom, or had the woman been stirring some soup instead of cutting the bread in the kitchen, or had the bread been already sliced before packaging, this critical event could not have occurred, and the life of this unfortunate man might have been extended by years, or even decades. It can be said that this is obvious, and I agree; but since the weight of circumstance bears infinitely the more significantly upon all our lives than does the weight of events, it seems inarguable that the repercussions throughout the field of jurisprudence are far-reaching."

Panic came and he thought wildly that it couldn't have happened, that it hadn't happened, that he'd been on some other road, on some other night, with some other companion. Then he knew that it had happened, and was made to know that the horror of being trapped by circumstance was as claustrophobic as that of being trapped by bars. Shivering with cold he felt the trickle of sweat on his skin and wanted to call out, but pride stopped him. Later there was some relief and the fever abated and he lay in the dark with his eyes open, watching the splinter of light through the crack of the door and listening to the wind's moaning, thinking again of the man who had brought him here. He needed to talk to that man, urgently.

He began shouting but there wasn't any strength in his voice, and he tried harder, till the blue-white light was flashing again behind his eyes, the pain rising and roaring louder than he could, and the dark knocking him down.

"Sorry, I—"

"It's okay, but I don't smoke anyway. Not those."

"You on pot?"

"Only when I get low."

"A girl like you shouldn't have to get low about anything."

"Oh God," she said, "this place. Yuck."

He put the pack down flat and tapped on it with his long lively fingers and she wondered if he was always like this, kind of vibrating with something inside, like a taut string.

"It isn't doing too well?"

"This place?" She gave a lopsided laugh. "You kidding?"

He looked around at the peeling paint and the missing light tubes and the jukebox with its "out of order" notice stuck across the glass, and she knew what he was thinking: This was the kind of place that made you wonder how the hell it kept going, then a week later you come past and see it's shut down.

"Was it your ma going?"

"How d'you mean, was it my—oh, right. It was different when she was here." She looked at him wonderingly. "How did you know that, Charlie?"

"I thought it figured."

"Gee, are you clairvoyant?"

"Who, me?" He gave a jerky smile, his eyes bright, flicking around at things. "Don't you get any help?"

"What kind of—oh sure. Couple of kids come in, mornings, but you know what they ask for? Three bucks an hour, in a place like Indian Rock!"

He pushed her glass toward her with his long thin fingers. She liked to watch his hands, they kind of danced when they did things, like when he'd opened the jewel case just now, gliding over it, flipping the catch.

"Here's to you, Rose."

"Sure. You too."

As she lifted her glass she saw the reflection of the ruby in it, right through the ice and everything, as if it were a dull red flame. She couldn't wait for tomorrow, for the customers to see it on her hand!

"You shouldn't have to work in this kind of place," he said.

"Great. But I do."

"How long have you–"

"Charlie," she said.

"Yeah?"

"You said you'd tell me."

His eyes went kind of nervy again and the smile got brighter and she thought no, he couldn't always be this way, he'd never stand the strain.

"Sure, Rose. I'll tell you." He flicked ash off and some of it fell on the jewel case and he blew it away, moving the case to where it wouldn't get any more ash, doing it slowly. It got her impatient.

"You said there was something you did, Charlie, you had to apologize for."

"Sure." He leaned a bit more toward her, folding his arms on the table, talking low. "It was having to stall you like I did, when we got in here, that guy and me. Remember?"

"I didn't know you were stalling about anything."

"Well I guess it seemed a little crazy, you know? I wanted to call a doctor, and he didn't, then you called one and I–well, you know, him in there on the floor and everything. I told you I didn't know who he was, remember?" He dragged on his cigarette, keeping the smoke away from her, a real gent, thrilling her in a small way because there weren't too many gents in Indian Rock. "Well I know who he is, all right."

He'd stopped smiling and she felt herself staring at him, waiting, because of the way he'd said it, quiet and slow. She couldn't wait any longer.

"Who?"

"He's someone important, Rose. I mean he's someone so important I can't even tell you."

"But you—"

"Listen," and he held her hands, mashing the cigarette out on the tin tray and bringing his hand back to hers and looking at her very straight. "I had to stall you, before, because I didn't know anything about you. Now I know enough to trust you. I think you're the kind of girl who can keep her—keep quiet about things when you know they're important. I really feel I can rely on you, see, and that's why I felt so mean, before, stalling you that way." He touched the ruby with his fingertip. "I'm glad you've accepted my apology."

She didn't say anything for a bit because of the way he was watching her, his brown eyes kind of glowing and not like a stranger's, and she was trying to think, too, why he'd had to give her a fabulous ring like this, just because he'd—

"But you'll have to understand a few things, Rose. This man is so important I still can't tell you his name. All I can tell you is that I'm his top aide, and that—"

"His what?"

"You know what an aide is?"

"Oh, you mean the people generals take around with—"

"Generals and other men of high standing. He—"

"Is he a—"

"No. He's a civilian, but in very high office. And what happened, Rose, is very simple. There was an accident, like I told you, and we—"

"Was it an auto accident?"

He looked down, and she knew he didn't want to talk

about that. She didn't know how she could wait for him to go on, because there was a kind of breathlessness starting inside her, like the little thrill when he'd waved the smoke away from her with his hand, but much bigger, and getting bigger all the time because she couldn't really believe what was happening—she'd been thinking Charlie might be someone like Howard Hughes or a famous producer or someone and now he was telling her the man in there was so important and everything, it was too much!

"I've told you I'm going to trust you," he said, pressing her hands to make her know he meant it, "but there are things I'm not going to tell you because I don't want you to have the responsibility on your mind, see? I don't know if we're going to be able to keep the reporters away from this place, and—"

"You mean—*reporters?*"

"Well, sure. You have to believe me, Rose—he's a very important man." He looked surprised that she didn't understand.

On a breath she said, "It's okay for you, Charlie, I mean you're used to this kind of thing. I just need to get my balance, is all."

"Sure, I understand that." He pressed her hands again. "The thing is, there was a little accident somewhere tonight and I had to get him to a safe place so he could recover, without a whole bunch of people around, you with me?"

"Yeah, I—"

"Okay, well, that was why he didn't want me to call a doctor. Naturally I felt the terrible responsibility, I mean the risk of complications, specially with a back injury, but"—he smiled ruefully—"he's the kind of guy who tells you to do something and you do it, you know, the greatest boss I ever had. He can feel there's nothing seriously wrong, and I guess he thought that if a doctor came and maybe recognized him from the papers or the TV or somewhere, the word would soon get around."

She was thinking right away about how the man had

looked when he came into the motel, with his thick mass of steel-gray hair and his big looks, not so much big in size but sort of commanding, standing there with his eyes red from the sand and with blood on his face, telling them not to phone, it wasn't anything serious.

"You know something, Charlie?" She felt the breathlessness again. "The minute I saw him come in here tonight I thought, now *where* have I seen that guy before!"

"Uh-huh? Well it's natural."

"I suppose it is, but it—it's kind of amazing too, don't you think? Well I know *you* don't think so but I—" she had to laugh although there wasn't anything funny, it was just to kind of let all the breath out, this whole thing was really too much.

"Is Pa in bed?" He took his hands away and lit another cigarette, his thin fingers moving sort of calculatedly, like a conjurer's.

"Oh sure." She looked across at the Koffee King clock that hung crooked above the hatch. "He's up at six every morning to go get the provisions from Morales."

"Thirty miles away?"

"Yeah."

"Isn't there a store at Indian Rock?"

"Only one. Ma used to go there but after she—when Pa took over he spit'n the man's eye over a ten-cent hike in his price for bread so now he goes sixty miles every day to get the bread cheaper, does that make any sense?"

Charlie was laughing again in that way of his, crinkling his eyes up and not making any sound. "I like your pa, you know that?"

She tried to see Pa as other people saw him, but they didn't have to scrape the hash browns out of the pan with the flames still on them, "hash blacks" Bob Dawson called them—*Hey Rosie, your pa got any hash blacks ready for me?*—and flushing the can after him every time because for sixty years he'd gotten used to a backyard privy, and picking up his dirty clothes off the floor because he said that was what women were for, people didn't know Pa the way she did.

"Oh, he's okay," she said, because her first pa had been a shit.

"We don't have to tell him anything, Rose."

"Who, Pa? Oh, you mean about him in there?"

"Yes."

"We sure better hadn't. He'd say it wasn't regular. Either we know the guy's name and address or he doesn't stay here, that's what he'd say." She thought for a bit, looking down at the ruby and the way it seemed to throw out a deep red light on the table when she turned it sideways. "Charlie?" She looked up at him. "You wouldn't be conning me, would you?"

He didn't say anything right off, but sat staring at her, kind of puzzled. "What was that?"

"I mean"—wishing she hadn't said it—"this thing's on the level, isn't it?"

He'd gone very quiet and it made her feel terrible, with this beautiful ring on her hand, and then asking him if he was a con man! How did she ever—

"I wish it wasn't on the level, Rose. I—"

"Charlie, I didn't mean—"

"I understand. Believe me, I understand. But I just wish I *was* trying to con you, for some reason, because this thing's hit me pretty hard and I wasn't ready for it. I have to make sure he gets enough proper rest, make sure he gets back on his feet okay without any doctor nosing around, and I have to keep the reporters away when people in Los Angeles start asking where the Chief has gone—that's what I call him, see. It's—"

"Sure, Charlie, I—"

"It's known in high places that he travels incognito now and again, just private visits to private friends, usually with his wife or one of his lawyers or one of his top aides, like me; but when something like this happens we have to get on to the situation very fast and—"

"Forget I ever said it, Charlie. Please." The more he had to explain, the more awful she felt.

"Okay," he said with his quick smile.

"I'll do everything I can to help. Really."

"I know you will." He looked serious again, stubbing out his cigarette, doing it carefully, watching till the last of the smoke had gone, like he was having trouble with what he was going to say next. "And that reminds me, Rose. I don't want you or your pa to get this wrong, because I mean you're running a fine little independent business here and—well, the Chief's going to want me to arrange for compensation, when he's left here. I thought I should tell you."

He was looking a bit embarrassed and she wanted to put him at his ease but she wasn't too sure what he meant.

"I don't understand, Charlie."

"What I mean is, the Chief and I are going to cause you quite a bit of inconvenience, having to keep him away from the public gaze and—well, you know—holding reporters off when they come snooping around, that sort of thing. I'm just telling you he'll want to compensate you for all that, by a cash offer. You don't have to think about it now, because there'll be—"

They both listened, but it didn't come again.

"You sure your pa's in bed?"

"Oh yes, but—"

"Does he look at the television when he—"

"The sound wouldn't be on. He's—"

Before she could finish he got up and went through the swinging door, quiet and quick like a cat, and she followed him across the lobby and along the passage to Room 7. There wasn't any light inside but she could see him bending over the man on the floor—the "Chief." She went in and crouched down too, worried, keeping out of the light that came in from the passage so they could see the man's face.

"He's okay," Charlie whispered. He sounded relieved.

"He's sweating."

"Sure, but he's okay."

He got up and they went out, closing the door quietly and going to the lobby so they could talk without having to whisper.

"Are there any TVs in the other rooms?"

"No. Just the kitchen and the café. I guess it must've been Pa, yelling in his sleep. He does that."

"I'm glad you mentioned it." He gave a quick smile but she could see he was worried about the Chief. "Is there only the two of you alone here, nights?"

"Except for the guests."

"Don't you have a dog?"

"Pa kicks them and they won't ever stay, but I have a shotgun and I don't sleep heavy, and he has a whole armory in his room." She heard the dishwasher cut off in the kitchen. "Where are you going to sleep, Charlie?"

"In with the Chief, in case he wants anything."

"Poor Charlie."

"Who me? I'm fine." But his smile was kind of jerky and she knew he was more worried about the Chief than he wanted her to see.

"If you need anything, give a knock on my door," she told him, "it's that room through there, marked *Private*. Did you keep the aspirin?"

"Sure."

"I'm going to tell Pa to get some codeine when he goes to Morales in the morning."

"You could do that." He got his wallet and took out a five but she shook her head because he was the most generous man she'd ever known, and she just couldn't imagine taking money from him, just for a small thing like codeine.

She said, "I'll put it on the check."

"Okay. Will I disturb you if I use the phone later?"

She shook her head—"Use it whenever you want."

He nodded. "Sleep well," he said.

"You bet." She looked at her hand, turning it slowly till the light burned red on the ring. "It's beautiful, Charlie. It's just too much." She kissed his face, surprising him, and went along to her room, leaving the door ajar and hearing him go into the café and help himself to more whiskey. Then he came back past, very quiet, and went into 7, hardly making any noise at all with the door, and then there was only the faraway banging of the sign in the wind outside.

He stood for a minute in the faint light streaming through the doorway, looking down at the Judge, the whiskey in his hand. Then he put the glass on the dressing table and went into the bathroom, fetching a hand towel and draping it around the lamp over the bed, switching it on and pulling the towel up a little more till there was only a glow in the room. Then he shut the door, pushing the extra-security lock home.

There was only one other thing he had to do but he'd wait for an hour till Rose was asleep. Loosening his necktie and dropping onto the bed, he thought of her, wishing things had been different tonight, or wishing she'd been different, some kind of a bitch who would have taken that piece of junk without any question, knowing he was conning her but not caring, so long as she finished up getting the whole box. With Rose it had been like giving candy to a kid. Christ, how did she manage to stay so innocent, running a dump like this?

Or maybe he'd got it wrong and she'd imagined he'd just been setting her up for a lay, and she was in there taking the pill and waiting for him. If so, there wasn't going to be any action, she wasn't his type. Okay, a lot of guys would go for her but she was too young and innocent; it'd be like stealing something from a kid, kind of. He liked them when they'd gotten to the age when they'd stopped showing their navel to a bunch of truck drivers and then kicking them on the shin every time they tried to pinch her ass.

He lay listening to the wind, feeling alone, even with the Judge right here in the room, feeling more alone than he'd ever felt before in the whole of his life, because he was going into something so new that it had him scared.

When he'd finished the whiskey, he lit a cigarette and thought about the man lying here on the floor and the woman lying out there in the wreck and went over the whole thing in his mind again, about what he should do, and what he shouldn't do, and what he was going to do. The picture hadn't changed very much because there were still things he didn't know and would have to find out, and in an hour he got off the bed and crouched down by the Judge and listened to his breathing and heard how steady it was, quiet but steady, and stood up and pulled back the security lock and went out, shutting the door and going along to the lobby.

There was a night-light burning above the phone and he dropped a dime in and dialed for Directory Information Nevada. While he was waiting he pulled out the driver's license and read the name and address.

"Information, can I help you?"

"Yes, I'd like the number for this person: Theodora Creaturo."

He had to spell it.

"What city?"

"Las Vegas."

She gave him the number and he put some quarters in.

CHAPTER FIVE

Hello?"

It was a woman's voice.

"Can I speak to Theodora, please?"

"Who is it?"

"I'm a friend of hers."

There was music in the background, and a lot of voices.

"That's funny, all her friends call her Theo."

"Well I haven't met her too many times."

She didn't say anything. Some people were laughing rather loud and it sounded like she was cupping the mouthpiece for a minute to talk to someone. Then the background came in again, but she still didn't say anything.

"Is Theo there with you?" Charlie asked.

"Who're you, friend?"

"You wouldn't know me."

He didn't want to give her a name because he didn't know if Rose was asleep yet or if her door was shut.

"Why don't we do something about that?" the woman asked him, and gave a low laugh.

"That's a great idea. Who do I ask for?"

"Marcia."

"At this number?"

There was some more laughter and she turned away from the phone, calling to somebody—"Tell him he should've grabbed her keys!"—or it sounded like that. Then she said on the line, "What was that?"

"Sounds like a good party you've got going there, Marcia."

"The greatest."

"I'm beginning to feel kind of left out of things. Can I get you at this number anytime?"

"Most times. If I'm not here, she'll take the message."

"Who?"

"Theo."

But it was a lousy party anyway, with everyone laughing their goddamn heads off, and she kept falling down and when he tried to help her up he found her leg was stiff and cold and she kept screaming at him and then it was dark, just a glow, and he felt his tongue in his mouth and the guy was kind of looming right over him, a huge man and very slow and Charlie said out loud, *Oh Jesus Christ!* and got off the bed and spun onto his feet with his scalp tight as he watched him.

"Judge! Y'okay? Judge?"

"Yes."

He kept on, very slow, to the bathroom, walking like he was asleep, holding himself stiff because of his back. Oh Jesus, Charlie said in his mind, finding his cigarettes and lighting up, the flame of the match blinding and leaving flashes when he blinked. The Judge had come past the bed, that was all, on his way to the bathroom, and he'd looked down at Charlie, waking him up, the way he was shuffling. Now he was using the john, and Charlie pulled the smoke in deep, feeling it bite, feeling the shake of his hand as he took the cigarette from his mouth and rested it in the lip of the ashtray, picking up the blanket from the floor, throwing the pillow back on the bed and spreading the blanket out, smoothing it flat.

He hadn't been ready for this. The Judge had been just a thing on the floor for a long time, something you had to step around and not disturb, and now he was back in the action and all those things Charlie had been saying to him in his mind would have to be said for real.

Stevens was cleaning up in there now and he waited, dragging on the cigarette, listening to the pressure go banging along the pipes as the man used the taps. Then there was silence while he dried himself, and after a bit the door came open and Charlie said:

"Good to see you back on your feet, Judge."

"Thank you."

He held himself very straight, taking care not to bend his neck, pulling the blanket back and propping the pillow on end, lowering himself to the edge of the bed and swinging his legs around, pulling the blanket up—"I can manage, thank you."

"Okay," Charlie said, and dropped into the chair, putting his feet on the end of the bed with his legs crossed, feeling the bruise on his shin where he'd caught it on the rocks down there in the ravine.

Stevens had taken off his expensive silk necktie and left it in the bathroom, and his thick hair was darker at the sides now, slicked back, wet from washing his face. He leaned against the pillow, his hooded eyes closed.

"I get you anything?" Charlie asked.

"No. But I'd appreciate it if you wouldn't smoke in here."

"Sure." He went over and ground the butt out in the ashtray, coming back to the chair.

"It makes me cough, and I have to keep still. Do you mind telling me your name?"

"Berlatsky."

"Have you ever seen me before, Mr. Berlatsky?"

Charlie saw suddenly that Stevens was watching him in the dim light, his dark eyes heavy and unblinking.

"I guess I haven't."

The man on the bed reached inside his coat and took out the wallet, holding it up in front of his eyes so he didn't have to bend his neck while he checked the money and the other things. Then he put the wallet back.

"I had to find out who you were, Judge."

"Of course. I would have done the same thing."

Charlie was sitting up a little straighter now because Stevens had noticed how he'd called him "Judge," and he'd realized there were only two ways for Charlie to know who he was, and one of them was by looking at his driver's license in the wallet.

"You had me worried, see. I didn't know how bad you'd got hurt and I thought I might have to call somebody."

"I understand, yes." He was quiet again for a while. "Did you go back and look for my car, Mr. Berlatsky?"

He'd seen his suitcase by the dressing table: that was the other way how Charlie could have known who he was, by checking the stuff in it.

"Yes I did."

"Why?"

"Listen, you said I had to look after you, remember? So I had to find out everything I could about you because I didn't know what the hell was going on, see."

"Thank you for bringing my case here."

"You're welcome." Charlie got up and went over to the dressing table and picked up the pack of Kents and remembered and put it down again, shoving his hands into his pants pockets. This wasn't the way he'd meant things to go: the man was throwing him questions like he was on the stand or something.

"Did you examine the contents of my case, Mr. Berlatsky?"

Charlie didn't answer right off—let the man wait. He saw the bottle of aspirins had gone from the dressing table, so Stevens must have seen it there when he'd gotten off the floor, and taken it into the bathroom. For someone living on aspirins he was managing to think straight enough.

"I went through the whole thing, Judge."

"Why?"

Charlie swung on him. "You better wise up, hadn't you? How do you think it looked to me, the way you were acting? Dead on your feet out of an auto crash and all you wanted was a motel instead of a hospital, didn't want a doctor, telling me we had to look after each other—or don't you remember the way it was when we hit this dump last night?" He stopped and turned away and said to himself he'd better cool down, play it slow. It was just that he was scared because when he'd come away from that phone in the lobby he'd finally known what he was going to do.

Stevens wasn't making it too easy. He wasn't just something on the floor anymore, he was sitting up in the bed and throwing questions just like he was a—well, that's right—like he was a judge.

"What time is it, please?"

"Huh? A quarter to two."

"Thank you."

Charlie came back to the chair but he didn't put his feet on the bed like he'd done before. Stevens had his eyes closed again and there was fresh blood oozing down his face because when he'd washed up in there he'd opened the wound again, and Charlie got up and found some Kleenex but Stevens didn't open his eyes and he had the feeling he oughtn't to disturb him till he did open them because he wasn't looking so good with his white face and the way he had to keep so still.

"It's time I thanked you, Mr. Berlatsky, for helping me, when my car left the road. I might well have needed immediate assistance."

"That's okay." He put the box of Kleenex on the bed where Stevens could reach them. "Your face is bleeding again, you better do something."

"That's good of you, yes." But he didn't move. After a time he said, "That was an unpleasant experience for you, finding my car." His massive head was turned a little on the pillow and he was watching Charlie.

"I've seen wrecks before," Charlie said. They looked at each other in the dim light. "And I've seen dead people."

A sound came out of Stevens, a kind of grunt, as if someone's fist had gone into his stomach, and it was a couple of minutes before he spoke again. "You must have wanted to call the police, and report the accident."

"Sure."

"Why didn't you?"

"How d'you know I didn't?"

"They would have come here."

"Anyway," Charlie said, "I'm going to call them pretty soon."

"Are you?"

"Well, I have to." He let a couple of seconds go by. "Don't I?"

Stevens closed his eyes and didn't say anything and after a while Charlie had to get up and walk around because that had been one of the things he'd meant to say to the judge and now he'd said it and it hadn't been too bad. It was having to wait for the answer that bothered him because it had to be yes or no, one or the other, and the whole thing hung on it, the whole of the beautiful goddamn scary thing.

The man still didn't answer and he couldn't stand the silence anymore so he picked up his cigarettes and went out of the room and along to the café, lighting up, hungry for smoke, pacing up and down between the tables in the bluish light coming from the tube over the ice-cream bin, listening to it buzz and feeling lonely and afraid, wondering what the hell he was doing here, one man, just one man, alone and walking up and down in a goddamn café in a beat-up motel in the middle of the night with his nerves in his stomach. How the hell did he get here, how did it happen? Some guy's voice, not here in this dump but out of the past, Sam Goldstein's, *well you know Charlie, don't you,* the green shade over his face and his eyes screwed up into little bright slits to keep the smoke out of them, *he won't ever call till he gets the ace,* dropping his ash and starting that wheezy cackle, *but oh brother, when he gets that ace in his hands he'll bet the whole o' the roll!* The hell with Sam, he's got nothing to do with this.

The sign was banging out there and he wondered why Rose didn't do something about it, tell her Pa to fix it, or one of those truck drivers; bang in the wind, bang till it got on your nerves. Okay, Berlatsky, you better straighten yourself out because this thing's only just beginning and it's going to get a hell of a lot worse; now start relaxing.

She'd left everything on the tray here and he took the cork out of the Old Crow and hooked the few small pebbles of ice out of the water in the jug and used her glass, feeling the stuff burn on his tongue. She'd left the ring here on the tray, the old one, and he picked it up, feeling the roughness of the scratched metal alloy, a piece of crud, it was a piece of crap; throwing it down, oh Christ I've got to go back in there, go through with it. You have to go through with it, Berlatsky, because you've got the ace, this time, the ace in your hand.

He left most of the whiskey, mashing the cigarette out and going quietly back through the swinging door, passing the phone in the shadows—*That's funny, all her friends call her Theo*—the sweat prickling on his skin as he went on down the passage.

The man's dark eyes were open, watching him come in.

"I needed a smoke, Judge. Guess they have me hooked."

"It gave me time to think."

Charlie sat in the chair, one leg raised, the ankle across his other knee, very relaxed.

"I have to call them," he said, "don't I?"

"The police?"

"Sure. I mean there's been a death."

He waited again but it wasn't so bad this time. He was going to hang in there, and it didn't make any difference how long it took. Stevens was still watching him, his head turned a little on the pillow.

"I didn't know the road," he said slowly. "I thought there was a curve ahead of me, then I couldn't see anything, because of the sand. I expect you know this road better than I do, Mr. Berlatsky, don't you?"

"Pretty well, I guess."

"Do you often stay here, at this motel?"

"First time I ever did. It isn't my style."

"I would imagine not. You seem the kind of man to have quite a rewarding position."

"You think so?"

"I come to know people rather well, in my profession."

"Then you're way out this time, Judge. Listen, you don't have to fool around—just gimme the questions and I'll answer those I want to, okay?"

"You'll understand that you have me at a disadvantage, Mr. Berlatsky—"

"Sure, but you go ahead. Just to make it easy for you I'll say my 'rewarding position' is selling junk jewelry and it gets me enough to live on providing I don't actually eat or anything. Take it from there."

Stevens turned his head away slightly and closed his eyes, quiet for a minute, maybe getting his strength again, his face very pale, some Kleenex sticking to the gash in his cheek.

"You have a wife?"

"Nope."

"Close friends?"

"You mean girl friends?"

"Not necessarily. Anyone you would trust with your last dollar."

"Hell no!"

"Anyone you would confide in, or go to in time of trouble."

Charlie thought about this, and didn't come up with anyone.

"I guess not. And I never realized. Isn't that awful?"

"It simply means you have an independent nature."

"Great."

"Have you always held down this particular job?"

"Sure." He got out of the chair again, not used to having a lot of questions thrown at him: it made you feel you were a kind of sitting target. "Except you don't exactly 'hold down' a job like that, you just have to hang in there and hope for a break now and then. I've sold just about everything there is—pantyhose, ball bearings, tropical fish, contraceptives, you name it, I've sold it."

"That kind of work," Stevens said, "is obviously congenial to you."

"Are you kidding?" He stopped walking around and stood looking down at him. "You knock on the door and put on a real big smile and when they open up you take your hat off and keep the smile right there while they look at you like the cat puked you up on the doormat, then you go through the spiel you've been through a dozen times today, fifty times maybe, and all they say is they'll have to ask their husband and you're back on the road with a flea in your ass and the time's going by, Judge, see what I mean? It takes time, they kind of eat it out of your day and it doesn't cost 'em a buck, and when the lights come on, you look in your wallet and count it up, and most of the time it doesn't take you long. And the next day it's the same, know what I mean?"

He didn't even know if the guy was listening: he had his eyes shut again.

"But you meet people, and—"

"Oh sure. That's why I don't have any friends—I'm so goddamn busy trying to sell 'em something I don't ever get to know them."

There was another silence and he took a few paces and looked at himself in the mirror over the dressing table and thought Christ you look scared, Berlatsky, and went and sat in the chair again.

"Have you ever been in trouble with the police?"

"Who, me? I'm too smart for that. I don't mean I get away with anything, I just mean I keep my nose clean because you don't have any trouble that way. I guess that's kind of new to you, isn't it Judge? The only people you get to see are the ones who've dropped themselves in the shit, one way or another, right?"

"We all tend to do that, Mr. Berlatsky. Some of us are more successful at it than others. Do you smell burning?"

"Smell what? Oh Jesus!"

He got out of the chair fast and pulled the towel away from the lamp, but bits of it were stuck there, getting brown. The room was very bright now and the lamp was directly above the judge and Charlie looked down at him and saw for the first time what this man was going through, with his white face kind of sucked inward by pain, the bright sweat and the dark blood and the purple-looking hollows under his eyes, lying here with it all on his mind, inside this head here, this skull on the pillow, the blinding sand and the sickening drop and the smash and finally the other thing. Quietly he said, looking down:

"Who was she, Judge?"

The man didn't say, and Charlie took the half-burned towel and dropped it in a corner of the bathroom and shut the door and took a leak and came out again.

"Would you mind putting this light out, Mr. Berlatsky?"

"Sure."

Charlie put it out and went into the bathroom and switched on the light in there and came back, leaving the door open, his mouth getting dry because he was going to have to do it soon now, get it over with before he finally chickened out and spent the rest of his life regretting it.

"Thank you."

"That's okay."

"Tell me one other thing, if you will."

"Try me."

"Do you have any particular ambition?"

"Who me?" He wanted to laugh but he was too scared. "Make a killing in Vegas, buy into a small business, same thing everybody wants, isn't it?"

He moved around the bed with his hands bunched in his

pockets and the nails digging into the palms and the sweat coming out on him as he said it again in his mind so when he said it for real it'd sound the way it should. Then back around the bed and suddenly he was standing over the man and thinking somewhere in the back of his head that he was always going to remember this night, with the wind and the blowing sand and this man looking up at him as he said:

"You need me, Judge. You need me bad. And all I'm asking is a hundred grand."

CHAPTER SIX

Beverly Hills Police Department, Sergeant Hollis."

"Oh Sergeant, this is Mrs. John K. Stevens, and I'm worried about my husband. He is Judge Stevens of the County Court—"

"Yes, ma'am."

"Well he should have been home by eight last evening and it's now two o'clock in the morning, and I'm worried because he'd be certain to call me to say he was delayed."

"I see. Have you tried calling any number where Judge Stevens might be?"

"He might be anywhere between here and Las Vegas—he spent the weekend rock-hounding, alone."

"You don't think he's simply decided to stay somewhere overnight, Mrs. Stevens, on account of the—"

"I really doubt that because he's due in court tomorrow morning and he always likes to relax at home Sunday nights. I—I tried not to call you, Sergeant, but I just can't sleep, and—"

"Okay, ma'am, we'll check this out for you and call you back. Is he driving his own car?"

"Yes. It's a new Cadillac Fleetwood, dark blue. The license number is JKS1."

"Okay, I have that. There's some pretty bad weather between here and Las Vegas and he probably took shelter in a motel or somewhere like—"

"But he would have called me, in that case."

"We have reports of telephone cables being down in some of the mountain areas and—"

"Oh really? I never thought of that, but with this awful wind—oh, I'm sure that explains everything."

"Don't worry, Mrs. Stevens, we'll check it out."

"Hello?"

"Are you Mrs. Stevens?"

"Yes. Did you find him?"

"Who?"

"My husband. Aren't you the police?"

"No."

"I'm sorry, I—"

"Your husband wants you to know he's perfectly all right, but he won't be home for a couple of days, okay?"

"A couple of—but he's to be in court tomorrow!"

"He says to tell them."

"But what—please ask him to come to the phone."

"He can't do that."

"Has—has there been an accident?"

"Nothing serious. He needs to rest up a couple of days, see."

"But please I—are you speaking from a hospital?"

"He just says don't worry, okay?"

"But you *must* tell me what—hello? Hello?"

"Beverly Hills Police Depart—"

"This is Mrs. John Stevens again and I'm very worried about my husband—are you the sergeant I spoke to—"

"That's right, Mrs. Stevens—"

"Well I just had a call from a man who said that my husband has had what he called a minor accident—at least he said it wasn't anything serious—but he said he won't be home for a couple of days and of course he has to be in court tomorrow, or rather today, and I just don't understand it."

"Well, it seems nothing serious has happened, so—"

"But the man wouldn't let him talk to me!"

"He may be under anesthesia. Which hospital is it?"

"The man never said. He just hung up."

"Didn't you get his name, or—"

"I tell you he just hung up, before I had time to ask him anything like that."

"He didn't say he was a doctor, or where he was speaking—"

"No. He told me nothing."

"Okay, Mrs. Stevens, I'm going to make a report on this for the duty officer—he'll be here in a few hours, at eight o'clock. In the meantime we're still checking out accident reports on Interstate 15 at Barstow and Morales, but so far there's no news of Judge Stevens' automobile being involved in any trouble."

"Well, I—I suppose that's something, but I'm worried about the way that man sounded, on the phone. He didn't sound like a doctor, or—you know—anyone responsible."

"Just leave it to me, Mrs. Stevens, and I'll go on checking. And if the man calls you again, please make sure and let us know right away."

"Yes—yes, of course."

Charlie Berlatsky turned the key in the lock and opened the door and felt the wind on his face as he crossed the auto court. He had to hurry because in three hours it'd be daylight, but if he took the Chevy he'd have to leave it at the roadside while he was down in the ravine, and someone might notice it and remember, and he didn't want any slipups or he could blow the whole thing. So he'd have to walk.

The fine sand stung his eyes and they streamed and the tears blew back in the wind and he bent low against it with his fists in his stomach to keep his coat from flapping open. Between the gusts there was bright moonlight and he was counting on recognizing the rock formation when he got there, and the thorn trees, because he'd been there twice already and with a bit of luck he might even find the beer can again.

"The last time I had a blackmailer before me, Berlatsky, I sentenced him to five years."

The bastard had been trying to get him worried, coming on heavy in those slow tones of his that made you think of something chiming, like a penitentiary clock.

Charlie had swung round on him—"Just what the hell are you talking about? You gimme that kind of spiel again and by Christ I'll leave you here on your own and let them bust you!"

"I would advise you to think a little more about your situation before you—"

"Listen, I've had time to do all the thinking I want, since I brought you in here. And I know the score, believe me." Stevens wasn't going to let them hang him if he could see a way out, or he wouldn't have told him they had to look after each other and he wouldn't have shot all those goddamn questions at him to check him out. "What are you going to do, Judge? Tell 'em you never saw her before, she was just thumbing a ride and you picked her up and then had an accident? It wouldn't work. There'd be two reports, a girl missing from Las Vegas and an unidentified girl in the wreck of your car, right? Creaturo was a hooker and you know what they do when a hooker kicks it—they look at her diary and they ask around her friends. You think your name wouldn't come up?"

Stevens sat propped in the bed with his eyes closed, the light from the bathroom silvering one side of his face and leaving the other in dark shadow, so it looked like a black and white mask, and Charlie didn't know if he'd passed out again, but he didn't think so. It'd been a shock for the guy to know he'd found out the girl was a tart, that was all.

"You going to tell them you picked up a couple of people and the man stuck you up and threw you out and drove off in your car with the woman and smashed it up in the ravine? That'd be okay, if they weren't your fingerprints on the wheel down there. There's plenty other things you could try, but listen, Judge, I've thought of 'em all and you know something? None of them work. Not one."

He could hear the way his voice sounded and it sounded okay. He was making this pitch as good as he meant to, but his hands were clenched like stones and dug deep in his pockets as he looked down at the man in the bed like you look down at something you're kicking to death before it can get up and bite; and now the man was opening his eyes and he had to turn away and walk around, scared again of what he was doing, the sweat running on him. Why couldn't they fix the air conditioning in this lousy dump for Christ sake, what was he doing here anyway? Stop looking at me like that, will you, like I'm something—

"You must realize that the word of a judge will carry infinitely greater weight than—"

"Listen, will you? Tomorrow morning I can walk out of here and there's nothing you can do to stop me. But you've got yourself on the hook and I'm the only one who can get you off. You want to go on sitting in that courtroom handing those punks a five-year stretch? See Berlatsky. You want to be governor of this state? See Berlatsky. Because there's no way you can get off that hook all by yourself. There's no way you can do it without me. *No way*. But if you don't want to pay what it costs, you just have to tell me, Judge."

He picked up the pack and shook the last one out. "The thing is you'll have to make up your mind pretty fast because if you want me to help you I'll need to hurry—you know what I've got to do and it'll take time." He put the cigarette between his lips and went to the door. "I'll give you ten minutes."

In the deserted café the light tube was buzzing and his face looked gray and unfamiliar in the fly-specked Budweiser mirror and he turned away quickly as if it was someone else's face, someone he didn't know, and he thought: Sometimes people do things they never believed they could do, and this time it's me.

He poured a shot of Old Crow and drank it neat, feeling it hit his stomach as he stood thinking about that bastard in there, and what he was going to do. It was funny because he almost didn't care which way it went: there was a kind of numbness in his mind, as if this thing was so big that it had kind of blown a fuse to stop him from going nuts. There was a cigarette machine by the door and he felt for some quarters and then changed his mind, he was trying to cut down, for Christ sake. Don't let it all go, Berlatsky, keep a hold.

When he'd finished his cigarette he went back through the lobby and along the passage, wondering if he could go through with it if Stevens made a deal, wondering if he was big enough to handle the thing.

The man in the bed hadn't moved. He looked dead.

"Judge?"

He couldn't be dead. He just looked like it.

"Very well, Mr. Berlatsky." The big dark eyes were suddenly looking up at him, their heavy lids drooping in private defeat. His voice was toneless. "Very well."

Charlie wanted to say no I'm not going to do it, I've changed my mind, screw it and screw you, you lousy bastard, surprising himself, wanting to run, just anywhere. Then the panic went away and he was standing looking down at Stevens and saying in a kind of flat voice:

"Okay Judge, it's a deal."

His mouth tasted foul because of the cigarette, and the panic.

"You'll appreciate the difficulty of raising such a large sum at short notice. My private means are far less substantial, in any case, than you appear to–"

"Listen, I saw the magazines so don't give me that crap. I saw the pictures of your place in Beverly Hills–I'd put it at half a million–and you've got stock in some of the biggest companies in the U.S.A. 'Substantial shareholder,' that's what it says in the magazines."

He wasn't losing his cool again like he did before. He felt as if he'd been through something and come out the other side where the world was a little different. Maybe it'd been the uncertainty, before.

"Be that as it may, Mr. Berlatsky, the fact is that I shall need several days to arrange things with my bank, and—"

"Get this." He leaned over the man. "When that cash is in my hands you can leave here. Not before. Now get that, will you? That's the deal and I don't make a move till I have your okay on it." The bastard was like a worm on a goddamn hook, but then they were like that, these legal brains, that was their job, taking a word or a phrase and throwing it around till they made it sound like something different. "This is the way it goes, Judge, and don't think I'm kidding. I keep my end of the deal tonight, see, and at nine o'clock in the morning you're getting on that phone and fixing up the money and listen, will you, you don't leave this place till it's in my hands. Let me put it a little more simply: I don't trust you. No hard feelings."

The man's eyes were closed again, and Charlie saw the silver sheen on the side of his face was very bright, like he was in a fever. They ought to put some air conditioning in this crummy joint, you could die of the heat in here.

"Very well. I'll call my attorney and ask him to—"

"Wrong. You'll call Mrs. Stevens, nobody else. I don't need any city shyster here trying to outsmart me. Nine o'clock you'll call your wife and tell her to raise the hundred grand, tell her if she doesn't co-operate you're going to be in bad trouble, okay?"

Stevens still had his eyes shut and he looked hollow and old, like you saw people in shock after an accident. Well that was just about what it was—there'd been an accident and he was in shock, and maybe the Creaturo kid had meant something to him—he didn't have to haul a hooker this far from

Vegas just to do the business. One thing this punk wasn't sweating about was the money: with a house like that and a Fleetwood and "substantial shareholdings" he could be taken for a truckload of greenbacks and not even notice the draft: he was getting away with it cheap.

"Judge?"

The eyes came open slowly, but they didn't seem to focus too well, they looked kind of glazed. "Yes?"

"I want your okay on this, before—hey, how many of those goddamn aspirins did you take?"

"What?"

"How many—*Christ!*"

Charlie hit the doorpost of the bathroom going in and his eyes cased the place in a series of flickers and he saw the bottle and jerked the cap off. The thing was still almost full and he took a deep breath and let it out again, then he tipped four tablets onto a Kleenex and put the bottle into his pocket and went back to the other room, still a bit shaken.

"Don't take too many of those goddamn things, Judge. There's four here, you want any more you just ask me, okay?" He sat on the edge of the bed and looked closely at the white silent face and thought is this the same guy I stopped on the road to help? Look what I'm doing to him now.

"You listening to me, Judge?"

The man opened his eyes and they looked at Charlie without any kind of expression, just a dullness.

"Yes."

"Okay. How're you feeling?"

"I need sleep."

"Sure. Okay, listen. I'm going out there now, see, and I'll be back here before daylight. You want anything before I get back, tell the girl, name's Rose." He got up and pulled one of the drawers out of the dressing table and stood it on end by the bed where Stevens could reach it. "Knock on the bottom of that, see, use your knuckles, she's not too far from here. You feel okay now, Judge?" There wasn't any answer. "Judge?"

"I would like you to do something for me."

"Sure, just tell me."

"Call Mrs. Stevens. Tell her that I'm all right, that she doesn't have to worry. Will you do that?"

"Sure I will." He took his sales itinerary book and one of the ball-points in his top pocket. "I need the number."

"Hillcrest 6658. Time is it? What time?"

"Ten after two."

"Thank you."

"You're welcome. I'll see she knows." He got off the bed again, looking down. "Listen, Judge. You try calling those lawyers while I'm away, or anyone at all, I'm going to ruin you. Hear that? Judge, you hear that?"

"Yes."

"Just want you to know the score."

He went to the door.

And now as the wind hit him and he bent against it he thought about the man in the bed, not scared of him anymore, sorry for him in a way because look, you're spending a weekend with a nice little hooker like a lot of people do and then the weather acts up and you run off the road into a lousy ravine and she gets hers, the poor little bitch, and even then you'd be okay, kind of messy but still okay, if you didn't happen to be a Superior Court judge.

That was tough shit but there was one thing about it: If it'd been any other guy but Charlie, anybody who knew what you should do, and what you shouldn't do, they would have made sure he got a doctor or an ambulance and then the police would have taken a look at the wreck and seen the girl and Stevens would've been done for, no question.

He pressed against the wind, his coat flapping. "Y'know something, Judge? You had some luck tonight, meeting a guy like me. Oh Jesus, you had some luck!" He laughed suddenly and was aware of it and realized the Old Crow was creeping up on him: after he'd called Mrs. Stevens just now he'd gone into the café and poured himself three shots in one glass and drunk it down straight because of what he was going to have to do, in the ravine. He began talking out loud again, about how he'd tell Stevens he'd been lucky tonight, it'd make him feel better about all this, "for one thing you could've been killed in the wreck and for another thing you would've had it if anyone but me had come along so what the hell are you beefing about, for Christ sake?" But it sounded lonely, with only his voice and nobody answering, sounded weird, and he shut his mouth and went on till he saw the rocks and the thorn trees down there on his left. He stopped.

"Okay Berlatsky, c'm'on."

But it was a while before he stepped over the edge of the road and made his way down, getting Stevens' flashlight out of his pocket and switching it on where the rocks made dark patches in the moonlight, going faster and faster all the time so he wouldn't chicken out and go back, filling his shoes with sand from the soft areas and slipping on some of the rocks, trying to dodge the chollas and the thorn trees, talking again sometimes, come on, this is your end of the fucking deal and you better go do what you have to, that kind of thing, the liquor sour in his stomach instead of warm like it should be, the howl of the wind growing less all the time as he went down, till the air was quiet and he looked around and saw the big rock near the group of saguaros that stood with their arms in the sky, black in the moonlight and tall, very tall, standing over him in the silence.

Goose bumps on his wrists, the hairs rising.

He'd almost stepped on her, not seeing the wreck was so close to these cactus here, the lower rocks hiding it till he was right up to it. The moon was clear in this area and he didn't need the flash and wouldn't have used it anyway, not wanting to see. There was a period while he stood here not doing anything, his mind kind of holding its breath, and then he reached down and slid his hands underneath her and for a time couldn't move because she felt so cold, the tall black cactus standing over him and the silence here and the dreadful sound of his breathing like a faint sawing because she was so cold and so stiff and so disgusting for a time couldn't move and then he picked her up in a kind of rage, sickened and looking away and not at her but remembering her eyes, the way they'd been, they way they'd still be now but he wouldn't look, staggering with her, with it, across the loose rocks with her arm not dangling the way it should, not hanging and swinging but held out stiff, catching at thorn trees and turning him sideways, his scalp rising away from the skull and shot with icy pins and needles as he tripped and fell across her, seeing her eyes as he tried to save himself, feeling her face against his.

Oh Christ, oh Christ, rolling away from her and throwing up and lying on the stones for minutes trying to think of other things and rubbing his cheek to warm it, to make the cold go away from it, the cold touch of her face. But it wouldn't go and he sat up, shivering, *c'm'on now, c'm'on*, his voice kind of whimpering. Then there was nothing to do except either go back up to the road and tell Stevens he'd chickened out, or get this thing finished and try and forget it, so he stood up and took a breath and reached for her hands and brought them together and dragged her the rest of the way, not looking down, never looking down but just the same seeing her eyes as he went on dragging, her feet making a scuttering sound across the loose stones, a shoe coming off, remember to bring it, her wrists cold in his hands and very small, like they would break, snap, if he didn't go easy, her perfume on the air or just still in his memory from when he'd fallen with her, the night quiet, just the two of us, intimate and disgusting and sad, she's so young.

When there was sand and soft earth among the scrub he lowered her gently, wanting to let her drop so he could be saved from another whole second of touching her, but holding out and letting her gently down and then turning away and scrabbling his fingers in the sand to clean them, his breath coming free again now he wasn't near the perfume anymore. Then he went back to the wreck of the car and looked for something but couldn't find anything better than the sheet of glass, the rear window that had snapped off along the edge of the door. So he brought that, and picked up her shoe on his way, and began digging at the soil alongside of her, using the broken window, till in an hour the hollow was deep enough and he rolled her in. She finished face-down.

That's funny, all her friends call her Theo.

Halfway through filling the hollow he wanted to stop, and plunge with his hands to find the shoe and bury it somewhere else, maybe near her feet or just anywhere, because after she'd rolled face-down he'd dropped the shoe in and it had landed on the waves of hair that covered her neck, and it wasn't the right place for a shoe to be forever, it was strange and undignified and pathetic and it was all he could think about while he was digging and scooping with the broken glass, her shoe being like that, a jigsaw puzzle where you had to make things fit, and no one would ever be able to, the soil and sand tipping in and the small stones clattering till she was gone.

His hand was slippery and he looked at it, gleaming and blackened in the moonlight, a deep dark cut across the palm. He dropped the piece of broken glass and walked away, suddenly more tired than he'd ever been in his whole life, keeping his eyes open by watching the tall saguaros go leaning across the sky as he passed underneath. When he reached the wreck he pressed his handkerchief into a pad and clenched it in his left hand to stop the blood, using the flashlight and swinging the beam around to check for anything of hers he might have left here. There was nothing, and for a minute he stood with his eyes shut, taking slow deep breaths till the colors and flashes behind his eyelids got gradually paler, dying away. Then he began climbing to the road.

The wind was behind him, going back to the motel, and he turned his collar up against the sting of the blowing sand, letting himself be half carried along through the moonlight, listening to the howl of the cables above him and not thinking, at last, of anything in particular, till he got to remembering what it was all about, this whole goddamn beautiful thing, seeing the string of gold figures high up and in front of him, like on a billboard—and suddenly he began laughing, shocked at first to hear what he was doing, because of her down there, then letting it go free till he was standing still, bent over, with his eyes squeezed shut and the big long emptying laugh coming out of him like it was something he had to get rid of before he could go on.

CHAPTER SEVEN

THE ENTRANCE DOOR WAS LOCKED and he jerked the handle again, worried and trying to think who could have done it, why they should want to keep him out.

Then the key was being turned and the door came open and Rose was standing there in her pajamas, her eyes big as she stared at him in the light from the café. She caught her breath.

"Charlie—what happened?"

"Just let me in."

She stood away, keeping her voice low—"I heard you go out and leave the door unlocked!"

"I knew I wouldn't be out long, so—"

"You were out ages! Oh *shit*—look at your *hand!*"

He made her go into the café with him because he wanted a drink, one final drink to burn the chill out of his guts, then the daylight would come and he could start forgetting.

"But where did you *go?*" staring at him wide-eyed, her long hair falling loose.

"I'm okay, I went for a walk and—"

"Oh now listen, I don't—"

"I'll tell you about it—"

"For God's sake come in the kitchen, Charlie, there's a first-aid kit and I know what to do, it's something I'm good at."

She made him wash at the sink, the blood streaming under the tap as the handkerchief came unstuck, her face serious as she worked on him, spreading the antiseptic and winding the bandage, crossing it around his thumb: he could see she'd had some kind of training. There was a mirror on the wall with half its silvering peeled away because of the steam from the sink and he could see his face in it, haunted-looking and with his eyes red from the sand, his hair mussed by the wind out there, he didn't wonder why she'd looked like that when she saw him come in.

"I can't stand the sight of blood," he said, "that's all."

"You look like a ghost, Charlie." She put the rest of the bandage away in the big metal kit, her breasts jumping a little under her pajama top as she moved, a flush on her skin because of the excitement with him looking like this and everything, and he thought oh Jesus how alive you look, how alive, not like her out there. "What did you do to your hand?"

He smiled ruefully. "Like I said, I went for a walk because I couldn't sleep, then when I came back I heard that goddamn sign banging, the way it bangs all the time, so I climbed on the fence and tried to do something about it, then I slipped and there was a piece of metal. You know something? You look real cute with your hair down that way, I mean really."

"I just don't believe you."

"Why sure, you look–"

"I don't believe it about your hand, Charlie."

She was leaning her back against the sink, her arms folded, watching him, her stone-blue eyes steady and quiet.

"Well, how else could I have–"

"I don't believe any of it. Not any of it."

In the silence the wind tugged at the top of the air vent, its sound hollow and fretting.

"Well gee, I–"

"Charlie."

"Yes?"

"No more lies." In a while, "Okay?"

"No more lies," he said, like he didn't understand but wanted to go along.

"I don't know what's happening, Charlie." Her eyes were serious. "And I'll tell you something. I don't want to know."

Thrown a little, he said with a shrug, "Okay."

She went on staring at him, like she'd never seen him before. "It's because whoever you are and whatever you're doing, it's making everything different for me, in this place."

"Okay, Rose," he said, and stopped thinking out an explanation for everything. She didn't want to know, and that was going to make his life a hell of a lot easier, the next couple of days. He took her arm and she went with him into the café.

"You don't know," she said calmly, "how I hate this place."

"Sure, it must be kind of—"

"It's a trap I've been caught in since Ma went, see. I've always helped, since I quit school, but since she went it was me who had to cope with Pa. He's okay, I mean he's kind to me, but oh my God, the same stupid thing every day, the hashed blacks and his dirty shirts and him cussing out the customers till they don't come back, and you know what we pull in? As much as we'd make shining shoes."

Charlie took the cork out and poured her a shot, giving her the glass and taking a pull straight from the bottle because there wasn't another glass here and she stared at the bottle and laughed suddenly—"Oh boy, have you been hitting it in the night!"

"Here's to you," he said, and clinked her glass with the bottle. He was beginning to feel good, because he'd got it over with.

"What do you think I am, Charlie?" She put the glass down, the liquor untouched. "This time of the day I'd get loaded!"

He looked at her, seeing her clearly for the first time since she'd let him in, liking the way she looked in her pajamas, her long fair hair hanging loose, the way her eyes got serious, the way she'd suddenly laugh, her mouth fresh and pretty.

"I think you're nice," he said. He was feeling good because he'd got it over with and his end of the deal was sewn up and all he had to do now was collect, and he thought of it again, a hundred thousand clams, and he laughed and it was different from the strange way he'd laughed in the wind out there.

"What's funny, Charlie?"

"Nothing's funny."

"But that's crazy," she said, laughing with him.

"What's wrong with crazy?" he said and she went on laughing and put her head on his chest and he held her and they stood there shaking together and not really knowing why, and when she brought her head up he kissed her and because of how she felt in her pajamas he began getting a hard-on, but he let her free herself when she was ready because he had to go see the judge and set up the day's business.

"The thing is," she said, "you don't look like the kind of a guy that'd do anything bad. I mean really bad. You know."

"How really is bad?" he asked but she was serious about this thing and didn't laugh with him this time.

"You could be wrong," he said.

"I know."

"Would you want me to tell you?"

"Tell me what?"

"If you were wrong."

She looked at him for a long time and said, "No."

He found some quarters in his pocket and went over and got a Kent pack out of the cigarette machine and opened it up, holding it to her and then remembering, pulling one out for himself and lighting it.

"I don't see why you don't want to know," he said. "Okay, you told me about this place and all that and I have the message but—I mean, women are curious, no?"

She gave a little flat laugh on her breath. "Don't get me wrong, Charlie—I'm crazy to know! It's just that if I knew, I might want it to stop—I might even try to make it stop, by telling Pa to throw you out of here or calling the police. But if it stopped, I wouldn't have this new feeling anymore, see. And I couldn't stand that."

"New—"

"Don't you see? I've been slinging hash for five years in this broken-down dump and about the most exciting thing that's happened to me is I get my ass pinched by men I'd rather see —well, they're okay I guess but listen, Charlie, there's suddenly you here and look at this fabulous ring on my hand! And I mean it stands for everything, the new feeling, with you and your—well—nice manners and that guy in there you call the Chief and going out in the night and doing things I just don't understand and I *like* that, see, I *like* the—the bigness of it because for five years the biggest thing I've had to spend my whole living day understanding is how to make the check out for a hamburger, know what I mean?"

Her stone-blue eyes were excited and he forgot to say yes he did, or no he didn't. He was thinking, too, that instead of having to kid this chick along with regular inroads into the Casino Royal Collection he could get her help for free and not only for free—she said she wouldn't even want to know the score.

"Charlie?"

"Uh?"

"You know what I mean?"

"Sure."

"Well—say something."

"Okay. I mean it's okay, that's fine with me, Rose." He took her hand. "You don't tell Pa to throw me out and you don't call the police and I can go on doing my thing for the next couple of days and when I'm through I'm going to give you something that'll make that ring look like you picked it up in a dime store when the lights went out, I kid you not."

He watched the sudden flash of joy in her eyes, then the rush of doubts—"But Charlie, if it's going to cost you that kind of money, what are you—I mean how—"

"You don't want to know. Remember?"

A slow nod. "Right."

"I have to go see the man now."

"Okay, Charlie."

He dropped his cigarette into the glass and it hissed out in the whiskey as he turned away and turned back, wanting to tell her just a little, wanting to share it, because of the size of this thing, because of how smart he was.

"Listen, baby. It's like things have been with you, I mean my own life, only it's been longer." He was holding both her hands, watching her eyes. "I've had a lot of chances, see, like the ones everybody gets as they go along, but I've always lost out, see, never come up with anything big-time—it's always been too late or some guy's let me down or—you know how it goes."

"Yeah, Charlie, I know," she whispered quickly, the excitement coming in her eyes, the excitement he was feeling, and she was watching.

"But this time," he was gripping her hands, "this time I can't lose, Rose. And this time it's the jackpot."

His head was foggy and it bothered him. Sometimes he thought he was awake, but he couldn't seem to focus his mind. The wind rattled a window but it was in his dreams because she called *Kenny* again, *oh Kenny*, the name she had for him, from his middle name, Kendrick, *I'm sorry*, he said, *I'm sorry*, the tears warm in his sleep and the wall growing bright, the officer looking down at him and asking how it had happened, the accident.

"Judge?"

It was the sand, blowing across the road. I couldn't see where I—

"Judge? You okay?"

Yes, Officer, but you're not a—

"Yes," he said and the light began hurting his eyes. "Switch it off, please."

"Switch what—oh."

The thin man went across and pulled the door, leaving only a narrow band of light down the wall.

"Thank you."

"Listen, Judge." Berlatsky was leaning over him and there was the smell of antiseptic. "It's all okay now, everything's okay. You understand what I'm saying?"

"Yes. It's 'okay.' "

"Listen, you have to know what I'm talking about, then you can sleep easy." He leaned closer, his voice softly excited. "They won't ever find her now. They won't ever know there was anyone in the car with you, understand."

"Yes." His head was clearing a little now. "I understand."

"Okay. I came to tell you. Now you can sleep."

"Yes."

Berlatsky nodded quickly, straightening up. "You want anything?" he asked. "I get you anything?"

"No."

"Okay." He turned away and then came back to lean over the bed again. "Everything's fine now, Judge. Everything's great."

Then he went away.

Stevens lay still, trying to think coherently.

The aspirin was dulling his mind and he felt remote from himself and his situation, but he knew from memory that he had taken aspirin and that his situation had been agonizing at that time. Also he knew that if this man were as good as his word there no longer existed any connection between Theodora Creaturo and himself, and therefore his situation had been changed. He was offered certain reprieve, possible acquittal, depending on how much humanity there was in Berlatsky's makeup.

If he had been less drugged he would have felt relief, even elation, because for the moment the ultimate agony had been at least postponed. The ultimate agony would be less to do with Barnes Morgan than with his own wife and children. Morgan had no feeling for him, though they referred to each other as "good friends" in public: John K. Stevens was simply his rival in the race for the governorship, and if the truth of this accident came out then Morgan would have him crucified, as a professional reflex action. He would be destroyed, left morally crippled, spiritually embittered, and disabled from ever again holding office of any kind where he could be useful to his fellow citizens—but that wouldn't be the ultimate agony. The ultimate agony would be shame.

His head was throbbing as he forced himself to think, and he turned it on the pillow, away from the band of light on the wall. His thoughts were mostly images, faces and voices, the faces of Evelyn, Jeffrey and Patricia, the voices of those who knew them, shocked as the news broke—*Los Angeles County Judge Involved in Call-Girl Death*—as his wife sat under the dryer in Marcello's, *We'd like you to know, Mrs. Stevens, that you have our sincerest sympathy*, as his son was called in to see Matthews, the head of his law firm, *Of course this won't make any real difference to your career with us, Jeff, but there are certain aspects we'll need to consider*, as his daughter walked across the campus with her books and her brave new world, *I didn't even know he was your father, Pat, till I saw your name—I know how you must be feeling*, their answers perfunctory, polite.

The wind cried past the building, and water gushed along hidden pipes, sounding from the next room, Berlatsky's. He would be washing in there, washing himself thoroughly, because there was something unclean about death. Had he said a prayer for her? She would have been amused if he had: her god had been Mammon. *Don't see things in me that aren't there, Kenny—I'm out for a good time, while I can get it!* She'd preferred men much older than herself, because they were usually richer, but in her shallow way she had shown a kind of pride in him, only yesterday reading aloud from that copy of *California Horizons* she'd bought because she'd seen his photograph on the cover.

Among the more informed citizens of Los Angeles, the city where he was born, it is claimed that John Stevens has already become a legend in his time, as a man of law, a man of justice, and a citizen whose notability derives less from his wealth and power than from the fact that so much of that wealth and that power has been liberally and generously put to use in the public interest, as witness the John K. Stevens Home for Autistic Children and the Living Arts Academy for Prisoners on Parole. For these and for so many other reasons, those people of Los Angeles who know him best have long ago conferred their own exclusive title on him, despite his protestations. They call him the Paragon.

His head was filling with slow fire, and he had to turn it straight again on the hot pillow.

Somewhere in the wall the pipes gurgled, and he thought again of Berlatsky. So many men had passed through his hands, subjects of his power to judge them, that he knew them from long experience; and he had seen in the eyes of the thin and nervous man who had helped him from the ravine two traits of character that had tremendous importance for him, if he were right. He had believed Berlatsky to be venal and an opportunist. That was why he had grasped at the only chance of survival offered to him, invoking Berlatsky's aid. *You look after me and I'll look after you.* He had known it was perfectly safe to make this proposition because the man had already shown he was ready to co-operate, by not calling a doctor. Since then it had become clear that Berlatsky had used his own brand of intuition, seeing in this notable stranger a man who would do anything to avoid public shame.

The water pipes grew quiet and all he could hear was the wind against the building as he slipped from consciousness again and the images began streaming, the gigantic cross rearing into the moonlit sky, black as a cactus, with Barnes Morgan staring up at him, a hammer in his hand as the hood of the Cadillac dipped and the rocks began spinning slowly and the lights smashed to darkness as she screamed.

Charlie was winding his watch, counting the turns carefully so as not to overdo it because today time was going to be important. Today he wasn't selling crap jewelry: he was running a lot of people's lives and some of them were big people and he lay on the bed feeling a kind of awe for himself. He wasn't scared anymore like he'd been all through the night. This thing he was running was gathering speed and he could feel the power in it, like the first time you sneak into your Dad's auto and drive it a few feet and realize the terrific power that's in you, just to be doing this, making this huge thing move along the ground.

And he could feel other things that he'd never be able to explain in words, but you could call it surprise, the kind that caught your breath, surprise that when you really made a pitch for something so big that you couldn't ever dream of getting it, you got it, just like that, because this time, for the first time, you'd dared to dream. You had to dream it first, then you went out and got it and it was all yours, hard and safe in your goddamn fist where no one could take it away. Surprise and something else, a kind of rage he couldn't help feeling when he realized just how big these bastards were, the ones at the top, the ones like John K. Stevens, a guy he'd have had to wait in line for a whole day to see, just to get near, if they ever let him get near at all. They were so big that people couldn't imagine they were made of flesh and blood, but if you knew the way, if you saw the chance, you could bring them down like a demolition squad brought down whole buildings.

Play it my way, Judge, or I'll ruin you. A kind of rage, not because it was so easy but because those god-almighty bastards made it look so difficult.

Charlie Berlatsky lay on the still-made bed in Room 6 with his nerves secretly galvanized by awe, surprise and rage, winding his watch and listening to the sounds in the building, identifying them so he would know what people were doing. At six he heard Pa go out the back way and drive off in the battered blue Olds he'd seen last night in the auto court (he'd asked Rose and she'd said whose it was, he'd asked about all of them out there) and soon afterward a toilet flushed somewhere and half an hour later a couple of guys went out: that was their late-model Mercury in the auto court and they must have paid on arrival and were leaving too early for breakfast.

There were other sounds and he listened to them and smoked the rest of the pack before he got off the bed and went in the bathroom and soaped his armpits because he hadn't stopped sweating since he'd got into this tacky dump, they ought to fix the air conditioning. The bandage got soaked and it was turning slowly pink and he squeezed it, feeling the wound throb, the glass digging in the sand like a blade and the sand going down, smothering, the shoe across her neck like that, he didn't want to think about it anymore, it was over with, the wound throbbing till he stopped squeezing and went back in the room and put his shirt on, having trouble with his necktie but persevering because he always liked to look smart, people had more respect for you.

There wasn't any hurry because the banks didn't open till nine but he put his white calfskin shoes on with one hand, checking his watch again at 8:21 and going out along the passage to the door back of the lobby marked *Private* and knocking on it.

She just said to come in. She was in her jeans and the striped sweater, standing by the window painting her nails, surprised it was him. Maybe she thought it was Pa, but he didn't think Pa would ever knock on a door.

"I couldn't get back to sleep," she said with a soft private laugh for him, "after we talked."

"I couldn't either."

"How's your–oh Charlie, it's bleeding again! What did you–"

"It's okay, I got it wet. What time does Pa get back?"

"Pa? Oh, any time now. It depends if he's picked a fight with the grocery man. See that?" She held out her left hand. "I got the mark off, where the old ring was. I wanted to do it before I put yours on my finger today." She kissed him and smiled. "You like my silver nail polish, Charlie?"

"It's real nice. Rose, the Chief has to make a call, pretty soon, so I want you to keep people away from the lobby, as much as you can, while he's at the phone. I don't want anyone recognizing him, get it?"

She stared, intrigued. "I'll do what I can. Charlie, you—you mean he really is someone big, like you said?"

"Sure he is. What made you—"

"I said I didn't believe any of it, remember? I meant—"

"Listen, baby"—he took her hands—"if you take what I told you as the gospel truth, you won't be far out, see? Remember I said there were things I didn't want to tell you because I didn't want you to have the responsibility on your back, and that still goes too. That guy in there is a really big wheel and we have to keep him out of sight for as long as we can, and don't forget that, or you could screw up the whole thing."

Her eyes grew big.

"I wouldn't ever want to do anything, Charlie."

"Fine. If we just keep—*Christ*," he said because the noise of the bell jangled right into his nerves, "what the hell is that?"

"Someone wants gas, that's all." She laughed because of the way he'd jumped.

"Okay. Okay."

She swung away and put the top back on the nail polish and came back past him to the door. "I'm going to fix your hand in a minute, Charlie—"

"You get many people for gas about this time?"

"Quite a few."

She went through the lobby and out the front door and he looked at his watch again: 8:27. For a minute he let his eyes wander around the room, seeing how trapped she was, how she'd opened up these walls to other worlds with pictures of movie stars and their plush Palm Springs homes—Redford,

Streisand, Sinatra—their smiles, their pools, their automobiles, only one photo among them with any reality, low down above her bed, a grizzled old guy in a Forty-niner rig, could be her pa, with a fine-looking woman with heavy blond braids, not smiling, and Rose herself a couple of years younger, her stomach bare and stuck out for the cameraman—it seemed she thought the navel was the thing they went for—then a big picture of the Desert Winds Motel with some big cars outside and fancy signs everywhere: That was before Ma died, he'd guess.

The bell sounded again and he gave a jerk and wished to Christ his nerves wouldn't act up this way when he had to keep his cool more than he'd ever done before. He went out through the lobby and saw a sedan pulling in behind the one at the pump, so there must be a pneumatic hose that rang the bell. On his way along the passage he heard someone in the kitchen and had to find out who it was, turning back and going into the café, looking through the hatch.

"Hi!" she said, a girl with dumb, friendly eyes, her mouth working fast on the gum as she tied the apron on. *Mabel*, the apron said. "You want sump'n t'eat?"

"No. Are you Mabel?"

"You bet."

"Hi, Mabel."

"Hi."

He went back through the lobby. Rose had told him about the two girls who came and helped here and it looked like that first car must have dropped Mabel off, maybe like it did every day around this time.

There was daylight in the windows of Room 7 when he went quietly in, and for a minute stood looking down at the man on the bed. His heavy-lidded eyes were shut and his face was sweaty and pale; his big hands lay beside him on the bed and Charlie thought how defenseless he looked.

He'd told himself in the past couple of hours that it was best not to think of the exact minute when he'd have to set the thing running, so it wouldn't play on his nerves, and he'd tried to think about other things, like the pictures on Rose's wall. But it hadn't really helped because he'd jumped like a cat every time the gas-pump bell had rung and now he was standing here with his right hand dug deep in his pocket and bunched in a fist because it was all kind of rushing in on him now in the last few seconds, the awe and the surprise and the rage and something more: the fear that he thought had gone out of him. Now it was back and his fist was clenched in his pocket, showing the things he mustn't show in his face.

"Judge."

He had to lean down and say it again before the man's eyes came open. It was a while before they could focus.

"Yes?"

"We have to do it now."

CHAPTER EIGHT

EARLY SUNSHINE WAS SLANTING into the green-and-gold living room of the house on Canyon Drive when Evelyn came downstairs soon after eight-thirty, already dressed.

"Maria?"

"*Sí, señora!*"

"I do not want any breakfast, thank you." She spoke slowly, enunciating carefully.

"*No?*" The girl's limpid brown eyes became doleful.

"I may be going out, at any time."

"*Sí, señora.*"

"Yes—Mrs.—Stevens."

"A'right, Miss' Steven."

"Has the mail arrived?"

"May? Please?"

"*Correo.*"

"*Ah, sí!* Yes!"

Maria fetched the letters, half running. She was the most willing girl they had ever had, and within three months she'd be speaking good English, and a month later she would leave, as they all did, because her mother was sick in Tijuana: in other words, someone—often a close neighbor—had offered her even more money, a color TV set and the whole of every Friday off as well as Sunday.

"Thank you, Maria."

"No eat, Miss' Steven?"

"No thank you." The girl's enviably beautiful eyes lingered on her as she began opening the mail. Evelyn usually slept later than this, coming down to breakfast in her dressing gown; but this morning she was early and already dressed and Maria was puzzled. She had been awakened in the night by the telephone, and had asked Mrs. Stevens if there was anything she could do: there was talk of an accident to the judge. "That is all, Maria."

"*Sí.*"

Three circulars and a statement from Bank of America; a sweet note from Pat, "missing you both," and a brochure from Marcello's announcing her privileged entrée to his new Boudoir Rose on Wilshire.

She wasn't expecting to receive any kind of written communication from the man who had called her in the early hours: she was looking through the mail because she had to wait, and had no appetite for breakfast. The warmth of the sun touched her shoulder and she moved more fully into it, chilly from lack of sleep.

The Committee of the Miss Beverly Hills Selection for this year would be honored if she would assist in the judging, as a leading ex-holder of "this most coveted of crowns in the world of feminine beauty." Thank you, gentlemen, but you should see what seventeen years and a sleepless night have made of your little Miss Ex-holder.

There were still a few more letters to be opened when the telephone rang and she picked up the receiver before the second ring, her heart suddenly quick.

"Yes?"

"Is this Mrs. Stevens?"

"Yes."

"This is George here, of Arco. We were kind of expecting to have the Caddy in about eight-fifteen. The judge said he —"

"Oh yes, I'm sorry. He—he couldn't manage to pass your way this morning. Let me call you later."

"Okay, Mrs. Stevens. Just so long as I know."

"Thank you."

She could still feel the insistent beat of her heart as she put the receiver down, and it was a minute or two before she could take the letter opener and start on the remaining letters. Slitting an envelope, she was aware of strangeness, a slow cold feeling that normal life was going on in its routine way, the mail to open, the garageman calling, while some other kind of life, some other passing of time, was secretly proceeding in a place where she'd never been—the place where John was, at this moment.

For the hundredth time she told herself to stop worrying like this. Nothing had happened to John, nothing serious. The man had meant what he said: it was a minor accident. (Had he said "minor accident" in so many words? She couldn't remember anymore, because she'd repeated his message in her mind so often that nothing of what he'd really said was left.)

A long letter from Jeffrey, one of those airy reports on his progress with his career in law, disguising his self-doubts of his ability. "Oddly enough," the senior partner had told her confidentially, "the son of a Superior judge, or at least *this* son of *this* Superior judge"—with a self-amused smile—"has to begin work under a disadvantage. You see, there's so much to live up to, and that can be daunting."

This time the receiver was in her hand before the first ring had stopped.

"Yes?"

"Mrs. John K. Stevens?"

"Yes." The thudding again in her chest.

"This is Lieutenant Cheever, Beverly Hills Police Department. I have this report, Mrs. Stevens, about your anxiety over your husband."

"Oh yes, Lieutenant?"

"Have you had any further communication from the man you mentioned, or from Judge Stevens himself?"

"No." The letter from Jeffrey was shaking slightly in her hand, and she dropped it onto the gilt coffee table.

"Well, we're sure here that you'll be hearing from the judge anytime. But meanwhile would you like me to come by in a half hour, Mrs. Stevens, so we could make certain we have the facts correct?"

"Why yes, I–"

"This is strictly routine, you understand–"

"Of course, Lieutenant. Yes, would you please come and see me? Just as soon as convenient for you."

"I'll be right along."

"Thank you. Thank you so much."

The phone seemed to slip a little as she replaced it, as if she'd forgotten how to do it properly. Because the lieutenant had been too reassuring and the fact that he'd decided to call her was significant and the fact that he wanted to see her personally was even more disquieting and her mind was beginning to race and she almost called to Maria but stopped herself, this was absurd, she mustn't panic like this. Surely it was a good thing that the police were so ready to help her, even though they were sure–as they pointed out–that John would be getting in touch at any time now. *The attitude of mind*, the book on her bedside table said, *toward any event must be appropriate to what is, not to what might be. Otherwise we shall find ourselves living through unreasoning hopes and fears instead of calmly coping with life as it comes.*

But oh God, it's so easy to read and say "how *right* that is," and so hard to do.

"Maria!"

"*Señora?*"

"I think I would like some coffee."

"A'right!"

A brief sad note from Fran Hudson saying the papers were finally through and she didn't know why she'd ever started it but she couldn't go groveling to Burle after all those things he'd said.

An invitation from Saks Fifth Avenue to view their fall collections at a private showing.

It rang and this time she picked up the instrument more slowly, her nerves dulled by the repeated cries of wolf.

"Yes?"

It was a woman's voice, asking for Mrs. Stevens.

"I am Mrs. Stevens."

"Thank you. We have a call from Mr. Stevens—will you accept the charges?"

A sudden wish to laugh. "Yes of course!"

"One moment please."

"Mrs. Stevens?"

Not John. It was the thin voice.

"Yes."

"Please listen carefully." The thin voice with that odd note of deference in it, as there had been before.

"Very well."

She had the feeling again that this wasn't reality, the gilt table, the sun on her back, the smell of coffee from the kitchen, that reality was here in this telephone, coming from somewhere else.

"I'm going to give you a number where you can—" he broke off and she heard some kind of bell ringing in the background. "I am giving you a number where you can call me if you need to. Write it down."

"Please let me talk to my—"

"In a minute. Make a note of this number—for his sake."

"All right." The silver Tiffany pencil sent reflected flashes of sunlight across the wall. "What number?"

"Area code 714. Number is 203."

Writing it down on the telephone pad she had the feeling that the other world, the real one, was coming out of the receiver and onto the paper here, through her fingers and the pencil, making her a part of it and giving her a sudden sense of reassurance. She was going to speak to John in a minute, so he must be all right and today mightn't turn out to be the nightmare she'd let herself imagine through the sleepless hours.

"I have that."

"Okay. If you want to call that number, ask for Mr. Rackman." He spelled the name. "Repeat that."

"Mr. Rackman."

Strangely difficult to say "Mister" to this man—she wanted to tell him to get off the line and let her husband speak. But she knew now that it wasn't a doctor, or anyone calling from a hospital. There hadn't been an accident, not of the ordinary kind. She could feel her heartbeat everywhere now, in her wrists, in her neck, and her breathing was quite loud in the room, as if she'd been running.

"Listen, Mrs. Stevens. If you tell anyone that name, or that number, it'd be very serious for your husband, get that. And I mean very serious. Understand?"

"Yes. Yes. I won't tell anyone."

"Okay. You—" She heard the bell ring again in the background, and when he spoke again his voice sounded nervous. "You do everything I tell you, and everything the Judge tells you, and we'll be okay. If you don't, things'll get very bad. I mean bad for him."

"Yes, I understand. But please let me—"

"Evelyn?"

John's voice but different and she caught her breath because he sounded—

"Evelyn, this is—"

"Yes. Yes darling, I'm listening."

"I am all right." Sounded so tired, so slow. "I hope you haven't been too worried about me."

"No. Darling, where are you?"

Then she could hear the thin voice in the background telling John something.

"Evelyn, there isn't time to say much. Please listen. I want you to bring me a sum of money, in cash."

"All right darling," her heart jumping because he'd said 'bring' and that meant she could—

"A hundred thousand dollars."

She knew she had heard correctly, but didn't want to believe it, believe what it meant.

"How much did you say?"

"One hundred thousand dollars, in cash. Do whatever you can to obtain it, Evelyn, as soon as possible."

She listened to the distant sound of Maria in the kitchen, putting a cup and saucer on the tray, and the chatter of a blue jay on the lawn outside as she stood in the shaft of sunlight, deathly cold. It was happening so often these days, the executives of American companies in Brazil, the children of wealthy families in New York and California, happening so often but only in the paper, the stories of the demand notes and the anxious waiting and the statements from the police, only always in the paper, until now.

"Evelyn?"

"Yes." Her voice not sounding like her own. "I'll get it for you, darling. I'll bring it, wherever you are."

"It has to be done."

"Yes of course. How will I know where to—"

"Call the number, Evelyn. Then we shall tell you where you have to come. You must do it today."

"Yes, as soon as—"

"Please call the presiding judge's office and have the Gomez trial adjourned. Speak to Fenwick. It should only be for a few days. Please don't forget to do that."

"I'm writing it down, darling," the silver pencil sending flashes against Maria's white linen apron as she came with the coffee, putting it down for her. "I'll tell Fenwick, yes."

"And I would like some Ben-Gay."

"Some what?"

"The tube of Ben-Gay, when you come. I've hurt my back slightly."

"John," gripping the receiver, "what kind of accident did you have? Please tell me exactly what—"

"I'm all right, really. Just a slight—Evelyn, I must go now. Do everything, my dear, and don't worry."

"But I—"

"Okay, Mrs. Stevens. The banks open in ten minutes, so you better be there. I'm going to—"

"Mr. Rackman, I demand to know the extent of my husband's injuries and what kind of medical attention he's receiving."

"He's okay, like he just told you. You don't—"

"He's a man of great influence and we shall hold you personally responsible for—"

"We have to hang up now. I'll just tell you again: You give that number to anybody, or call the police or try and bring anybody with you when you come, and it's going to be serious for him, believe me. Remember that."

The line clicked dead.

Just after 9 A.M. Lieutenant Cheever, in plain clothes, slotted his unmarked car against the curbside on Canyon Drive and got out, walking past the mailbox as the attractive woman in green began backing her two-door Cadillac down the driveway. He waited till she came abreast.

"Pardon me, ma'am. Are you Mrs. John K. Stevens?"

"Yes." She looked almost scared.

"I'm Lieutenant Cheever, Beverly Hills Police Department." He flashed his I.D. for her.

"Oh yes, I—something came up, Lieutenant, and I tried to reach you at your office but you'd left already." Her face was pale under the makeup and he was aware of some kind of appeal in her hazel-green eyes as she looked up at him from the driver's window against the sun. "I located my husband."

"Where?"

It seemed she didn't expect the question.

"Oh he's—perfectly all right except for backache and I'm going to meet him and—and bring him home."

She glanced deliberately along the street, ready to back out and be on her way. Cheever was interested.

"Well that's fine, Mrs. Stevens. We felt sure you'd be hearing from him pretty soon. Did he call you himself?"

"Why—yes, yes he did—"

"Or was it the man who called you in the night?"

"Man? Oh him."

"You felt worried about the way the man sounded, so the report says. He didn't sound like anyone responsible."

She tried to smile and didn't manage. "Well you know when you get a phone call in the middle of the night, Lieutenant—you sort of imagine things that don't exist. But I really appreciate your coming by—"

"What kind of accident was it?"

"Oh just a—a minor one. He strained his back, that's all."

"Guess he was lucky."

"He certainly was."

She looked at her small gold watch.

"Was there any damage to his car?"

"Only slight."

"Uh-huh." He let his gaze wander across the lawn, admiring its freshness under the morning sun. "We didn't pick up any report of an accident involving Judge Stevens' Cadillac. We covered the whole of the area you mentioned." He looked down at her in time to catch her reaction.

She glanced away, testing the glove compartment to make sure it was closed, glancing up again. "I didn't realize how much trouble I was causing you all, Lieutenant. If you'll excuse me, I'm late for an appointment with my hairdresser. Thank you for being so kind—and so very efficient."

"Part of the job, Mrs. Stevens. And we don't too often get a judge on the missing list." He stood clear, looking up and down the street, nodding that it was okay to drive out. "Call us again if you need us."

"Thank you."

She managed a real smile this time, relieved he was letting her go. Nice eyes, kind of flecked in the sunlight, and a very nice hairdo, done yesterday, he'd guess, didn't need doing all over again, so soon.

"Wow—that's quite a lot of money!"

"I know," she said.

He was watching her and she tried to keep away from the light, but the windows were so bright this morning. You can do a lot with some good makeup but you can't alter your expression.

"Let's just step into my office, Evelyn—we can talk better there."

One of the telephones rang as soon as they had sat down, and he lifted the receiver.

"Manager." He took off his glasses as he listened, leaving a deep red mark across the bridge of his nose, pinching it between his thumb and finger. "Have Bill deal with this one. And Betty, I don't want any calls in here till I let you know." He cleaned the lenses with one of the small square cloths he kept in the drawer, watching Evelyn with his naked-looking brown eyes. "You said a hundred thousand?"

"Yes. I know it sounds—well—"

"A lot of money!" He laughed easily. "What's old John going to buy himself, an airplane?"

"He didn't say why he wanted it." She tried to laugh with him but it sounded awful and she hoped he didn't hear—but he heard, all right. Roger looked like a soft lovable bear, the kind of man you felt you could tell almost anything; and that was why people did, and that was why they were so surprised, years afterward, at the way he remembered things. "I don't have a good memory," he'd told her once. "People say they have bad memories, but there isn't any such thing —it's just that they don't listen. I listen."

"And you say he wants it in *cash?*"

"So he told me. He—he was rather insistent about that."

He didn't say anything for a minute, concentrating on his glasses and then putting them back on, dropping the lens cloth back in the drawer.

"Like some coffee?"

"I don't have time, Roger, but thanks."

He laughed again, gently. "You mean you came here to grab a hundred thousand dollars and run out again just like that?"

"Well, yes, I—"

"You'd give those two guards a heart attack!"

She wished he didn't laugh so often. Today she didn't feel like laughing.

"Well," he said slowly, watching her until she looked at him and then glancing away, "I don't know, Evelyn." A sudden bright idea—"Maybe we should call John about this, what d'you think?"

She was ready for this. In the middle of all the fright and confusion her brain was trying to map its way through, one step at a time, deaf to the sounds of nightmare going on around. She said simply:

"He's in Chambers."

"Oh."

"That's why he asked me to come and see you."

"Difficult case?"

"Yes," seizing the chance, "very difficult."

"Gomez," he nodded. "Don't they say he's in the Mafia?" A quick smile—"I shouldn't talk that way to the wife of a judge!"

"It's all right," she said wanly, going along with the joke.

She was learning so much today and learning it so fast. She had been so sure that all she had to do was step inside the bank, see the manager—who was a personal friend of the family's—and walk out with a hundred thousand dollars in her handbag. John's standing with the bank was substantial: he had dealt with this branch for twelve years, eight years before Roger was posted here as manager. She had thought there wouldn't be any question, any difficulty at all, but the situation was already clear to them both after these first few minutes: she was having to lie and lie desperately and he knew it and was trying to think of the best way of saying look, Evelyn, you're in some kind of trouble and I'm a friend of yours and I'd like to help.

But there wasn't time.

She asked sharply, surprising herself, "I don't understand the difficulty, Roger."

He smiled gently, easing his glasses.

"I thought you didn't. Well, the first problem is that John doesn't have a hundred thousand dollars in his account with this bank. He's too smart for that. Of course I can arrange an immediate loan, using his stocks as an official collateral, but that would take a few days."

"A few–but Roger, you've known John for more than four years now and–" She broke off because her voice was beginning to sound shrill.

"It isn't that, Evelyn. It's–"

"But I mean if there were some kind of–well–"

"Emergency?"

"Well, yes."

He was driving her out of cover and she began hating him, at the same time thinking it so strange that in the last few minutes she had begun hating a friend of the family's she'd known for so long. From the other world out there, the real one where the real things were happening, she could feel a kind of pressure wave acting on her, driving her to lie and deceive, unable suddenly to meet the eyes of sane and responsible people: police officers, bank managers. She was beginning not to know herself.

It has to be done, John had told her on the telephone.

"You see," Roger was saying, "for security reasons we don't carry large bills to the amount you mention. And you wouldn't want small ones, would you? And even if I could let you have that large a sum in cash I wouldn't let you out of here without an armed guard." He folded his soft hands, watching her.

She said tonelessly, "It has to be done."

"The next currency order," he sighed apologetically, "won't be through till Wednesday."

"We need it now, Roger."

She was learning, too, just how unsubtle you can get when the pressure comes on, how easily you can lose your flair for diplomacy when time starts racing and you can only just keep your feet.

"We could raise it," he said reluctantly, "inside of twenty-four hours, with a special order to the Federal Reserve vault. Certainly we could do that."

Somebody knocked on the door and he didn't say anything and they went away.

"That's no good," she told him.

She was thinking of other people now: Clive Brenner, their family lawyer, wealthy in his own right; Ros Westland, her close friend, an heiress; the Tuckerfields, the Martins, George Bassett of the supermarket chain. Any one of them would help her at the lift of a telephone.

It'd be very serious for your husband, get that. And I mean very serious.

There wasn't any point and there wasn't any time to observe the niceties now. Roger was a friend and he should know that as a friend of a family like the John K. Stevenses he had his obligations.

"Roger," she said, feeling herself being pitched forward into dangerous utterance, "suppose I told you there was an emergency?" She stopped there, letting the plea rest, afraid to add anything because she didn't know the answer to the one question: Which would be worse for John—to allow delay in raising the money, or to raise it by pressing Roger to the point where he would realize the truth and possibly tell the police?

"An emergency," he said, pulling the cloth from the drawer again, too worried now to parade his gentle reassuring smile. "You mean an emergency that could be alleviated by the immediate availability of a hundred thousand dollars in cash?" He took off his glasses but didn't look at her, concentrating instead on what he was doing.

"Yes."

It was all she could say now because in his quiet way he'd pushed her to the point where she couldn't lie or deceive anymore, where she had to tell him the truth.

"Well," he said slowly, "I guess we could order a special run for you."

"What is that?"

"We could make a special Brink's armored run to one of the Federal Reserve banks."

She could feel the sudden thudding of her heart.

"How long would it take?"

He put his glasses back on, looking at her with his thoughts somewhere else. "We could do it right away."

"Then do it, Roger." She had to control her voice. "Do it now, please."

His soft stubby fingers began drumming along the edge of the desk. "I'm sure you have things you can do for an hour," he said. "Shopping, or—"

"Will it take that long?"

He gave a tired smile. "That's pretty fast, Evelyn. Apart from the formalities, there are things like traffic signals. Come back in an hour and I'll do all I can."

CHAPTER NINE

CHARLIE HUNG UP and stood beside the big man in the makeshift booth and for a while he couldn't move or say anything. It had been a strain, worse than he'd thought it would be, much worse, the way she'd sounded so scared and the Judge having to tell her not to worry. He hadn't wanted to listen to them—it had been like getting a crossed line and hearing voices and feeling he oughtn't to go on listening.

Rackman's Delicious Pies, the ad on the wall said, must be ten years old, a picture of a pig poking its head through a lot of pastry and grinning about it like a goddamn idiot, didn't even know it was dead, a whole mass of numbers doodled around the telephone list, *Freda* in a red felt pen, a heart with an arrow through it. The way he'd stood here listening to them and kind of wanting to help, wishing he could do something for them because they sounded so worried, it didn't make any sense.

"You didn't have to tell Mrs. Stevens I was in danger," the big man said. "It would have been sufficient to—"

"For Christ sake, I had to make her see I wasn't kidding, didn't I?" He felt mean, and knew they only had contempt for him: they were out of his class, way out, and that was funny, how he had them in his hands, could break them if he wanted, yet he was still outclassed, nothing he could do about it.

The Judge was leaning forward with his neck held stiff

and his big hands supporting him against the coin box and Charlie pulled him away, holding his arm as they began walking back to Room 7, having to take it slow, like helping some poor bastard across the street.

"I don't need your help, Mr. Berlatsky."

Charlie took his hand away. "Okay, but just don't keel over, Judge." He could hear a car pulling out of the gas-pump area, then Rose coming back and crossing the lobby and going along to her room, maybe to put the cash away safe where she kept her shotgun. He noticed the wind hadn't rushed through the door when she'd opened it, and the sign had stopped banging.

"I should remind you," Stevens said in his slow tones, "that my wife won't find it at all easy to obtain a sum so large, in cash."

"She has to. You told her."

"They were only your instructions that I should tell her."

"Listen, a guy like you can dip his hand in and come up with a hundred grand just anytime he wants, don't try to kid me. I told you, I saw those magazines."

They didn't talk again till Charlie had seen him back onto the bed, sitting upright against the pillow. The Judge wasn't sweating anymore and his skin wasn't so blotchy, and Charlie was glad, because he didn't want the poor bastard to suffer; that wasn't the idea, he didn't want to hurt either of them, him or that classy-looking wife of his in the mansion on Canyon Drive—in the magazine she looked like an ex-model or a show girl or something but with plenty of style—they were just kind of temporary associates, him and the Judge, doing a deal together, looking after each other just like he said. There wasn't any need for anybody to get hurt.

"You feel like some food now?"

"No thank you."

"Something to drink? I mean I'll get you anything you want, you just have to say."

"Thank you, I don't need anything." His heavy-lidded

eyes were almost shut and his head lay against the pillow like it was part of a monument, carved out of rock. "I should also remind you, Mr. Berlatsky, that if you deliberately harass Mrs. Stevens when you talk to her again I shall have the police called here. The charges against you are now very serious."

Charlie didn't answer right away because it was hard to believe what this guy was saying.

"Well Jesus Christ!" He would've laughed but he was too angry. "I'm the man who pulled you out of that goddamn ravine, remember? I'm the man you told to stay around so we could help each other, okay? And all that's happened so far is that I've done my end of the deal and believe me it made me sick to my stomach having to bury that fancy little hooker of yours out there and now you have the fucking nerve to say you'll call in the police if—"

"Mr. Berlatsky." His voice came out of him like out of a drum. "You misunderstand me. I find your assistance highly convenient but not *essential.* In other words I am quite prepared to submit to circumstances and reveal what I have been party to, if you push me too far. Please bear that in mind."

"Okay." Charlie had his right hand dug hard in his pants pocket and he could feel the other one throbbing under the wet bandage. "But just how far is 'too far'? That's one helluva question, isn't it?" He leaned over the bed and stared at the big beaten-looking face of John K. Stevens, not hating him, not liking him, just seeing him as another human being on his way through life, a man caught on a hook and wriggling. "How far do I have to push you, exactly, before you throw everything away, everything you've got, how far *exactly?*" He shook his head slowly, thinking about it. "Oh boy, that's really a difficult question, isn't it?"

The dark eyes showed for a minute under the hooded lids, looking up at him. Then they closed wearily.

"Yes, Mr. Berlatsky. Very difficult."

She dropped the wet stained bandage into the trash basket by her dressing table and tore the blue paper off the new roll, getting some scissors.

"Who's Mr. Rackman?"

"It doesn't matter who he is. The only thing you have to remember is if there's a call for him, I'll take it."

She looked at him with her eyes suddenly serious, then began snipping at the bandage. "I wasn't trying to find out anything, Charlie."

"Sure."

In a while she said, "They told Pa he couldn't have any codeine without a prescription."

"Okay. Did he want to know who it was for?"

"Pa?" She laughed suddenly. "You could ask him to get a snakebite kit and he wouldn't want to know who'd got bit!"

"What does he think about?"

"The TV."

"All the time?"

"All the time." She began crossing the bandage around his thumb. "He's like me, Charlie, see. This place'd send us both into the nut house if we didn't have something else to think about. But I can't look at the TV as much as Pa because he's got it right above the hatch in there." She swung her head to look at him, her hair suddenly dazzling as it caught the sunlight through the window. "Then you walk in, Charlie, the biggest TV show I ever saw in my life."

"That so?"

"Like I told you. I don't want to know what you're doing, I just want to know you're doing it, whatever it is."

"Sure." He looked at the photographs of the movie stars and their lush Palm Springs homes. Pa had the TV and she had the wallpaper here. It figured.

"I left the old dressing on, Charlie, even though it's damp, because if I pull it off the wound it'll open it up again."

"Okay. You're doing fine."

He felt a warmth for her, a kind of gratitude, not because of the first-aid thing but because he needed her comfort, the young smell of her and the sight of her competent hands and the friendliness in them, the way she was excited by what he was doing, without asking too much about it. Since he'd hung up in the phone booth his nerves had been getting so bad that if that gas-pump bell went again he'd hit the roof and Christ knew where these scissors would go.

He hadn't expected it'd be such a strain talking to Mrs. Stevens and now there was another thing he hadn't expected —the strain of waiting around like this, of doing nothing, just waiting for her to call "Mr. Rackman." In the past twenty minutes he'd gone the whole course and back again, first telling himself the Judge was right—she wouldn't be able to raise the money right away and he'd be stuck here for days till the cops got wind of it and he had to get out and lose the whole of the jackpot—then telling himself the Judge was just trying to stall him: that phone would ring any minute now and pour a hundred thousand goddamn beautiful clams right in his lap and for the first time in his life he'd be a winner. Just the ring of that phone out there in the lobby was going to make the difference between spending the rest of his life trying to sell junk to dumb-assed housewives and setting himself up in a nice little place along the Mexican coast and letting the rest of the world go screw itself. Jesus, no wonder his nerves were shot.

The only thing was to think about something else.

"That your ma there?"

"Huh?"

"In the photo."

"Oh. Yeah."

"She looks a nice woman."

"Ma was okay." She cut the bandage and snipped it in half from the end, making a knot, looking at the photograph while she tied it. "It was cancer."

"She was still young."

"Right." She looked away from the wall. "It's kind of funny, I didn't know who she was, in the end, you imagine that? Because it took almost four months and she was along at the hospital in Morales, and I went there to see her every day, never missed, thirty miles and back, like Pa does for the bread but that's only because he's a nut."

She put the unused length of bandage back in the blue paper and dropped the scissors into the drawer, using her raw pink hands with a kind of confidence like he'd noticed before, wanting to do things right. They were raw and pink because of the cleaning she had to do here and the thought came and went, without him really knowing, the thought that in the little white house along the Mexican coast she wouldn't have to do any cleaning because there'd be a local girl for that.

"It must've been tough," he said.

"Worse than that. It was boring. You imagine?"

"Well, when people—"

"I mean every single day, and feeling so good about not ever missing, because it was all I could do for my own ma, you know? But it was always the same—'She's bearing up,' or 'Not too bad today,' the same kind of words till I could say them for myself without having to ask anybody, and all the time knowing she wasn't going to get better anyway, having to pretend all the time, it finally got me down. Does that sound awful?"

"I guess not, Rose. It—"

"Well, I think it does. But after a while she kind of stopped being my ma and turned into that patient up there in the hospital, a part of it, like one of the nurses, and I began thinking why doesn't she just go and die and get it over with, and let other people get on with living, like they're meant? I shouldn't think there was anything worse in the world for any person to do, I mean have those kind of thoughts about their own ma. Least I don't cuss at her, though, like Pa does, for dying."

Charlie saw her eyes were wet and he didn't know what to say because he wasn't used to thinking about people the way they really were, especially women. He only saw them as people who were going to be dumb enough to buy his line of crap or who were going to slam the door in his face and leave him eating tacos-to-go that night instead of sitting down at a McDonald's. The judge had asked him if he had any friends and he couldn't think of any, and he'd never realized it before.

"I guess you did everything you could for her, Rose."

"You know what I found out? You can't ever do enough, least not enough to stop you blaming yourself afterward."

"There wasn't anything more you could've done."

"That's what they all say," she laughed softly, "but one day somebody's going to tell me I was a stinking little bitch without any heart and it'll be such a relief." She took the blue paper package into the bathroom and opened a cabinet, her voice clear and hollow because of the acoustics. "When are they going to call?"

"Uh? Who?"

"The people who are going to call Mr. Rackman?"

"Anytime."

She came back slowly, her arms folded across the blue striped sweater, eyeing him with quiet excitement. "Is that why you're so jumpy?"

"For Christ sake stop watching me always will you?"

He saw her look of shock as he turned away, making for the door, surprised his flash point had gotten so low, hearing her softly saying:

"It's just that I never saw anyone like you, Charlie."

"Okay," he said as he went on out, "so now you have."

At nine-fifteen by his watch he heard her talking to some guys at their breakfast in the café so he went into the lobby and thumbed the phone book and called Pacific, Airwest and American, getting their flight schedules and writing them down in the back of his sales itinerary book: three direct flights a day from Los Angeles, two one-stops—both at Ontario, California—and a noon plane change at Las Vegas.

His hands were shaking as he wrote and he felt a wave of something like self-contempt. There wasn't anything to get so steamed up about, he'd done a job for a big wheel and now he was getting paid off, that was all. He hadn't kidnapped the guy or anything, Stevens was perfectly free to walk out of here and he knew it. It was a deal between two people who understood each other and there wasn't any need to feel so uptight about it. Any normal guy would be hugging himself, getting a lucky break like this, Jesus, if he hadn't stopped his Chevy last night to do someone a good turn he wouldn't have gotten into this thing anyway, it was a kind of reward for humane services, you could say.

But just the same his hand was shaking as he wrote in the book and he supposed it was the strangeness of doing something like this for the first time, something this big, this important to him, he just didn't know how to handle it. Then he'd better goddamn learn instead of standing here with the sweat coming out of him and the ball-point shaking in his hand. He hung up as soon as he could because she could call him anytime and the line had to be clear.

Pa had dumped a heap of Morales *Gazettes* on the box by the reception desk and he dropped a dime in the tin and shook out the sports page, finding the Santa Anita charts. Rocky Mountain had come home at seven to one and he could've called the track for Chuck to get him on if he'd known she was running; Christ, he'd missed out again. Then he wanted to laugh because Chuck wouldn't have trusted him for more than ten bucks and that would've gotten him seventy so what the hell, he was already on a dead-sure winner and the payoff was a hundred grand!

He threw the paper down on the heap and looked straight into the policeman's eyes as he turned around, hadn't heard him come in, thinking about Rocky Mountain, something like a flash of iced lightning going down his spine.

"Hi."

"Hi there."

California Highway Patrol, polished belt and the gun moving against his hip as he pushed the swinging door open—"Hey Pa! You got any hash blacks for me today?" and the other guys laughing.

At twenty-one minutes after nine the main desk at Los Angeles County Courthouse received a call from the Wilshire Boulevard branch of City Bank.

"I'd like to talk to Judge Stevens."

"He'll be in Court Three—one moment, sir."

The line was switched.

"Court Three—Can I help you?"

"I would like to speak to Judge Stevens, please."

"Yes—who's calling?"

"Roger Staples, City Bank."

"Yes, Mr. Staples."

She came back in ten seconds.

"Judge Stevens hasn't arrived yet. The court won't convene till ten o'clock. Will you call again at a quarter to ten?"

"Are you sure the court's going to convene as usual today?"

"Why, yes sir, it's Monday."

"Would you please check on that for me? It's important."

"Well, I haven't heard anything—just a minute please."

It took longer than that and Betty came in with three currency receipt drafts for him to sign and went out again.

"Mr. Staples?"

"Yes?"

"You're right." She sounded more surprised than she wanted to show. "The court's been adjourned for today."

"Thank you."

"Is this Judge Stevens' residence?"

"*Sí, señor.* Yes."

"Is Judge Stevens there, please?"

"No. Is not here now."

"Thank you."

"Is a'right."

"Weinstock, Simon, and Brenner—may I help you?"

"Thank you. Is Mr. Clive Brenner there please?"

"May I say who's calling?"

"Roger Staples."

"Thank you, one moment."

She came back almost directly to say that Mr. Brenner was on another line and could he return the call?

"No, I'll wait. It's rather urgent."

"I'll have a message put on Mr. Brenner's desk, Mr. Staples, to that effect."

"Thank you."

They were very efficient: Clive saw to that.

He buzzed for Betty and she came in and he told her that if Mrs. John K. Stevens called or stepped in he wanted to know at once, whatever he was doing.

"Okay, Mr. Staples."

Her eyes looked better this morning, she'd been having a bad time with them, the smog allergy. Faint voices on another line, someone asking for an early appointment, Friday. A phone ringing in a distant office. A soft voice, *yes sir.* Suddenly Clive.

"Roger, I'm sorry I kept you waiting—I was talking to New York. How are you?"

"Fine, how are you, Clive?"

"Pretty good. Tell me about this 'urgent' memo I see here."

Suddenly Roger felt a fool and wished he'd not been so precipitate—now that he had the Stevenses' attorney on the line his suspicions seemed outlandish. Surely it was the kind of domestic crisis that blew up even in the best of families, and he was going too far, calling their lawyer.

"Let me just give you the facts, Clive, then you can laugh the whole thing off for me and I'll go back to my work."

"Sure, let's do that."

"Okay, John Stevens isn't at home, he isn't at the courthouse, the Gomez trial has been adjourned for today, and Evelyn has just been here asking for a hundred thousand dollars in cash for John, who needs it in an emergency."

The silence went on for so long that he had to ask if Clive was still there.

"Yes, I am. Did she say what kind of emergency?"

"No."

"Did you give her the money?"

"No."

"Did she want it in a hurry?"

"Yes."

"When did she want it by?"

"Now."

"Has she left the bank?"

"Yes."

"Do you know where she's gone?"

"I told her to come back in an hour, do some shopping."

"What time was that?"

"Let's see, about ten or eleven minutes ago."

"Can I come and see you right away?"

"I wish you would."

"Fine."

Soon after ten-thirty Roger sent out for more coffee but Clive Brenner lifted a hand.

"It makes me nervous," he said.

"Me too," said Roger.

Neither of them laughed.

Roger sat behind his desk watching one of California's youngest, shrewdest and most smoothly running attorneys doing his job, which was thinking, the filtered sunlight from the windows giving a sheen to his dark healthy skin and gleaming on the discreet gold pin, the gold wafer-thin wrist-watch, the fine gold rims of his glasses, their lenses slightly tinted as a gesture to the Southern Californian sun. Clive looked his best in white shorts and T-shirt at the Beverly Hills Tennis Club, but he looked pretty good anywhere, not notably handsome but exuding so much tanned and golden health that he made you feel like you'd just come away from the dentist.

He looked for the third time at his watch.

"I'll be getting along."

"Maybe she just—well—got caught up with a friend or something," Roger said anxiously. He didn't want Clive to leave him with this thing on his back.

Clive swiveled his dark narrow head to look at him directly, as Roger had seen him do in court at a moment when he had something cogent or unexpected or annihilating to say.

"The only friend she has right now is the man who can give her one hundred thousand dollars in cash. She didn't think it was going to be you. Right?"

"You think she's trying to raise it somewhere else?"

"That is what I would do in her place."

"But Clive, I told her I'd do all I could."

"Did you mean it?"

"Well, not really, no, but—"

"I'd say she knew you didn't mean it."

Roger shrugged. "That might be true. But I thought I could help her more by trying to find John first."

Clive didn't reply. He was off on a new thought train, gazing at his slim folded hands, the gold signet ring catching the light. Roger knew he won many of his cases partly by a simple device: in examination he would let a silence begin and go on till the witness couldn't stand the strain anymore because he could hear his last words ringing louder and louder around the court, damning him, driving him to break this dreadful silence in an effort to redeem them. It was then, as he began speaking again, that he realized it wasn't his last words that were going to damn him, but these.

"I don't like to think I did the wrong thing, Clive. They're friends of mine and naturally I—"

"I would have done as you did."

"You mean that?"

"Of course." Clive stood up, getting his briefcase as Roger came round the desk.

"You know them better than I do. I suppose she didn't just decide on a mad spending spree?"

"No."

"And they're pretty—well—solid together, as far as—"

"Yes. If Evelyn wanted some money she'd ask John for it, and if he wanted it himself he certainly wouldn't send her to fetch it, not without a security man." He shook hands briefly. "Keep in touch and please call my office immediately if she visits you again, or telephones."

"You think she will?"

Clive opened the door. "Frankly, no."

At 10:36 Evelyn came down the steps of the Golden State Mutual Savings and Loan, her lime-green handbag under her arm. The sun was a glare and she put on her dark glasses, crossing the street at Beverly Drive and walking two blocks on the south side to the coffee shop and going in.

Suddenly ravenous, she ordered ham and two eggs on rye and drank two cups of milky coffee with it, feeling terrible that she was sitting here wasting time eating, but knowing that if she didn't have some protein she'd be likely to faint at some time during the day when she most needed her strength.

"I'd like some pie, please."

"Sure, honey. What kind?"

"It doesn't matter."

"Well, we have apple, pecan—"

"It really doesn't matter."

Her hunger seemed endless.

The telephone was at the back of the place and she called the John K. Stevens Living Arts Academy for Prisoners on Parole, canceling her weekly visit for this morning; then she called Miriam Stoner to put off their tennis foursome this afternoon with Phyllis and Toni, saying she'd turned her ankle a little, coming down some steps. Then there was the terrifying moment when she had to move from this world to the other, from the trivial concerns of charity visits and tennis foursomes to the reality of the world where she would, please God, find John.

At the bank she had asked for twenty quarters and now she took some from her purse, lining them up along the edge of the coin box, eight in a row, leaving the rest of them ready in case she needed them, her heart beginning suddenly to thud, sending its rhythm pulsing behind her eyes as she tried to steady her breathing, *the attitude of mind must be appropriate*, the book on her bedside table said, *to what is, not to what might be*, taking the leaf of notepaper and reading the number she had written down so peculiarly long ago as the thin voice had dictated it, the voice of the man she hated so fiercely that the feeling almost frightened her.

Taking the phone from its hook and lifting her right hand she realized, as the tip of her finger touched the dial, how tremendously important telephones were, how important this one was, its dial worn by people's fingers, right down to the dull brown brass, clicking away as she sent it slowly spinning, *otherwise we shall find ourselves living through unreasoning hopes and fears*, how absolutely right that is, how very logical.

"One more quarter, please."

"I'm sorry."

"That's okay."

The machinery jangling, and nothing more to do now, *instead of calmly coping with life as it comes*, so very right, the ringing tone beginning and the sudden urge to hang up in case something had happened that she wouldn't want to hear, ever to hear, standing and waiting, listening, caught in the limbo that lay between here and there, here where she was and there where she would be going. But he wasn't answering, there was only the ringing, measured and slow, designed by technicians who had decided precisely how long, how long each ring should last, and how long, how long the interval of silence, not answering, but this was the right number, ringing, the one he gave her, ringing, with nobody there to—

"Hello?"

Jerk of her breath.

"Is this Mr. Rackman?"

"Yes."

CHAPTER TEN

In room 19 of the Los Angeles Police Department's Operations Headquarters, Bureau of Investigations Group, Commander Hellman came from behind his desk and wandered across to the bookcase in the corner and stood gazing into the bottle. The time was 11:37.

Inside the bottle sailed a three-masted New England schooner under full canvas, as she had been sailing through most of Bill Hellman's life, and he looked at this beguiling scene whenever he felt the need for peace in his mind to prepare him for a spell of serious thinking. This was such a moment. On his desk one of the telephones rang and its sound was cut off abruptly as Lieutenant Brady took the call out front. A rhythmic chopping noise was becoming louder above the building, three floors higher, but Hellman ignored this too, if he heard it consciously at all: the patrol and liaison helicopters took off and landed on the roof pad throughout the whole of each day and he would probably notice them only if they stopped.

The sea was serene and the wind was fair, a few whitecaps flecking the choppy blue, the schooner's sails filled and pulling gently at their cables, the bows lifting from a shallow trough in the waves as she flew gracefully onward, *Maid of New England*. For her cargo she carried only the private and secret thoughts of this one man, freight that would never reach landfall.

His reflection left the glass as he turned away.

"Brady!"

"Yes, sir?"

"I want to see Lieutenant Delano."

"He just left the building, sir."

Brady stood in the doorway, hands behind him.

"Where'd he go?"

"Hotel Richmond, sir, the arson case."

Hellman thought a moment.

"Then get me Forester."

He moved back to his desk, his small feet planted with unthinking precision, toes turned slightly inward. His feet had moved with this precision along the streets of this city when he'd started out as a kid cop; then they had moved into the various buildings of the Los Angeles Police Department and taken him higher, always a little higher, year after year, so that his head was now a bit more gray and a lot wiser. On his way up he had made more friends than enemies, more hits than misses, and as many mistakes as it took for negative feedback to supply his personal guidance system with sufficient data to keep him on target. This target was not necessarily the office reserved for the chief of Operations HQ, where he now sat down behind the desk. Probably he had never thought of any kind of target in his life, and if he were asked to think of one he would be likely to say it was something farther on, somewhere "out there." Possibly he would never reach it, any more than the *Maid of New England* would ever reach landfall. He was wise enough to hope for that.

He was on the phone when Lieutenant Forester came to the doorway and waited quietly, a thin intelligent academic officer of twenty-six with a reputation for making incredibly educated guesses while everyone else was immersed in the yellow pages.

"Brady," the commander was saying on the intercom, "I want you to check those reports for me as a preliminary. I have to go to the dentist in twenty minutes."

"Yes, sir. Did it get worse in the night?"

"None of your damn business. Now, Forester."

"Good morning, sir."

"Listen, I wanted Delano to do this but he's not here, so you'd better get it right. Sit down. There's a man just left here who's the personal attorney to one of our Superior Court judges. Give it to you briefly, listen hard."

He spoke for three minutes and fifteen seconds and Lieutenant Forester made five notes in his book, which was typical: most of the others in this bureau would have made a couple of dozen.

"Right, you can get the addresses and the other stuff on your way out. See them at Beverly Hills first and try to see Cheever personally but don't call him off a case or go chasing him all over town: I just want you to absorb whatever action they've taken so far and then apply it to your subsequent findings. Talk to Staples at City Bank and ask him to contact me here if Mrs. Stevens calls him or shows up."

He had a thought and pressed the intercom.

"Elizabeth?"

"Yes sir?"

"Call the Bel-Air Tennis Club and ask them if Mrs. John K. Stevens had a court booked for today or if she was down to play with someone else. If the answer is no, don't do anything. If the answer is yes, ask them if she's canceled her game. If yes, tell me. If no, call them at hourly intervals to ask the same question."

"Till when, Commander?"

Forester saw him frown. Sergeant Elizabeth Brown was the only member of his own staff who called him Commander and he hadn't yet found how to stop her.

"Till they tell you she's canceled her game." He shut down the box and said to the lieutenant, "After you've seen that bank manager go and talk to the Stevenses' accountant and ask him where Mrs. Stevens might be expected to go to raise a large sum of money in cash if she couldn't do it at City

Bank. She may have a savings account, or more than one. Questions?"

"Yes, sir. Do you want me to keep in frequent contact with you as I get information, or play the whole thing through and make—"

"Keep in close touch."

"Okay."

"If I'm not here the only other place I'll be is the dentist's: not our own man, he couldn't fit me in. Call me there if you turn up anything that can't wait, right?"

"Right, sir."

Forester sat with his hands folded neatly on his knees.

"Don't you want to make a note to get the name and address of the dentist on your way out?"

"No, sir."

"Got a head like a damned computer." He swung his chair on its swivel and looked across the panorama of downtown buildings, putting a question of his own to himself because the last part of Forester's mission could turn out tricky. The question was whether to postpone his appointment with the dentist and do this last job himself or rely on this boy to cope on his own. After a short struggle he came up with an answer he knew was right. This case had his deep personal interest—though it wasn't an actual case as yet and pray to God it never would be. He had known John Stevens for quite a few years, naturally enough, since many of his cases went into the Los Angeles Courthouse for their adjudication; and he was taking unusually long steps in this inquiry for three reasons. One: John and Evelyn were personal friends and he knew them well enough to have certain fears raised in his mind, based on their attorney's report. Two: As a wealthy man with substantial investments, John and his family ran more risk of extortion by menaces in any one of its forms than other people. Three: As a Superior Court judge with a political future, and especially as the judge president of the Gomez trial with its Mafiosa connections,

John was peculiarly vulnerable to demands on his influence. The fact that Evelyn appeared to have received a ransom note didn't necessarily mean that demands of a different kind wouldn't be made as well.

This initial inquiry was therefore important, and as usual Hellman was tempted to handle the sensitive phase himself. But then *every* inquiry was important, and on the wall behind the desk there was a framed motto. *If You Think Any One Case is More Important than the Others, Please Get the Hell Out of Here*. And in one small sack of the cargo in the *Maid of New England*'s holds, never to be opened, was the thought that the notice on the wall was mainly for himself, to jog his memory. A corollary to this principle was that if the lower ranks weren't ever trusted with responsibility, how were they going to make any progress?

"Forester," he said, swinging his chair round, "I want you to finally visit the Stevenses' home on Canyon Drive and ask for Mrs. Stevens and try to break down any reticence on her part and get her to answer as many questions as you can. You know what the situation is, and you'll frame your inquiry accordingly. Be clever, subtle, sensitive and aware. It's likely she won't be home anyway, but there's a maid there. Ask to see any of the day's mail that Mrs. Stevens may have left around, and look particularly for any *envelope* that doesn't have a letter to match it. If there is one, put it into a bag and bring it. Right?"

"Right, sir."

"Finally we want a photograph of Mrs. Stevens. If she's there she won't give you one so don't ask. If she's not there ask the maid to show you any that are around, and use close-up and flash and we'll print our own copies." He looked thoughtfully at the lieutenant for a couple of seconds. "In giving you these instructions I'm taking certain liberties, and I'll be responsible for them, not you. That doesn't mean I have to get my ass kicked just because you've been stupid enough to let it happen. Questions?"

"Not right now, sir."

"All right. Action."

He was on the phone again before Forester had got up from his chair. "Elizabeth?"

"Yes, Commander."

"Get a full description of Mrs. John K. Stevens' personal car and have patrols alerted citywide. I just want to know where she is and the car is not to be stopped. Right?"

"What about tailing, sir?"

"We'll put a tail on if it seems appropriate at the time the information comes in. Also start checking press picture files for a photograph of Mrs. Stevens and if you find one make contact with Lieutenant Forester and tell him we don't need one from him: you know his itinerary."

He put the phone down and stared at the opposite wall for a minute. You could never be right. You had to make a snap decision in cases like this, hoping to beat the clock while you checked out the scant evidence available and set in motion whatever activity you felt was appropriate. But if you did too much they'd want to know who panicked and if you did too little they'd want to know who was asleep. You could never be right, and the only thing to do was compromise.

He picked up a different phone.

"Jackson?"

"Yes sir?"

"I want you to put out an all-points bulletin."

"Go ahead, sir."

"Believed missing, Judge John K. Stevens, driving new dark blue Cadillac Fleetwood license number JKS1 somewhere between Los Angeles and Las Vegas. Subject requested to contact this office as soon as possible. Read it back."

The line crackled faintly as he waited for her to speak.

"I have the money," she said.

There was another silence.

"You raised it pretty fast."

She hated his thin voice.

"I asked for a special run on a Federal Reserve bank."

The smell of coffee was strong: the percolators were kept heating at this end of the counter. She thought she would never like the smell of coffee again.

"Are you still in Los Angeles?"

"Yes," she said.

Silence again, then she heard paper scuffing.

"Listen. There's an Airwest plane leaving L.A. at eleven-fifty, Flight number 303. To Morales. Be on that."

"All right."

"And don't forget, you come on your own and you don't tell anybody or say anything or do anything stupid. Then we'll all be okay. If you play it straight, you don't have to worry, Mrs. Stevens, believe me."

Quietly and without thinking she said:

"You bastard."

A word she couldn't remember using since college.

Because somehow it was worse when he tried to show sympathy: it was incongruous, and made him evil.

"I know how you feel," his thin voice said.

"How shall I recognize you?" she asked.

The rest of the quarters were still lined up along the edge of the coin box, and the movement of her handbag knocked one of them off and it jingled on the floor. Her bag was hooked over her arm, and she must remember not to leave it anywhere, always keep it on her arm.

"You don't have to," he said. "Stand near the Airwest check-in."

"What shall I do if–"

The line clicked dead.

"Hello?"

He'd gone.

She took the quarters and picked the one off the floor and put them in a special compartment in her bag, one that she never used, remembering what she'd thought when she had bought it in I. Magnin last fall: how stupid to put all these complicated compartments when there's nothing one can keep in them.

Going out to the street, she felt shaky, and for a moment—

"Oh excuse me!"

"What?" Startled, her heart thudding.

"I think you forgot to pay!"

The woman looking curiously at her, taking in her dress and shoes.

"Oh, I—I'm sorry, yes."

The check was in her hand, screwed up into a ball, and she tore it a little before she could smooth it out, needing to hurry, conscious of being watched, suspected.

"Here—please pay it for me, will you?"

"I'll get your change. There's—"

"I don't want any change—I have to hurry. Thank you—thank you so much," the glare of the sun in her eyes as she started down the sidewalk, for a moment not in the least knowing where she must go but knowing she must hurry, the sidepiece of her dark glasses prodding her temple as she put them on awkwardly, having the weight of her bag on her arm.

There was a Yellow Cab at the crossing and she passed it and came back, bending to talk through the window. "Are you free, driver?"

"Yes, ma'am!"

She got in, too quick for him to get the door open for her, and sat back, feeling the strangeness of the different-shaped seat after the Cadillac, and wondering for an instant what she was doing here. Then her thoughts came together because she was getting angry at her own lack of initiative in a crisis.

"Can you get me to the airport in time for the Airwest plane to Morales?"

"What time's it leaving?"

She was still not thinking efficiently.

"Oh–eleven-fifty."

"You have your ticket already, ma'am?"

"No, I don't."

"Well anyway, we'll give it a try. The freeway's pretty good, this time of day."

She closed her eyes, leaning her head back and feeling the acceleration as the taxi got under way. She would call Arco and have them pick up her car and take it home. She wouldn't ever have been able to drive to the airport herself, feeling like this and having to go fast.

"Thank you," she said.

"Huh?"

"I said thank you."

Charlie Berlatsky hung the receiver back on the hook and stood there in the booth in the lobby and after a minute bunched his right hand into a fist and drove it slowly against the coin box, the flat of his knuckles hitting it square and hard enough to hurt a little as the secret laughter began bubbling up inside him and the whisper came hissing through his teeth, "Oh . . . *Jesus,*" his hand making slow flat jabs at the metal box, "Sweet . . . *Jesus,*" his knuckles hurting enough to relieve him a little, control him a little so he wouldn't get that feeling he had in the roadway that time when he'd stood out there in the dark and the blowing sand, bent over the helpless laughter that had come shaking out of him; it mustn't happen now or they'd come trooping out of the café and look at him and tell somebody to come and pick him up and take him to the nut house.

In a while he came out of the phone booth and stood with his back to the desk, leaning his arms back on it and looking around for something ordinary to think about because if he thought about the other thing he didn't know what would happen, have to take it slowly, kind of ease his mind into it so there wouldn't be too much shock, leaning back on the desk and looking around at the peeling paint and the notice about visiting the Quaint Old Ghost Town of Legendary Indian Rock and the sand on the floor and his own feet as he looked down, his own white calfskin shoes with the rips and jags in them, the creases, not quite, would you say, not quite the kind of shoes you'd expect to see on a man who was worth . . . one hundred . . . one hundred thousand . . . one hundred thousand dollars?

I have the money, she'd said.

Just a voice on the phone and what did it mean, it meant that Charlie Berlatsky had hit the jackpot after forty-three years of being a loser. He began wanting to laugh again and couldn't seem to stop it this time so he just pulled the door open and went outside and walked through the auto court with his right hand shoved in his pocket and his left thumb hooked in the slit, walking steadily till he came to the road and just walking on, letting it come out now, the laughter, letting it come out of his chest in long quiet jerks in time with his footsteps as he looked up at the sky and saw how big it was today, how really enormous, the roof of a whole goddamn world, he'd never noticed it before, a blaze of dazzling blue flung from horizon to horizon and all his, all his own to walk under, the laughter coming out of him in long steady jerks as he walked under the roof of his whole new world and had to shut his eyes because it dazzled him, weaving a little like a drunk because he couldn't see, having to look up again and taking a deep breath as the last of the laughter came out and died away and left him weak and spent with it, his legs slowing, stopping, till he stood alone in the road and the rising heat of the sun thinking *Berlatsky you've made it, you've made it, you've done it at last.*

It took him a minute to realize there wasn't any wind. The wind had died and the air was soft and still and gold, the desert flowing from here where he stood to the far horizon and meeting the great wide blue in a thin line, shimmering in waves of heat. He stood watching it, the warmth of the day around him, thinking of her voice and the way she'd said it, so simply, feeling sorry for her because this thing had scared her so much, more than he'd imagined it would. And the judge in there, in that tacky beat-up dump over there with the sign hanging still at last, a big man on a bed with a lot of pain in him, down on his luck, his pretty little chick dead and gone and his wife scared to hell and oh Christ, Berlatsky, what've you been doing to these people, you better make it up to them now you're all right.

Walking back, slowly back, not laughing anymore, he thought well what the hell, they were off the hook just as soon as she got here. He'd treat them nice while they finished the deal and then he'd blow and go far, far away and they wouldn't ever see him again and all they'd lose was a hundred grand and to them that was only money. The heat of the sun was on his back and he walked faster, turning onto the tire-streaked auto court. It was only money to them but for him it was a different way of life, maybe some place near Acapulco, nothing grand, just a little white house with a patio and a palm tree and a girl with him, someone young and this time for keeps, not like the others, Cynthie or Marge or Chicago Phyllis or that horsey bitch Dolores, somebody real this time, a girl he could love and look after and show around at the casinos, a girl for his whole new world.

It wasn't much cooler inside the motel but at least there was a roof on.

"Hey Mabel, gimme a beer!"

"Amber?"

"Sure."

There were only two guys in here, hard-hats, that was their Dodge pickup outside. The cop had gone, thank Christ, they ought to make a little more noise coming in a door, those slobs.

She wiped the froth off the tray.

"Didn't I see you in here before?"

"Sure you did, Mabel. I own this goddamn place."

Her jaws stopped dead on the gum. "When d'you buy it?"

"Oh listen," he said laughing, "you think I'd be crazy enough to buy a dump like this?" *But he could, he could if he wanted.*

"What's wrong with it?"

"Huh? Oh it's great, really. Where's Rose?"

"She's around, I guess."

"She in the kitchen?"

Mabel laughed with all her gums. "Get in there too often an' Pa'd throw her out, you better believe me!"

He just had to talk to somebody who'd understand, not exactly tell anybody, just talk to them so he could say things that'd show how he was feeling, otherwise he was going to blow a fuse. He drank up his beer.

"I bring you another one?"

"Nope."

He tipped a quarter to see what it felt like and it felt absolutely great. He went out of the café and along to where her door was marked *Private* but she didn't answer when he knocked, so he went down the passage but there was only a little chicana with bright black eyes and legs like frankfurters, carrying an armful of dirty sheets.

"You want anything?"

"I'm looking for Rose."

"She ain't here," and through the other door marked *Gem Shop*.

He didn't see her right away because she was standing so still among all the postcards and trays of stones and Mexican silver and stuff, a square of sunlight burning on the floor by the window. She was looking at him without saying anything, just watching, holding something bright in her hands, the sunshine coming up off the floor and making a kind of glow all around her.

"Hello Rose," he said. It was the sort of place where you talked quietly, dust on everything and everything old, a tray near him full of rusty spurs and horseshoes, and a box of arrowheads. You could feel this was a ghost town.

"Hello," she said.

She didn't smile or anything, and he remembered he'd snapped at her the last time, he couldn't remember about what.

"I was looking for you," he said.

Her stone-blue eyes were very clear, watching him.

"For me?"

He came down the three steps to the earth floor.

"Well, sure."

She waited for him to come closer, watching him all the time with her clear stone-blue eyes. The thing in her hands began flashing as he passed through its reflection and he saw it was some kind of medallion on a silver chain.

"What did you want me for?" she asked him.

He shrugged. "To talk to. What's that thing?"

"This?" She held the thin chain high, and the medallion spun slowly in the sun like a silver fish. "It's the sign of the Thunderbird. Look." She caught it and showed him the engraved Indian figure. "Know what it means?"

"No."

"Everlasting happiness."

"It does?" She seemed pretty solemn about the whole thing.

"Yeah. That's what I want for you, and that's why I chose it."

She took his right hand and made him open it and dropped the medallion on his palm, the thin silver chain flashing as it coiled. She was smiling. "It's for you."

"Well—well that's really nice, Rose."

"It's Mexican silver. I've been here quite a while, trying to find something you'd like." She showed the ruby ring on her finger. "After the kind of jewelry you're used to, I couldn't expect to find anything in this place, imagine. But it's the message that gives it something. I know all of them, the meaning of the Indian signs—crossed arrows for friendship, morning stars for guidance, a lasso for captivity, they're fascinating and I've studied them, have you?"

"No."

She took the medallion and put the chain around his neck and her mouth came close and he kissed her, the sun against his eyes through the loose cloud of her hair, the warmth of her bare arms going around him, the smell of her body and beyond it the smell of the ancient earth under their feet, and what she'd said, everlasting happiness, and her wanting something to give him, standing so quietly in here alone, thinking of him, when he'd come in.

He was stiffening and pressed himself against her so she would know, and for a time she didn't do anything. He could feel her thinking and waiting and then she threw everything over and her hands began helping him because of his bandage, the zipper of her jeans making a quick rough sound in the stillness as she jerked it down, her mouth still on his and their tongues alive, her straw-yellow hair against the sun and then her soft murmuring beginning. Their feet shifted on the earth and she was ready and smooth and generous, helping him all she knew, eager and quick, the polished gemstones rattling faintly together in the trays where she leaned, arching herself for him, her eyes closed and her lashes soft and fair and sometimes opening to look at him, cloudy and remembering and closing again as she whimpered, not caring, saying his name over and over, Charlie, oh Charlie, suddenly crying out and shuddering and turning her head away, her eyes squeezed shut, his attention so full of her, like he always did it, needing to see everything, that he hadn't thought about himself, and now he let go and the sun burst and the polished stones rattled and spilled behind her and she cried out in pain but he didn't know because there was only this to know.

"*Charlie, Charlie,*" pulling herself away from the shelf and straightening and waiting awkwardly, till in a while he drew away and tried to steady her and she hung on him limply.

They stood like that for a long time, her tears drying and her breath like a child breathed, not wanting to wake.

"You okay? Rose?"

"Yeah. My back," and she laughed gently and he rubbed it for her, where it had been pressed against the shelf of trays. "Oh, Charlie," she began, like everything she wanted to say was in his name, "oh, Charlie."

"Your back hurt?"

"Okay now. You okay, Charlie?"

"Sure."

"Let me do it for you."

His hand was throbbing again because he'd had it pressed against the edge of the shelf, Christ she'd been beautiful, swing high and to hell with everything else, the door not even locked, something bright on his chest, the medallion.

"You look great with your hair like that."

"I did it for you."

"I mean instead of braids."

"That's what I mean," she said, laughing softly, "oh, *wow*," leaning against him, exhausted.

There were patches of color on the dark earth floor, rose quartz and tiger's eye and turquoise, and a label, the wrong way up, *25¢ each*. Dust was floating in the sun where it made a square on the floor.

"I don't know," she said against him, "what I'm going to do when you go. I don't know, Charlie."

"What you're going to do?"

"Yeah. I mean really." She pushed away from him suddenly, sighing, combing her long hair back with her fingers, looking out through the grimed window where the sun came, standing with her back to him, her thumbs hooked through the belt loops of her jeans and her shoulders hunched. "Oh shit," she said, "I only just thought of it, see." She turned around and looked at him suddenly, her eyes still pink from the crying, looked at him like she'd never seen him before, but it couldn't be that, then he got it, like she wasn't ever going to see him again. "I just wish you hadn't come here, Charlie," going to the door with her feet scuffing on the three steps, a dark stain on her jeans, opening the door and going out and shutting it behind her.

"Rose!"

It was just that everything had kind of happened at once and he hadn't had time to relate with what she'd just been saying. Women were like that, it didn't matter what they were doing, they went on thinking, and now—

"Rose!" he called out, hitting his toe on the bottom step and jerking the door open. She was going through the lobby to her room to clean up a little or something, a thick red line across her back between the sweater and her jeans where she'd been pressed against the shelf; it must have hurt bad. "Rose," quietly this time, not wanting anyone else to hear as she turned and looked at him with her face kind of blank.

"Yeah?"

Like he wasn't anybody she knew.

"*. . . she go an' have to die for, with all this work to do, leavin' me to—*"

"*Pa!*" she yelled with her eyes bright, "*cut that out, you hear me?*"

Charlie knew she'd loved her ma, before her ma had turned into just something at the hospital, like one of the nurses.

It was very quiet suddenly, the whole place, and he could imagine Pa and Mabel and the two hard-hats in there all looking at nothing, shutting their ears. It was very quiet.

She turned away and he whispered.

"Rose."

She looked back, impatient.

"Yeah?"

He beckoned to her but for a minute she kind of sagged, like she felt she had too much to deal with, not moving, watching him like she was trying to remember him. "What d'you want, Charlie?" She came toward him with her face clearing a little, sort of questioning, as if she was ready to help if there was something he needed. He went back down the steps into the gem shop and she came through the doorway and stood looking at him.

"How did you mean," he asked, the door still open but no one could hear in the café, "you don't know what you're going to do when I go?"

Her face went blank again, lost-looking.

"Are you crazy?"

"Listen," he said, "shut that goddamn door." He waited till she had. "You mean you'd miss me?"

She frowned like she didn't understand.

"Are you kidding, Charlie?"

"I just wish you'd try and talk straight, Rose, what's in your mind, I mean I don't want to get it wrong and say something stupid. The thing is, you don't even know me."

She slid down the door and sat on the top step, he guessed her legs were aching, like his, because of how they'd done it. She leaned her head back so she could look up at him and rest at the same time.

"All I know about you," she said, "is all I want to know."

"Okay, then why don't you come with me?"

"Yeah," she said with a funny little laugh, "why don't I?"

He waited for her to finish what she was saying or say something more but she was done, apparently, and he didn't understand what was in her mind.

"Rose, what the hell are you talking about?" He crouched on his haunches in front of her. "Listen, you remember I was telling you how I've always been a loser because there's always something happens or a guy lets me down, remember, and I said this time it's different, I'm going to win, and this time it's the jackpot? Remember?"

"Sure," her head angled back against the door, watching him through her narrower eyes, listening, "yeah, you told me."

"Well, listen," but he had to stand up and move around a little because of the big sky he'd seen out there and the whole new world and he couldn't say anything sitting on his hams, "listen, Rose, I'm moving out of here tonight or maybe tomorrow, so why don't you come with me? You like Mexico, down the coast around Acapulco? I'm buying a little place down there, see, with a nice view and somewhere near a racetrack because I've worked out a system, and—well—I guess that's all there is." But he couldn't keep from sounding excited about it and he wanted to say it, say the actual words, *I'm moving out of here with a hundred thousand dollars in cash and that's how I'm going to set me up and start living*, but she thought he already had that kind of money because of being a top aide to a big wheel and giving her an expensive-looking ring and everything. He had to be careful what he said but the thing was it'd be great to take her with him—she was young and not bad-looking and Christ she knew how to do it and that was very important.

She didn't say anything but she'd leaned her head away from the door and her eyes were wide open, watching his face.

"I'd give you a good time, Rose." He felt for the pack and tapped out a cigarette and lit it, the smoke of the match leaving a streak of blue across the sunlight. "You could have whatever you wanted, I mean really, you'd just have to ask, the price wouldn't make any difference, see, I only want you to understand you'd be okay for things; I'm not trying to sound like a big-mouth, you know? Really, I could give you a great time, the new house and everything."

In a minute she said, "Charlie, are you trying to *persuade* me?"

"Huh? Well, sure."

She nodded slowly. "And you can't find anyone better than a waitress out of a fifth-rate motel?"

"I don't know anyone nicer than you, Rose."

She watched him for a couple of seconds and then closed her eyes like the light had gotten too strong. When the tears began coming she scrambled up and fumbled around with the door, getting it open.

"Rose, you okay?"

"I'm not sure how I can handle this."

She didn't say it clearly and he heard the slam of her door on the other side of the lobby before he'd kind of got it pieced together, what she'd said.

CHAPTER ELEVEN

IT WAS A SHOCK because Stevens was a big man and he was standing up instead of lying on the bed and Charlie had to stop short as he came in or he would have bumped right into the guy. His nerves gave a jerk and it was a minute before he got his breathing right again.

"Judge, you okay?"

"Yes."

The leather suitcase was open on the floor with one end of the muscle-exerciser hanging over the edge, a couple of pairs of socks and a magazine and some underwear. There was steam coming through the bathroom doorway and Stevens looked pink-skinned, his thick hair still damp around his ears. He was naked to the waist and not flabby, all muscle and chest, and Charlie had the fleeting thought that if Stevens wanted to he could bust him straight through this wall and leave a hole, even with a stiff neck.

"She's coming," Charlie said.

"Pardon me?"

"Your wife. She's on her way."

"On her way here?"

"Sure."

The big man had become quiet, looking down at the clean shirt he'd taken out of the suitcase, his heavy eyelids low and hiding what he was thinking.

"Is she?"

"Gonna be here"—Charlie checked his watch—"in an hour."

The Judge stood perfectly still, just holding the shirt.

"So soon?"

"At the airport, I mean."

"Morales?"

"Sure."

The heavy head swung at last to look at him.

"Did she telephone you?"

"Well listen, how else would I know?"

"By telephoning her."

"Oh, sure."

"You didn't harass Mrs. Stevens again, Berlatsky?"

"Certainly I didn't!" The man's eyes were so steady, hard to look at for long.

"Good."

"I went out of my way to tell her there wasn't any need to worry, okay?"

"Thank you. Why did she telephone you?"

Charlie turned away and got a cigarette and remembered and put the pack back in his pocket, hitching one leg onto the edge of the dressing table, not answering right off because he still wasn't used to it and had to get a quick grip on himself, otherwise he'd say it with a kind of laugh.

"She has the money."

The Judge looked away and was quiet again for a minute.

"I see."

Charlie got off the dressing table, the handles swinging and knocking, "Well that's okay, Judge, isn't it? I mean we can tie up the deal and then I'm going to get out of this place and leave you off the hook." He waited. "Isn't that okay?"

Stevens nodded slowly.

"Excellent. Mr. Berlatsky, I would be obliged if, as a personal favor, you didn't mention that there was a passenger."

"Huh? Oh sure, Judge."

"I want to tell her myself."

"Listen," Charlie said, "I didn't go out there and bury that kid so I could blab about it afterward." He saw Stevens' eyes close for a minute and felt sorry for the guy: Theodora Creaturo had meant something to him and if it hadn't been for that goddamn wind blowing the sand around—well there wasn't anything they could do about it now.

He began putting the clean shirt on, moving slowly like he was under water. "Thank you," he said, "but I can manage."

"Sure."

Charlie wanted him to feel better about everything. He was so full of this terrific sensation himself that he wanted other people to share it with him. He didn't want anybody to feel sad. But of course the Judge had been shaken up by this whole thing and it had been a lousy shame about the kid; sure, he understood that.

"You feel like something to eat, Judge? I get you something?"

Stevens didn't answer because he was standing dead still with his face squeezed, waiting for the spasm to pass. He'd overdone it, washing up and putting the shirt on, his back still not right. Charlie wanted to do something for him but the man didn't like being helped.

"She'll be bringing some Ben-Gay, huh? Do you good."

He checked his watch again. It was a half-hour drive to the airport and he was going to leave here in ten minutes, giving himself time to deal with any kind of emergency like picking up a flat or something, Christ, he didn't want to be late for *this* rendezvous!

Stevens was lifting his massive head and his face was slowly clearing and in a minute he went on buttoning his shirt. "If there were some eggs," he said, "and some coffee."

"Sure. I'll go get it for you."

The gas-pump bell rang as he ducked out, and Rose was going through the lobby pushing a handkerchief into her jeans, throwing her long hair back as she went through the main door to the auto court, and he stopped, halfway along the passage, and thought hey, there goes my girl! He'd got a new girl, Rose, and she was nice and this time for keeps and he couldn't quite get a grip on the idea yet because everything was happening so fast: Just last evening he'd been driving down this road and if it hadn't been for the wind he maybe wouldn't have pulled in to this motel at all, he'd have gone straight past and found somewhere better, the Sandpiper or Shankey's or that place near Barstow, but he was here and that was his girl, Rose, and they were going to live in Mexico together and it was hard to believe, you could say that again.

The little chicana was in the café talking to the two guys with the truck and he could see the other girl through the hatch.

"Hey Mabel!"

"Yeah?"

"Couple of eggs, sunny side up, hash browns and toast and what've you got, jam or Jell-O or something, and cream, okay? And plenty of coffee, on a tray, for Room 7."

"Take awhile, we had a fuse blow."

"Pa fixing it?"

"Yeah." She gave a laugh, maybe meaning you should see that old guy up a ladder trying to find the gismo.

"Soon as you can make it, okay?"

"You bet."

"Everything nice, see, cloth on the tray and napkins, he's a friend of mine."

He checked his watch and went along to his room and picked up his straw hat, using a clothes brush, putting the hat down and dusting his shoes with some Kleenex, slicking back his hair and fixing his necktie in the mirror and going out, having to go back and pick up his hat again, his hands shaking a little as he put it on, standing in front of the mirror. You look better, Berlatsky, not scared anymore, you've made it now and it's what you said it'd be, the jackpot.

Going out to the auto court he wound his wristwatch a couple of times, make sure it didn't stop, he had to be there right on time and everything had to be the way it should. There was a truck full of horseshit at the pump, taking the stuff from the one-acre-and-horse-privilege community the other side of Indian Rock, and he thought of Dolores and wanted to laugh—*just think what that bitch has missed!* A hundred grand and a place on the coast and everything; she'd have done anything for a life like that.

The driver was still in the cab and Rose was standing watching the meter, her back to Charlie and not hearing him come up.

"Hello, sweetheart."

She swung round and just stared for a minute, holding her breath and then suddenly laughing, the sun in her eyes, shaking her hair back, and he thought she looked lovely.

"You look lovely," he said.

"Oh, Charlie," with a glance toward the cab in case the man could hear, then looking at him again with love in her eyes. He'd seen it before and knew what it meant and thought how serious a thing it was, how powerful it made you, kind of responsible. You had to handle it with care, like carrying something very fragile and not wanting to drop it. He'd seen two women look at him this way, Cynthie and Marge, and he'd had the same feeling, but each time he'd dropped it, the very fragile thing he'd been carrying, and the pieces were still somewhere back there, the way he'd come. He didn't want it to happen again.

"Listen," he told her, "Mabel's going to take him some food, okay?"

"What did you say?"

He had to tell her again and she smiled.

"Make sure he gets it, Rose. The guy hasn't eaten in a long time."

"Sure, Charlie." The gas checked off and the nozzle gave a jerk but she didn't take any notice.

"I'm going to the airport, Morales, and I'll be bringing his wife back with me."

"Whose wife? Oh, right."

"If she misses her plane or anything she might call the motel, asking for Mr. Rackman. Just take the message, okay?"

"Yeah." She bent down and took the nozzle out of the tank, fitting the cap back on. "Charlie?"

"What?"

"It's for real, isn't it?"

"For real?"

"What you told me. Everything you said."

"Mexico, and–"

"Yeah–yeah, that."

"A hundred per cent, sweetheart."

She caught her breath and then laughed again in that way she had, and he wondered why he'd ever thought she wasn't his type of girl, when she was so delightful.

She put the money in the black tin box in the closet, near where she kept the shotgun, catching sight of the photograph on the wall, a thing she never ordinarily did, only ever seeing it when she decided to look at it, mostly Sunday mornings because it had been a Sunday morning when her ma had died. She supposed something was making her look at it now, maybe because she was going to leave Pa again, like she'd done twice before, only this time she wouldn't be coming back.

The last time she'd stayed away a week, calling him twice to see how he was making out and hearing in his voice the things he refused to admit, that the place was in a mess and he was losing customers, *you think it takes a woman to run this place? That's what your ma used to think, but women on'y git 'n the way*, listening to him going on and knowing what was really happening and coming back, coming all the way back from San Diego at the end of that week and finding the trash cans full of burned hash browns he'd had to throw out, and the little chicana, Pepita, keeping away because she couldn't listen anymore to his dirty language and the noise he made when he smashed the dishes, coming back all the way to this damn place and settling in again, feeling there was something wrong with her because she seemed to be chained to it, couldn't seem to be able to break away.

The sizzling started again and that meant he must have fixed the fuse. There was a thumping noise too and she gave a yell:

"*Stop shaking that jukebox!*"

A couple of seconds of quiet and then Ron called back:

"Well it works *sometimes*, Rosie!" calling her Rosie just to make her mad at him.

Standing in a row, her and Pa and Ma, looking at the man with the camera. Ma had gone and now she was going, and there'd only be Pa here and that was tough to take, but she was going to leave him every cent she'd saved up, almost eight hundred thirty dollars, to start him off paying for the new girl he'd need to take her place. She couldn't do any more than that, leave him all she'd ever saved in her life. The times before, she hadn't left him anything because she'd needed it herself, to set herself up somewhere, but this time was different: there was Charlie, *you could have whatever you wanted, you'd just have to ask*. This time she'd have everything in the world.

She felt breathless and had to lean on the wall, the head of a thumbtack pressing into her shoulder—a lot of the pictures had been fixed with thumbtacks because they were real glossy photographs with signatures on, not just pictures she'd cut out of magazines. One day she'd have a photograph, a huge big one taken for her specially, of Charlie, so even when he wasn't around she could look at his thin funny face with its secret kind of smile, and his bright quick eyes that went flickering around and noticing things even while he was talking.

So this is how it hits you, she thought, this is what it does to you, making you feel weak so you can't breathe and have to lean on the wall, this is what I hoped would happen to me one day while I was still young, and now it has, and I know what they've been talking about since the world began, and all I don't know, like I told him, is how I'm going to handle it.

At twelve-fifteen Charlie drove the Chevy through the gate and parked the car and walked into the main building of Morales National Airport and felt how cool it was: after all night in the Desert Winds he'd forgotten what air conditioning was like.

He checked his watch with the clock on the wall and set it back one minute, seeing a flower shop and going over, Jesus, ten bucks a dozen but what the hell, he wanted to make her feel less bad about things. Giving her carnations would show her that everything was okay now, it was just a deal between friends.

"Hey mister!" he said.

"Yes?" The man in the white ducks turned back in the doorway.

"Is this your wallet?"

"Why, yes!" Charlie handed it to him. "Thank you–I really appreciate that!"

"Anytime."

Charlie counted his change and took the carnations, his hands a little shaky still because she might not get here or they might try something on him, but it was just his nerves, he knew that.

The arrival time was on the board, 12:25, and a little before that he went outside again and stood in the parking lot to watch for the plane. The sky was a perfect blue with not a single cloud anywhere, and heat waves shimmered along the tops of the cars, the sun sparking on their chrome, dazzling him. There was a kind of silence, the kind where small sounds made you realize how quiet it was, and he could even hear a mockingbird calling somewhere over the desert where the runway came to an end. Standing here with flowers, watching for a plane, he felt he was on vacation, meeting a girl, excited, like it had been with Marge all that time ago, and he began thinking of a whole lot of things in his past life, minutes like this, waiting for someone; the time when he and Cynthie and the kid had sat in a meadow in Wisconsin, listening to the larks and then looking at each other and laughing because they'd enjoyed the sound so much; the time when Blue Bimbo had come in at seventeen to one at Arizona Downs and he'd had fifty on to win; and other times and things he'd done and places he'd been happy in. And he thought maybe it was because he'd gotten so stuck in a rut trying to rake in enough bucks to make him a living it hadn't left him any time to think these things, and he could think them now, letting them drift into his mind, soft and colored and exciting, because that part of his life was over and there was a new one beginning.

He took a deep breath and laughed a little, his eyes full of the sky as he stared across the buildings and the control tower, waiting for the first faint smudge of the airplane.

After a while he had to look down because of the glare, and tip his straw hat lower across his eyes. Over by the fence there was an old guy in work clothes, pushing a cart and looking for more newspaper and other stuff to pick up, where it had been blown by the strong wind last night, and he thought dear Jesus, what's that poor bastard going to be able to tell Peter at the Pearly Gates—I spent my life picking up garbage other people left around, anything else you want to know?

From the main building he could hear a voice on the P.A. speakers and looked up again and saw the faint shape in the sky, still half-lost against the blue but getting sharper, floating lower, taking on color, the yellow of the Airwest line. He watched it for a while, not wanting to look away in case if he did and then looked back it wouldn't be there. He watched it, breathing deep and slow and feeling the warmth of the day inside of him, the yellow growing bright and the sun flashing once across the pilot's windshield as the wheels came level with the tops of the distant hangars and the plane became watery-looking in the heat-shimmer.

12:26 by his watch.

He didn't move fast, there was plenty of time. He moved slow, strolling between the parked autos, finding his wallet and pulling out a dollar and dropping it on the ground by the fence here where the old guy would pick it up, sliding his wallet back, feeling how thin it was and thinking he'd need to buy a new one, a little larger, because right now there was only a five-spot and three ones left in there and he never carried much more than that. In the future he'd make a point of keeping fifty in his wallet, maybe a hundred; it gave a man style when he paid for things, and people respected him, like they did when he wore nice clothes.

The smell of hot tar and a bus gunning up somewhere near the baggage area, the sun on the steps and through the swinging doors and into the cool, *Of course this is the Maharajah Collection, inspired by the ancient jewelsmiths of India, and frankly the prices are a little high for your needs from what you tell me, but let me suggest what we could do*, the high singing of the jet as the Airwest came nearer, swinging into the parking bay outside, *we could try this one on, because it has some very tiny scratches just here, can you see them? Sure, they're only tiny*, the people crowding slowly across to the waiting zone, a couple of kids with packs on their backs, waving to someone, a porter with a dolley, *but if it fits okay we could maybe bring down the price a little, say, 25 per cent, because frankly it worries me, keeping an imperfect piece in the collection. I'll tell you what we can do.*

They were coming through, the main group of passengers, and Charlie slipped his hand in his pocket again and looked at the photograph, the one he'd torn out of the magazine, the one showing Judge and Mrs. John K. Stevens and their golden retriever on the lawn outside their home in Beverly Hills, a good-looking dame with nice clothes—knew how to stand, knew how to smile. She'd be here because she knew she had to be, and if she'd missed the plane she'd have had time to call him before he'd left. She'd be here, somewhere in this bunch of people coming through now.

So I'll tell you what we'll do, we'll go throw this whole goddamn collection right in the garbage can, because that's where it belongs, see, that's what it is, it's garbage, it's junk, it's trash, and you must be about the most stupid goddamn bitch I ever talked to, except that slew of stupid goddamn bitches I talked to yesterday, and the day before, and the day before that, so you can go screw yourself, understand, you can just go screw yourself till it hurts and if you ever want to throw away your hard-earned money on trash like this you better go see someone else because Charlie Berlatsky, as of now, is out of town.

A rabbi, two kids with him, neat white collars and shiny shoes, somebody's birthday or funeral or what the hell, a girl like a mountain, sixteen, sucking on a candy bar, some guys in stetsons and a chicano with a long black cigar, one of the crew, with two rings and a ginger moustache, a woman in green, a big man—a rancher in a broad-brimmed hat laughing his head off with the other guy—the woman in green walking across to the other side of them, not with them, on her own, a big stylish handbag looped over her arm, lime-green to match her shoes and she was coming closer, it was harder than he'd thought it would be, because she wasn't smiling like in the picture and he should have asked what color she'd be wearing. Two other women over there, a teen-ager with them, woman in black, a chicana, a girl with her hand in a boy's, a tall brunette with her husband, no others, no other women on this flight, none that hadn't already gone to the baggage claim. It had to be this one, the one in green, her eyes screwed up a little like it was too bright in here, her face rather pale, the bag looped tight around her arm as she passed him quite close.

She went straight to the Airwest check-in and stood there looking around, and he drew a deep breath, not moving, watching the other people, the men, the big one and the rancher and the boy and the others, seeing where they went, noting how they walked and how their clothes were cut, looking for shut faces and busy eyes, not seeing any like that.

He gave it five whole minutes, seeing where they went, then took a better grip on the flowers and walked across to the woman in green.

CHAPTER TWELVE

Evelyn stood waiting.

The dizziness had passed off. It had started in the plane and she'd almost had to ask the stewardess for something, spirits of ammonia or whatever they had for stupid women who couldn't handle a crisis. She felt better now, though a little shivery with nerves.

She found her sunglasses and put them on, wondering why she did it, because it was less bright in here than outside. Nerves again, perhaps, or she instinctively wanted to hide herself as much as possible from these thugs. She couldn't see them, unless the two Mexicans over there by the coffee shop had been sent by Mr. Rackman. He didn't sound Mexican on the telephone.

Safe behind her sunglasses she watched them for a minute. They wore good suits and were talking together amiably, smiling. She thought they were probably businessmen, representatives. She knew that the moment she saw Rackman and his group she would recognize them for what they were: dangerous thugs. There was a stamp to people of irredeemable criminality, as she had come to realize over the years. Only a month ago she had seen the man Schumaker in the court when John had sentenced him to life for kidnapping: there'd been a total lack of expression in the man's face, a tacit arrogance in his being utterly unmoved either by what he had done or by what was going to happen to him after conviction. A man of Rackman's type, who would seize a fellow human and demand ransom for his release, would bear this same stamp she had seen in others.

This was why she couldn't stop shivering. Before, she had seen these men only across a courtroom, trapped animals calmly submitting themselves to judgment simply because they had no chance of refusing. But even in their very compliance it was clear to everyone else in the court that if men like these were able to reach a knife or a gun they'd slash or shoot their way out if they could, the violence in them exploding like a bomb. So she shivered, standing here alone and cut off from her friends, because she was here to make intimate contact with men like those, and surrender to their power.

Looking around her from one person or group to the next, she realized they weren't here in the main hall. There was only a group of teen-agers, a big man with a rancher's hat, a neatly dressed man holding flowers for someone, and two boys carrying kites. Everyone else was on the move and busy with their own affairs.

The first doubts came but she dismissed them because this was Morales and she had arrived on the flight Mr. Rackman had given her. She was only a few minutes late so they wouldn't have come and gone again. For some reason they must be late themselves, and as she began watching the main doors she felt frightened again because any hitch or delay could mean that something had happened to John.

When they came—if they came—they would have guns on them, she knew, but that didn't worry her unduly. The only thing that worried her, terrified her, was the thought that they might hold a gun to John and ask her to do something impossible. Standing here in her cool linen dress among these other people, for a moment touching a curl in the elegant hairdo that Marcello had given her Saturday she reflected again that later, somewhere, when these other people would not be on hand to help her, she was perfectly prepared to submit herself to rape or torture if it would save John from harm. Rape was a matter of spiritual revulsion more than anything, and she would be able to shield herself on a level where they had no power over her; in the event of physical torture she knew she would faint quickly, for the first time finding this tendency an advantage.

It had been thinking this out for herself on the plane that had made her dizzy, but she had persisted, wanting to know her own strength before it was assailed, because she knew that men vicious enough to take a female hostage would sometimes vent their spite or simply their lust, unable to resist the abuse of a helpless slave. In three cases over which John had presided this kind of thing had led to unintended death.

The thin man with the bouquet of carnations was obviously here to meet someone he didn't know, because he was now coming up to her, raising his hat and smiling.

"Mrs. Stevens?"

As she stared at him she felt everything go out of mental focus because this didn't make any sense. This wasn't Mr. Rackman, or one of his thugs; yet nobody else would know her name.

"Yes." She was aware of her distant voice saying it.

"I'm Charlie Berlatsky."

He held out the flowers for her.

She looked at them, a wild hope coming that John had already been released. Up at his thin smiling face.

"Did—did my husband send these?"

"No, Mrs. Stevens. They're from me."

In a moment she said, "Who are you, please?"

"Charlie—"

"I know but I mean what is your—why are you here?"

There was a flicker of surprise, then he said, "Oh sure, you know me as Mr. Rackman. I forgot."

She went on staring at his lively eyes, his pleasant and rather elfin face, trying to think why his voice was so different from the one on the telephone, why she hadn't recognized it the instant he spoke. Vaguely she thought it must be because this man couldn't possibly be the one on the phone.

"You," she said slowly, "are Mr. Rackman?"

"Yes. I had to use the other name, see, just for the phone calls."

"I see."

"Was it a nice flight?"

"Pardon me?"

"Good trip, was it, from L.A.?"

"Yes. Yes, thank you. Is—is my husband all right?"

"Sure. He has a little backache, right here at the top of the spine, just temporary. Did you bring the Ben-Gay?"

"Yes. What happened?"

"Huh?"

"What happened to my husband?"

"Just a slight auto accident."

"Are you lying to me?"

"Am I—well, of course I'm not lying, why should I?"

The dizziness was coming back and she took hold of herself, standing more upright, taking the flowers from him, wanting to behave normally because it would help. It was just that she'd been waiting here with her nerves in a fever and now there didn't seem to be anything terrible to cope with, and in a strange way it was a kind of letdown.

"Is John in a hospital?"

"No. We're at a motel."

"Is he confined to bed?"

"No, he was getting dressed when I left there, asked me to fix him up with breakfast."

She had a sudden and almost irresistible urge to sleep, just fall down and sleep. He was saying something again.

"I'm sorry?"

Quietly again he said, "Did you bring the money?"

"Yes."

He gave a quick laugh.

"Okay, let's get in the car."

Charlie held the pack to her but she shook her head.

"You mind if I do?"

"Not at all."

He lit up and noticed she wound the window down an inch, and the slipstream began whistling as he sped up along the entrance ramp to Interstate 15.

"Were you involved in the accident?" she asked him.

"Who me? No. Oh, this"—he gave a short laugh—"I did that with a can opener." The smoke was drifting across her because the gap in her window was creating a vacuum, so he opened his own.

"Who else was in the accident?"

"Nobody."

"He didn't hit another car?"

"Nope. He was riding alone and went into a dip, that's all. There was sand blowing across the road and we couldn't see too good, that was the whole trouble."

"*We* couldn't see? Where were—"

"I was right behind him. That's how I saw him go off the road."

"You went to help him?"

"Why, sure."

She was quiet for a time and he sat thinking again what a beauty this Mrs. Stevens was, not young anymore, okay, but then she was the type who didn't seem to be affected by her age: it was all in the eyes and the way she moved, all in the style. She had class. She must have stopped them dead on the street when she was twenty.

"When you said, on the telephone, that 'things would get very serious' for my husband, what did you mean, please?"

"Well, I guess—well, that's exactly what I meant."

"What would you have done to him, if I hadn't agreed to do what you instructed?"

"Done to him? I wouldn't have done anything at all!"

She turned to look at him. "But I don't understand. On the telephone you threatened me with—"

"Well okay, Mrs. Stevens, I guess it could've sounded that way, but I only meant what I said: that if you didn't co-operate, things'd go pretty bad with the Judge."

She was still watching him. "You're not holding him under any kind of duress, Mr. Berlatsky?"

"Listen, I'm not that kind of a guy. You better just wait and let him explain everything, okay? You just relax and take it easy and everything's going to be fine."

She was quiet again and they didn't say much for the rest of the ride. He sat thinking about that big green handbag, imagining the look of the stuff inside it, whole bundles of it, new and crisp, thinking about what it could do, was going to do. You could buy a nice little place for twenty-five grand over there where things were cheaper, and for fifty you'd buy yourself into a mail-order business or a franchise, get yourself a guaranteed income, enough to play the ponies and come out smiling. He didn't want to think about it or he'd start laughing again and she'd think he was nuts.

When he swung the Chevy into the auto court she said:

"Is this the place?"

"Yes. Not the kind of place the Judge stays in normally, you can say that again. But we were kind of running for shelter, out of that wind."

He got out and threw his cigarette down, still half-smoked, so as not to make the Judge cough in there.

"We take these flowers in?"

"Oh yes, they'll need water." She took them from him. "Aren't they beautiful?"

"Kind of nice against that dress."

"Thank you." She seemed to hesitate as they began walking to the motel entrance, then said too easily, "Is there anyone else here with you, Mr. Berlatsky?"

"Anyone else?"

"I mean—well, associates."

He gave a quick laugh. "Only the Judge."

She laughed with him a little and it didn't sound right because she wouldn't see what was funny, maybe she was still scared of him and was trying to yes him along. He didn't like that—people shouldn't be scared of each other.

"He's okay, Mrs. Stevens, really. Some backache and a bit of delayed shock, but he wouldn't even let me call a doctor for him. Couple of days and he'll be in great condition again. You don't have to worry about a thing, like I told you before."

"All right," she said, not looking at him.

He opened the door for her and followed her in.

"*. . . themselves women's libbers but they don't even know how to cook, it bugs the bejesus outa me, y'know that?*"

There was some more but the sizzling drowned it.

"Down along here, Mrs. Stevens," neat in his pin-stripe suit and feeling chivalrous, escorting the lady to the room where his associate was waiting, thinking at the back of his mind it was crazy, all you had to do was shake the tree and down the stuff came, all over the ground, a hundred thousand, crazy, you could say that again.

He knocked at the door of Room 7.

"Come in." Very low, a voice like out of a big bass drum.

Charlie opened the door and stood back. She didn't go right on in, but just stood there looking. Across her shoulder Charlie saw the Judge standing in the middle of the room, looking like a real gent now with a necktie on, and his sport coat, holding himself upright with his feet together, waiting, as if he'd been waiting ever since he knew his wife was on her way. His face was still pretty white and the gash on his forehead was puckered and turning black, and there were damp splotches on his sport coat where he'd been trying to wash the blood out, but he had a smile on his face, and Charlie hadn't seen him like that before, only in pain and worried stiff, and he could see now how much charm this guy must have when there wasn't anything bad on his mind. Too, it took guts to get out of that bed and wash up and put his clothes on without any help, his back the way it was, to be standing here ready for when she came, so she'd see he was perfectly okay, and in a funny kind of way Charlie felt touched, and proud of him.

"Evelyn, my dear . . ."

Then she ran into the room and held him and began crying, just shaking without making any noise, and Charlie shut the door and stood outside in the passage thinking no, they're not all bastards, not all of them, they're people like us, underneath all that money and power. He could hear Mrs. Stevens crying now and it embarrassed him to be here listening so he went along the passage as far as the lobby.

Rose saw him from the café and came out, a soft shine in her eyes. She had a dish towel in her hand.

"Was that his wife, Charlie? In green?"

"Yes." He took her hand. "Okay sweetheart, how long d'you need to get packed?"

She drew a breath, her eyes coming open wide. "You mean you're ready to go?"

"When you are."

"Well gee, Charlie, I–I didn't realize!"

"I had to wait till she came, see. Now we can go."

She drew her breath in again, looking around her like the whole place was kind of disappearing in front of her eyes, and it made him realize the same thing was happening to him: He was watching the whole of his past life disappearing and a new one beginning, while they stood here in the lobby of a beat-up motel in the desert, holding hands, like they'd rubbed Aladdin's lamp and asked him to carry them both away to paradise.

On a breath she said, "How long can you give me, Charlie?"

"Can you make it in an hour?"

"An *hour!*" She went on staring at him and then laughed suddenly, like out of joy. "Well I can try!"

"Have you told your pa yet?"

"No—I'm going to leave him a note."

"Okay, and listen"—they had to whisper because the swinging door to the café was open—"you don't have to pack everything you own, I mean just the things you value, see, because I'll buy you all the new clothes you want, everything you could ever need, okay?"

"Oh Charlie . . ." She leaned against him with her head back and her eyes closed, smiling, trembling against him, dreaming of what he said. He squeezed her hand, letting her go.

"Make it an hour, Rose."

She opened her eyes and nodded quickly, tears of excitement coming as she threw down the dish towel she was carrying and broke for her room. He stood there a minute, thinking how fast things had happened, it was hard to believe, then he went along the passage and knocked on the door and there wasn't any answer and he knocked again and Stevens called to come in.

He was still standing in the middle of the room, facing the door. His wife was using her compact, leaning across the dressing table, glancing up at Charlie as he came in and then looking back into the mirror, dabbing at her face where she'd been crying.

"Okay?" Charlie asked them.

"It was kind of you," Stevens said in his deep slow tones, "to meet my wife with flowers. Most kind."

"Not at all, Judge." The big green handbag was on the bed and he went over to it, putting his hand on the rich polished leather. "I'd like to settle now, okay?"

Mrs. Stevens clicked her compact shut.

"I couldn't get the money," she said.

CHAPTER THIRTEEN

Commander Hellman was back in his office by twelve noon, smelling of cloves and with his lower facial nerves, left side, still numb from the anesthetic.

"Brady!"

"Yes sir?"

"What's been the action?"

"Reports are on your desk, sir."

Lieutenant Brady stood in the doorway.

"I can see that. What else?"

"Delano sent for prints; there's been a new lead on the North Hollywood killing and one of the motor patrols smashed into a storefront avoiding a kid."

"In pursuit?"

"No, sir."

"Right."

Brady wandered out to his front desk.

Six reports, only one of them from Lieutenant Forester.

Firm of Shaw and MacIntyre, accountants, state the Stevenses have account with Golden State Mutual Savings and Loan, Beverly Hills. Will check there for withdrawal.

A voice somewhere in the reception office was asking if the boss was back and someone else asked didn't they see him come in? Two seconds later one of his intercom sets began flashing.

"Well?"

"Yes, Commander"—couldn't that bloody woman call him

'sir'?—"Mrs. John K. Stevens canceled a tennis game she'd had booked for this afternoon at the Bel-Air Tennis Club."

"What time?"

"What time was the game booked—"

"No, what time did she cancel it?"

"Between eleven and noon, sir. I was calling the club at hourly intervals."

"Right."

"Can you take a call from Beverly Hills?"

"Who?"

"Lieutenant Cheever."

"Yes."

Three minutes later the lieutenant was on the line.

"Listen, Cheever, I've got your written reports up to the time when you went to see Mrs. Stevens personally. Tell me about that."

"She was just leaving the house, sir, on Canyon Drive, when I arrived there. I questioned her about the reports she'd made earlier but she seemed rather nervous, and in a hurry."

There was a pause.

"I'm listening. Go on till I tell you to stop." Those Beverly Hills Beauties were always so shit-scared of rank.

"Yes sir. The first thing I noticed was that when she said she'd located her husband, and I asked where, she evaded the question: she just said he was all right and that she was going to bring him home. The second thing was that she said there'd been slight damage to her husband's car, and when I told her we'd had no report about an accident to that particular car she looked kind of confused. I was watching for her reaction on that. Third thing, sir, was that she excused herself by saying she had an appointment at the hairdresser's, but I'd say she'd only had it done pretty recent. I think that's all, sir."

"Right. Nervous, evasive—scared, would you say? Actually frightened?"

Silence for a couple of seconds.

"Yes sir, or at least I'd say she could have been. I'd never met the lady before, so I wasn't able to—"

"All right Cheever, you've been a help. If anything else occurs to you, call me."

He hung up and swung his chair around and looked at the downtown buildings through the solar-glass window and didn't see them because all he could see were John and Evelyn at the Los Angelinos' Charity Ball that night, Saturday of just a week ago, John quietly and courteously throwing off the ass-kissers who'd been moving in on him since the day he'd said he might relinquish his post and enter the race for governor, Evelyn smiling to everyone, putting them at their ease, always listening and never saying much. Where were they now, for God's sake, those two? And who could ever find them if he couldn't?

A button lamp began flashing behind him and he caught its reflection on the glass and swung around and hit the switch and said, "Well?"

"Yes, Commander. Mrs. John K. Stevens' Cadillac Eldorado sedan, license plate 94-HZU, has just been stopped on Santa Monica Boulevard by a Beverly Hills patrol. The man driving is George Willison Fedders and he says he works at an Arco station, and that Mrs. Stevens called him a while ago and asked him to pick the car up for her and take it to her home."

Hellman took a deep breath because these reports were getting worse the whole time, driving him to the one conclusion he didn't want to make.

"Patch me in to Communications."

"Yes sir."

He picked up the green telephone and heard her come on the front-office line and ask for the connection. A lot of background came in: static and voices and a siren somewhere in the city. Elizabeth asked for the patrol car and got it.

Hellman spoke, telling the officer who he was. "Where did this man pick up the car?"

Against the background noise of the street traffic he could hear the faint voice of the officer, putting the question. Then he spoke clearly.

"He picked it up from the parking lot of the Golden State Mutual Savings and Loan, sir, on Wilshire."

They were getting worse, these reports, worse all the time.

"Where did Mrs. Stevens call the man from?"

The question got a negative: Fedders didn't know.

"Did she give any reason for leaving her car there?"

Negative.

"Has she done this before, asking for her car to be picked up?"

Negative.

"Did she say anything else at all?"

Negative.

"Tell Fedders he can take the car to Canyon Drive."

He put the receiver down.

Several possibilities: She'd been ordered to make contact somewhere to hand over the money and they'd taken her on board their own car, or she'd been instructed to leave her car and proceed by other means, or she'd been alerted by Cheever's visit and had decided to keep the police off her tail; other possibilities, several others, none of them reassuring.

He went across his office, taking small measured steps, and stood for a while gazing through the glass at the *Maid of New England*, perfectly still, and when he'd finished he thought, okay, when you break a case too slowly they want to know who was asleep, and when you break it too fast they want to know who panicked. Well if he was going to get it all wrong again this time that was his lookout and they could just go screw themselves.

"Elizabeth?"

"Yes, Commander?"

"Get Captain Savana in here and I don't care where he is or what he's doing. Tell Communications I want a direct signals line, and throw out an immediate priority check on all airports, railroad stations, bus terminals and car rental firms in the greater Los Angeles area for any sign of Mrs. Stevens and make sure every cab driver in this town gets to see a picture of her as soon as possible. I want her picked up."

It was very quiet in the room.

The early afternoon heat, striking almost straight down at the roof of the building, made small cracking sounds in the timbers as they were stressed. Some way off, probably in the motel café, some men were laughing, and in the bathroom here a tap dripped with a light musical sound.

They stood perfectly still, the three of them, their attitudes frozen by what she had said. Stevens and his wife were watching Charlie Berlatsky, and he looked from one to the other of them, beginning to tremble. They both noticed the way he was beginning to tremble, and he was aware of it himself. His eyes were very bright. He said almost in a whisper:

"You couldn't get the money?"

"No."

"You didn't try."

Stevens hadn't moved, but he seemed ready to move at once if his wife were threatened. She said:

"Of course, I tried."

She watched the thin man and saw how feverish he looked and wondered why he needed that large sum of money so badly. John had told her nothing yet; there hadn't been time.

"Judge." Charlie's voice was hoarse, and he didn't seem able to talk above a whisper. "Did you know she wasn't going to bring it?"

"No."

He stared Berlatsky back, seeing the despair in the man: his shock was so great that he wasn't thinking about the actual loss of the money but of blaming someone, taking revenge. There was no other reason for asking that question.

Charlie looked at Mrs. Stevens, seeing she was pale, her

eyes still pink from crying. Something inside him, like a hot black animal, was wanting to spring and kill her.

"You said," trying to steady his breath, "you'd got the money."

She didn't move but seemed to be backing away from him, just with her eyes, like she couldn't recognize him anymore.

"I went to the bank," she said, "but they—"

"*You told me you'd got it—*"

"Berlatsky, I warned you—"

"She said she'd—"

"I told you it would be very difficult, don't you remember?"

The Judge had moved and Charlie hadn't noticed and now the big man stood quite close to him, watching him carefully. Their sudden voices seemed to have left a kind of echo.

"They managed," Evelyn said hesitantly, "to give me a little, at least. It was—"

"How much?"

"Three thousand—"

"*Three?*"

He wanted to hit her again, smash her. The sweat ran hot down his body. She was kind of drawing back from him again, without moving. The Judge stood over him, big and dark.

No one spoke.

A bell rang somewhere outside.

Nothing pretentious, just a little white house with a palm tree, and a woman like—

"Why don't we all sit down, Mr. Berlatsky?" Stevens said in his low quiet way.

"Christ!" Charlie spun on him. "I should've known I couldn't trust you bastards! I thought you were the kind of people I could trust, take your word for something, thought you'd got class, making a goddamn monkey out of myself while you two bastards were laughing your ass off behind my back, oh Jesus, oh *Jesus*," swinging around and away from them, not wanting to see them or he'd smash them, smash them for this, the sweat running on him and stinging his eyes, the whole of his body feeling empty, shaking, the whole of him shaking, standing with his face to the wall and shutting his eyes, I'm ready to go, he'd said, ready when you are, I can buy you anything you could ever want, oh Jesus, what can I do?

There was a noise behind him, someone was moving, but he didn't take any notice, didn't want to know, only wanted to get a hold of himself somehow, get back to where he could think, try to think what to do.

"Mr. Berlatsky."

Spoken low and quiet like you spoke to a kid, and he swung round with words hot in his mind, in his mouth—"You just listen to me, you goddamn"—and broke off.

Stevens was holding the green bag, and on the bed there were six thin bundles of Treasury bills laid out in rows of three.

"Mr. Berlatsky, here are three thousand dollars in cash. When did you last earn three thousand dollars for a service rendered in less than a day?"

Charlie looked at the bills, and his mind kind of slipped because this was the way he'd seen them in his mind so many times but they weren't the same, they didn't add up to anything. He looked at the Judge.

"We made a deal, remember? A hundred thousand."

"Certainly. But don't you understand—"

"I kept my end of the deal, remember?" Beginning to shake again, talking through his teeth. "Now you keep yours, okay? Now you keep yours, or by Christ I'll have you smashed, Stevens."

The quiet came again and he heard, felt his own breathing, too fast, have to slow down, she was turning to look at the Judge.

"John, can I know why—" She shrugged the rest with her hands.

"Later, Evelyn," he said.

Charlie swung on her. "You want to know what happened? I'll tell you. We made—"

"Berlatsky—"

"We made a deal, see, and if you don't want him smashed then you better tell him to keep his word, that's all I'm saying, keep his goddamn word." He looked straight at the Judge. "Like I just kept mine."

Stevens looked down.

"Mr. Berlatsky," she said, "it was all they'd let me have, at the bank. I went from one to another, trying to save time, but they—"

"Okay." He was feeling steadier now, and knew what he had to do. "Okay, maybe I believe you or maybe I don't, but I don't give a damn either way because listen"—he looked away from her to Stevens—"I don't care what they say at the bank, I don't care if it's difficult, I'm just telling you I'm going to leave this dump at noon tomorrow and if by noon tomorrow I don't have a hundred thousand dollars in my hands I'm going to call the sheriff of this county and tell him there's a wrecked auto down in that ravine. And I won't leave anything out."

He went to the door, feeling for his pack of Kents, imagine not finishing that cigarette in here because it might've made this bastard cough, you could do too much for people, for Christ sake, you could make a goddamn monkey out of yourself.

"Mr. Berlatsky." The Judge made a gesture toward the bed. "We shall try to meet your demands, but I can't give you any guarantee. At least we can offer you three thousand dollars, here and now, and in cash."

Charlie struck a match and lit up, looking at the rows of new green bills. "The deal," he said as he opened the door, "was for a hundred grand."

Leaning at the dressing table, Evelyn wondered, as she did on these rare occasions, why human tears should be salty to the taste.

She hadn't shed many, just a few that had escaped while she was taking the first shock, the strangeness of things. She hadn't, as her mother would put it, "made any fuss." A certain sense of unreality was now trying to stop her thinking properly, because if a friend of hers, Peggy or Miriam or someone, asked her why she was crying like this she'd have to say well, John didn't come home all night and I didn't sleep a wink, then I was told he'd been kidnapped and was being held for ransom, then I couldn't raise enough money for them, and finally he told me himself that he'd smashed up his car and killed the prostitute who'd been with him for the weekend, and now we have to keep everything quiet so that he doesn't get thrown off the bench and lose his candidacy for governor. And the funny thing is that I can't help remembering that I'd cooked a curry for him on Sunday evening from a new recipe, hoping he'd like it.

Using her handkerchief again she reflected that a sense of humor was sometimes the only thing that stopped you going mad.

He'd had the grace, at least, to spare her his apologies: that would have been too easy. He was standing somewhere behind her, waiting to hear what she was going to say, now she'd been told everything. She knew he'd be looking solemn and rather noble as he always (my God, how quickly you learn spite!) as he always did, with his big hands clasped behind him. As a matter of fact she wasn't going to say anything, not about that part of it anyway. She couldn't say anything, could she, about something it would take her a few days even to believe?

"John."

"Yes?"

"I brought the Ben-Gay."

"That was kind of you."

She leaned away from the dressing table and went to her handbag and found the tube, dropping it onto the bed. She ought to have put it into a plastic bag first: it had stained the lime-green leather.

"I expect there's someone here who can do it for you."

"Of course," he said.

She passed him, going to look out of the window. (It said in the book she had been reading that looking out of windows in a strained situation expressed the subconscious desire to escape, if only visually.)

"I'm a little foggy," she said, "because I haven't had much sleep, so please bear with me. You're not actually being held here in this place, are you?"

"Not physically."

"I mean why can't we go home and take this man with us? Surely he can wait for a day or two in a motel while we get the money for him?"

"He's frightened we might try to trap him, once we are back among our friends. He's anxious to lay his hands on the money and get away as soon as he possibly can—I'm sure you saw that."

She closed her eyes and tried to think logically, her brain functioning like a small clear voice trying to make itself heard above the appalling hubbub of other noises—the sounds of disbelief and anguish and protest against what life was suddenly doing to her.

"If they arrested him—the police, I mean—would he expose you, out of spite?"

"Probably. But even if he didn't, it would all come out under interrogation." He took a pace, but not nearer her. "If the police get wind of this, as they may have done already, and if by consequence they arrest Berlatsky, we shall be—I can't for the moment think of a better word—we shall be finished."

She turned to look at him. "How about 'destroyed'?"

Their eyes met at last and he was the first to look away. She could smell the Ben-Gay on the bed: it was an old tube, half empty, and the smell was quite strong in the room, the heat of the day bringing it out. It was a homely smell, to her, as it probably was to most people: liniment was what families used on each other when they couldn't reach the spot themselves; it went with sympathy, and kindness, and love. But there was pain in his face and in the way he moved, and normally she'd have had him lying on the bed by now (on your tummy, darling, and try to relax) and would be healing him with her gentle hands. Why on earth did a man suddenly become so loathsome and untouchable that you couldn't even heal his pain, when he'd simply spent a weekend with another woman?

"Don't you think," she asked, her brain busy with its logic, "that even if we paid him this money, he mightn't badger us for the rest of our lives, demanding more and more?"

In a moment he said: "That would be human of him."

"Or do you mean inhuman?"

He looked at her fleetingly. "In all my experience, Evelyn, I've never found a borderline between the two." He thought about this for a moment, then dismissed it. "I've had a long time, you know, lying here trying to think what to do; and more than once I thought about simply surrendering—not to him but to circumstance. But there's a kind of honesty in that man, a willingness to trust and be trusted—look how he took your word for it that you had the whole of the sum he asked for, bringing you here to find me without even checking your bag. And look at the way he turned down three thousand dollars, in bills, right in front of him. Berlatsky is a venal opportunist, but he seems to possess a certain code of ethics."

"How would you know?" Quick off the tongue, quicker than thought, oh God, they were right, hell hath no fury. . . .

He said nothing to this.

"How much risk is there," she asked him, managing this time to think before she spoke, "of the—the woman being found?"

"Not very much. I think he would have done the best he could to earn his money. To a man like him, a hundred thousand dollars is probably the largest sum he could ever think of possessing."

"How much—it's just occurred to me—would you have given him if he'd demanded more?"

He considered, staring at the floor, his heavy brows raised. "To protect all of us—Jeffrey and Pat as well, of course—from gross humiliation? To safeguard my nomination for governor? I suppose half a million. There can be no real limit, can there, if the funds are available?" He looked up at her on a thought. "Why didn't you go back to the bank, Evelyn, as Roger suggested? Didn't you tell me he promised to order a special delivery?"

"He only said he'd see what he could do. I got the feeling that he wouldn't have let me take away so much money in cash, in any case, and also I felt that I'd pushed him far enough: Roger would want to help us and he could see there was an emergency. He may have told the police, even, I can't be sure."

He was pacing a little, his shoulders held stiffly. "That's our greatest risk, if—" then some kind of spasm took him and she caught her breath, seeing it, wanting to go to him, astonished by her immediate resolve not to move, not one inch, toward him. His face was squeezed in pain and he stood there, making no sound at all, and she waited, and waited, and when the worst seemed to be over she tried to speak as if she hadn't noticed what had happened, and felt victorious, and ashamed.

"What should we do? Call Clive?"

"Yes." His voice hardly carried.

She turned away, to wait again, giving him time to recover.

"Would Clive bring the money?"

"Oh yes."

"He's brilliant. He might think of something."

"It doesn't take a brilliant man to see we've no choice of

action. This situation, you see, is too simple for it to contain any areas for modification."

"Supposing we told him he couldn't have the money unless we went home first to get it?"

"He knows we can send for it. Clive will order a special delivery and warn the bank to keep his confidence."

"But I think you should see Dr. Barnsely as soon as you can. You'll need X rays and professional treatment."

"Tomorrow," he said. "I'm as anxious as Berlatsky is to conclude this matter quietly here, and let us go our own ways."

"Will you have to report the accident to the police?"

"No. I shall simply call a garage and have them salvage the wreck, so that it won't attract attention later. The police would have to be called only if there were an injured person involved." He was silent for a moment. "For our purposes, that is not the case."

Evelyn turned away quickly as the random image came into her mind: the face of the stranger who had not only been injured, but mortally, a sensuous face, lingering-eyed when it looked at men—but no, not really, she'd met some of these girls in the courthouse when they'd become involved in more serious charges and they weren't sensuous, or even attractive, most of them; they looked cold, deprived in some way, selling the only thing they possessed because they had no joy from it, unloving and unable to be loved, and there she was now, this one, pushed hastily out of sight as an embarrassment, her last rites the terms of what that man had called a "deal."

"What was her name?" without meaning to ask.

He was quiet again for a while.

"Theodora Creaturo."

"It sounds beautiful," listening to herself speaking again without thinking first, as if she were someone else. "What was her real name—Aggie Smith?"

He looked down, not answering in any way, and she became a little frightened at the thought that over the years she'd turn into an embittered harridan snatching at every chance of demeaning him, each of her tawdry victories stored away, like dust gathers.

"So we'll call Clive, is that right?" her tone brisk, getting back to the facts. She must start curbing this new and miserable urge to hurt him.

"Yes," he said. "I must do what I can, for our pride's sake."

"You mean you have some left?"

It was quite startling, unnerving, how she did it without thinking; and she realized it was giving her pleasure to hurt him like this. Was that going to be her future, then, if she decided to stay with him, her days endlessly devoted to the pleasures of spite? If so, she'd better start doing something about it while she was feeling suitably numbed.

She found the half-crumpled tube of liniment.

"What was it exactly," she asked him, "whiplash?"

"It feels like that."

"Can you get your coat and shirt off, if I help?"

He looked at her, but she didn't see his expression because she was busy taking the cap off the tube and putting it on the bedside table. Now he was turning away and going a few uncertain steps toward the blank wall, his hands hanging by his sides, a small triangle of torn cloth falling away from a tear in his coat at the back. She waited, not thinking about anything in particular, just everything, the whole unbelievable new world she didn't want to enter, and would have to, and after a while she realized he was crying, almost in silence but not quite managing, and realized too that it hadn't been pleasant for him, any of this, and that what she was doing, in offering to help him with his pain, must seem to him a hope of redemption when everything else was lost.

Good old Ben-Gay, she thought, the family friend, redeemer of those without hope: they ought to use it in their ads. But it still wasn't nice, despite her desperate little jokes, to see him standing there doing that, a man as big as he was gentle, loved for his humanity and his readiness to become embattled in behalf of the luckless in life, his big shoulders quietly shaking and his face turned to the wall, a man as weak as others were weak, and paying for it, oh God yes, paying for it in terms by which a hundred thousand dollars was so much tinsel, difficult for her to stand here and do nothing, not to go to him and give him comfort.

"You know," she said, mostly to herself and not really caring whether he listened or not, "I was terribly frightened, in the night, because I thought there'd been an accident and you'd perhaps been—well, anything, I mean killed, and I thought, all the time, that nothing would ever matter to me, however bad, if only you were still alive and all right and I could see you again." She sat on the edge of the bed, the tube in her hand, watching his big body growing gradually still. "And if that isn't true anymore, now that my prayers have been granted, it'll mean I was just cringing in front of God for what I could get, and that's not a very flattering picture of myself. So I'm going to work on it."

After he had come to lie face-down for her and she had squeezed some of the liniment onto her fingers, she thought over what she'd been saying, because it had sounded rather complicated to her present foggy mind, but it wasn't really. It just meant that nothing else ought to matter now, because John hadn't died in that accident. Though of course, in so many ways, he had.

Captain Savana went on looking at his folded hands for another couple of seconds and then took the toothpick out of his mouth and snapped it in two and dropped the bits into Bill Hellman's trash basket.

"Is that the whole bit?"

"Yes."

"Okay sir, where d'you want me to start?"

"You can't start anywhere yet. Till we get some more leads, it's a Mexican standoff: nobody can move."

Nick Savana nodded. "Do we know this lawyer, Brenner?"

"I hadn't seen him before."

"They don't often bring us in."

"He can still leave us out."

"If he gets any closer himself?"

"It'd be a common pattern. The closer they get, the more they think they can handle it themselves."

Savana got up and slid his hands flat in his back pockets and pulled his arms behind him, looking out across the city.

"Is the Gomez trial one of the angles on this?"

"We don't think so. We think it's a straight snatch for the bread."

"Some small people then."

"Why?"

"A hundred grand doesn't sound like enough bread for a man like John K.—"

"Oh sure, right. It had us chasing shadows, first go off—it looked very much like a Gomez connection or the gubernatorial thing with a hundred thrown in just to get some easy money at the same time. Now we're thinking differently because the background doesn't fit: no phone calls or notes or the usual media pitch."

Savana got another toothpick and stuck it between his bright white teeth and said, "What about Mrs. Stevens?"

"If we can possibly pick her up I'll ask her to take a lie-detector test but I think she'd refuse and I think she'd be right. We don't think this is a Gomez connection but we're assuming these people are dangerous, and we know they've already scared the hell out of Mrs. Stevens."

Savana watched the time and temperature digits changing at the top of the South Western building: 02:31–85°. "Is the FBI in on this yet?"

"They've had a routine advise."

"Are they going to sick that jerk McFarlane onto us again?"

"McFarlane was killed in a shoot-out in Nevada a couple of weeks back."

"Oh really?" Savana's bright eyes came wide open. "That's

a shame." He was in the Special Investigation Section and liaised with the local groups of federal agencies more than most people did, and Joe McFarlane was okay—had been okay—except he'd gotten the idea he'd been called down off the Cross to straighten things out for everybody. Now maybe he'd get back up.

"Yes?" Hellman said into one of his phones.

Savana stood listening, hands in the back pockets of his pants and arms angled behind him, his fancy houndstooth sport coat hanging open and the sunlight glinting on the butt of his holstered Smith and Wesson, his squat head tilted back and his thick feet well astride on this part of the earth's surface as though it meant that if he didn't necessarily know what he was doing he at least knew where he was at.

"All right Forester," Hellman said into the phone, "I want you to stand by so I can call you. Give me the number." He wrote left-handed on a pad and hung up and looked at Nick Savana. "Mrs. Stevens drew three thousand dollars from the Golden State Mutual Savings and Loan twenty minutes after she left Bank of America."

"Three."

"Three."

"Her feet are going to get tired," Savana said.

"She may be running out of banks."

"You mean people like them can't go into a bank and come out with a truckload of the stuff?"

"Not actually. Ordinary branches don't keep that kind of money handy for just one customer to cash: they'd have to send for it. Also the public mood is quite aggressive about kidnapping since it came into fashion: it was the Stevenses' bank manager who tipped off their lawyer, and their lawyer who came to us." The intercom light began flashing and he cut it in. "Yes?"

"Oh Commander, we have this from downstairs. Mrs. John K. Stevens boarded Airwest Flight 303 at eleven-fifty this morning and landed in Morales, California, at twelve twenty-seven."

"She alone?"

"Yes sir."

"Carrying anything?"

"Just her handbag."

"Have Morales police circulate her description to all patrols." He cut the switch and looked at the pad on his desk. "I know what I think," he said to Savana. "What do you think?" He began dialing a number.

"She wants to find her husband so she told them she had the money but she didn't say how much."

"All right, so now what'll they do?"

"Ask for the rest."

The ringing tone began.

"All right, how'll they get it?"

"Send for the family lawyer."

Hellman nodded as the ringing tone stopped.

"Weinstock, Simon, and Brenner—can I help you?"

"Is Mr. Brenner there?"

"May I ask who's calling?"

"Commander Hellman, Los Angeles Police Department."

"Thank you." She came back in five seconds. "Mr. Brenner just stepped out, sir."

"Where did he go?"

She took another five seconds.

"To the bank."

"Which bank?"

She came back and said, "The Security Pacific National."

"On Beverly Drive?"

"Yes sir."

"Please have Mr. Brenner call me when he gets back."

Savana had turned and was looking down at Hellman as he gave her the number and hung up and began dialing again.

"Bank?" Savana said.

"Bank." The line opened. "Forester, get across to the Security Pacific National Bank on Beverly Drive and look for Clive Brenner, lawyer, thirty-five, about five-ten, black hair thinning, suntan, gold-rimmed glasses slightly tinted, trim and in very good shape, athletic-looking, tan suit, white or cream shirt, can't recall, probably briefcase or bigger case, going too fast? All right, he went to the bank a few minutes ago from his office, also on Beverly Drive in that area, check in the book, Weinstock, Simon and Brenner. I want you to find him and stick with him wherever he goes and send me your movements when you can. I'm giving you support: two men. Lock onto him, Forester, I mean that."

He hung up and got Elizabeth on the intercom.

"Pick two men who can recognize Lieutenant Forester and get them out to that bank in support surveillance. Throw out a watch at Hollywood-Burbank and Los Angeles airports for Clive Brenner, destination believed Morales, California. And hear me: that man is not to board any airplane without two men in tow, and they have to keep with him taking the greatest possible care he doesn't know. Tap what manpower you need and send Walker if he's available."

He cut the switch. "Brady?"

"Sir?"

"Have we got a chopper up there?"

"No sir."

Lieutenant Brady stood in the doorway.

"Call one in from patrol and have it stand by."

"Yes sir."

Hellman looked up at Savana. "Who are you taking?"

"Miller and Lucas."

"They on standby?"

"Yes, sir."

"All right. Brenner's got a big staff and I doubt he often goes to the bank in person. Any luck, we shouldn't be long."

CHAPTER FOURTEEN

Must be kind of creepy!"

"Living in a ghost town?"

"Yeah!"

"It's okay, I guess."

Rose put down his ripple fudge sundae and made out the check.

"D'you hear the ghosts of the Indians yellin', nights?"

"Only some nights."

"Wow!" He grinned excitedly with three teeth and freckles. "You hear 'em *some* nights?"

"Maybe only when I'm dreaming."

Then the cop came into the lobby and she went for some coffee but he just stood there in the doorway with something in his hand.

"Miss."

"Yeah?"

"You ever seen this man?"

He showed her the photograph, and at first she didn't think it looked like anybody she'd ever seen, but suddenly she knew it was the big man in Room 7 and her breath kind of stopped and she just stood there staring at the photo trying to think what she ought to say and wishing to God Charlie was here.

"This guy?" she asked feebly, and felt the cop watching her. He was a California Highway Patrol, but not the regular one, Tom Bleecher, who rode this area. She couldn't think of doing anything except go on staring at the photo held in his big bony hand with the split nail. All she knew was that Charlie wanted to keep people from seeing the man in there, because it'd mean reporters and everything and he didn't want that, so she shook her head. "I guess not," she said.

"You never saw him?"

"No."

She had to look up at him then because he was putting the picture away, and she tried to get the right kind of look in her eyes because she knew she tended to give away what she was thinking.

"You work here?"

"Yeah. My pa owns the place."

"Where's he?"

"Through in the kitchen."

"Mind if I go through there?"

"Sure, go ahead."

It'd be okay because her pa was deaf and by the time he'd got around to lipreading what the cop was trying to say it'd be just one big hassle, and anyway Pa hadn't ever seen the man in Room 7.

"D'you have any ancient arrowheads in your gem shop?"

"Huh? Sure."

"Can I go look at 'em when I'm through with my ice cream?"

"Yeah."

She went and hit the jukebox a little, like everyone else did, because sometimes it played, and she wanted some music, anything to stop this silence with her voice still going on in it saying no, she'd never seen the man.

The cop came back and asked for the registration cards and that scared her too, because they were picked up regularly by Tom Bleecher and this wasn't the right day. But she couldn't ask him why he wanted them; it wasn't even easy to look at him in the eyes and she was just praying he'd go without thinking of any more questions.

"Do you have a guest here," putting the registration cards into his zip-case, "who was in any kind of an accident?"

He looked up again now, right at her, and she couldn't look anywhere else, it would seem kind of evasive.

"No," she said, "we don't."

He just stood watching her till she had to turn away and start back for the café, like there wasn't anything more to say.

"How much are the arrowheads?"

"Uh?"

"How much are the arrowheads you said you have in your gem shop?"

She heard the patrolman going on out.

"Twenty-five."

"Gee, that ain't so much for a real ancient Indian arrowhead, is it?"

"There's plenty of them around, I guess."

She could feel her heart beating away like it was out of control, because she hadn't ever lied to a cop before except about how long she'd been parked and that kind of thing, and he'd stood there very tall in his big boots with his eyes on her and not moving a muscle, just watching and listening while she lied, and even in this heat she could feel the goose pimples on her arms.

"Do any of them still have blood on them?"

"Huh?"

"Do any"—he broke off to look up as the helicopter crossed the window—"do they have blood on them?"

"On what?"

Somebody was calling her name, softly.

"On the arrowheads."

The noise of the helicopter was fading.

She turned and saw Charlie.

"No, they don't."

"Can I go look at 'em an' take this with me?"

"Sure."

Charlie as standing in the lobby, jerking his head for her

to come, and she put the tray down and went across the café. The kid went dodging past her with his sundae.

"Rose," Charlie said, "can we talk in your room?" He looked ever so uptight, with his eyes jumpy and strained.

"Okay," she said, and wondered how she was ever going to tell him.

He followed her into the room at the back, lighting a cigarette, his long fingers shaky, looking around for somewhere to drop the match.

"In here," she said, not wanting to look at him because of what she had to tell him. A thread of smoke went up from the match and then disappeared.

"Did you get your things packed, Rose?"

He talked quietly and very quick, close to her, watching her eyes.

"Sure, Charlie, but–"

"We're not going yet, not till tomorrow. So if there's anything else you need to pack, you can take your–"

"Charlie," she said, "I–" but didn't know how to say it. "Listen, I–"

"Rose," he said very quick, catching her arm.

"Well I–I want to go with you, Charlie, don't think I–"

"*Rose*," he said, scared-looking.

"Why don't we sit down a minute–"

"You've got to tell me, Rose."

"It's just–I mean can I wait here till you get there, to Mexico or wherever–"

"Wait here?" Staring into her eyes.

She nodded, putting her forehead on his shoulder, loving him, not wanting to upset him this way.

"I'm getting scared, Charlie, that's all."

"Scared?"

"There was a cop in here."

She felt him draw tight like a string.

"When?"

"A couple of minutes ago. He–"

"What sort of cop? Rose?"

"A CHP, not the regular one who–"

"What did he want?"

"He showed me a picture of the man in there–"

"The Chief?"

"Yeah. He asked if I'd ever seen him."

Charlie was quiet for a bit, like he was trying to get his courage up to ask, then he said, "What did you say?"

"I said no."

She felt the tension go out of him a little.

"What else did he ask you, Rose?"

"If we had anyone here who'd been in an accident. I told him no, and he just took the cards and went on out. He–"

"What cards?"

"The guest registration cards. We have to–"

"Was that normal? I mean would a passing cop ask you for them?"

"No. I guess it was because he had the photo, and–"

"Okay. Okay."

His thin hand was gripping her arm, hurting, making her worried the way it was trembling, and the way his eyes had been so jumpy, and the thing about the cop, and how he'd had to yell at the two people in there, raising his voice so she'd heard from the lobby, calling them bastards and he couldn't trust them and things like that–everything that was happening now was a worry to her.

"I'll do anything you want, Charlie, but–" She broke off because he'd turned away and wasn't looking at her and didn't even seem like he was listening, thinking of something else. Then he turned back and faced her and she got scared again, seeing how kind of lost and empty he looked.

"Rose."

"Yes, Charlie?"

"Have you changed your mind?"

"No," she said. "I want to come with you more than anything, ever." She wanted to hold him, but he was standing so stiffly, just looking at her, like from a long distance. "I love you, Charlie," she said, and his eyes changed then, and went softer, and she knew she'd said something that meant a lot to him. "It's just because the policeman came, see, and I didn't know what I should tell him. I hadn't ever thought the police would come here and—"

"Okay," he said, and came close again, stroking her hair with his bandaged hand, the smoke from his cigarette beginning to sting her eyes. "Okay, Rose. Listen, there's a plane leaving tomorrow for Mexico and I'm taking it. Then as soon as you like you can follow me out there, if you really want to."

"Don't keep saying it," clinging to him, "it's just that I got scared when—"

"Sure. There isn't any problem. Believe me."

He'd put down his cigarette someplace and was holding her against him with both his hands and she didn't say anything else. It hadn't only been the cop asking her things, it was the way Charlie was acting too, so uptight he couldn't even stop trembling, and what was happening in Room 7, the way he'd yelled at them. She'd tried to tell herself she didn't want to know what Charlie was doing, but now the police had come into it she felt this whole thing was getting too big for her to handle.

"Everything's okay, Rose."

"I know," she nodded, safe against him, not wanting to move, ever again to move in case it made something happen that would stop them being together like this, because it was all she would ever want for the rest of her life, to be with Charlie.

Sheriff's Captain Paul Hobart was in his office when the Air Section of Morales Police Department sent a call through at a few minutes after two in the afternoon. He was presently looking at a report made by Officer Knox, a motorcycle patrolman, to the CHP office and passed on to Hobart. Liaison between the county sheriff's forces and the Los Angeles Police Department was increasingly strong since the APB had gone out from Commander Hellman of that city.

"Cap'n?"

"Yes?"

Pete was looking through the operations hatch.

"Radio, sir."

"Okay."

Hobart reached out with a hand almost black from the sun of many seasons, and held the message at arm's length. This time next year he'd be settling into his first pair of reading glasses, Doc Baker had told him. The hell with Doc Baker.

SK3 overflying South Indian Rock Highway on routine patrol at 2:01 P.M. sighted wreck of overturned auto dark blue make unidentified Californian plates—

"Patch me in," he called through the hatch. "Air Section."

He picked up the local connection and said, "Who's that?"

"Sergeant Comero, sir."

"Where did your crew sight this wreck?"

It was all down there on the radio report, but he was getting into the habit of picking up a phone instead of reading things.

"Close by Milepost 17, sir, down in the scrub on the west side."

"They didn't make a second run?" If they'd made a second run they would have picked up the make but maybe it didn't matter too much anyway because this report was getting real close to the earlier APB from Los Angeles.

"No, sir. We have a TSO on the Judge Stevens inquiry, so the pilot just went on flying to his routine pattern."

"What time did you get that standing order, Sergeant?"

"At 12:03 direct from Commander Hellman's office in L.A."

Hobart asked three more questions and got the answers he'd expected and hung up and read the report from Officer Knox of the CHP again to make sure he got it right.

In replying to both my main questions the young woman

showed a definite apprehension, and it is my opinion she was lying or concealing information. Acting on orders I gave her no reason to believe I suspected her in any way. I left the motel, taking with me the guest registration cards, receipt attached. S. W. Knox, Officer Patrolling Area Indian Rock and 15 to MP 873.

"Pete!"

"Cap'n?"

"Find Lieutenant Vorhees and ask him if he can join me here inside ten minutes."

Another level of squelch began sounding from the radio room.

Hobart got up and looked at the map on the wall, tilting his dark head back so his eyes could focus on the details. Milepost 17 was five miles south of Indian Rock, and the nearest building was the Desert Winds Motel. That wouldn't have meant a thing if it wasn't for the report from Patrolman Knox, just like fried chicken wouldn't have meant a thing without the Colonel: a whole lot of life was putting two things together and making them stick.

"Lieutenant's on his way, sir."

Hobart reached for his stetson and was outside in his own unmarked sedan a few minutes later when Vorhees hit base and climbed in with him. On their way south the captain thought to call up an information message for all local units so Hellman would pick it up on his next time around the circuit. He figured it best not to wire L.A. direct because if this wreck wasn't the Stevenses' car he'd look like a lemon.

Vorhees sat beside him listening to the radio calls, a short bullet-headed block of a man, younger than the captain but on his way up a lot faster because he couldn't relax.

"This inquiry's kinda building up, ain't it?" he said as they peeled off the freeway and hit the back road south.

"L.A. says it looks like a snatch."

"A judge, no less."

"There's no point snatching no-accounts."

13 to Morales.

Go ahead, 13.

I have a speeder, MP 28 on Nevada Road northbound.

Report your actions, 13.

"Is L.A. sending someone?" Vorhees asked.

"Yes. A Special Investigation captain."

"Christ sake, don't they lay off till we take a crack?"

"The Judge is a resident of Los Angeles, Frank, so it's their pigeon if they want it."

Come in, 17.

Somebody just hit a truck, Milepost 45 southbound, and it looks like we'll need a wrecker and rescue squad.

Standing by, 17.

At half-past two Captain Hobart swung the car off the road about a quarter mile north of MP 17 on Indian Rock Highway, running it deep into the trees where it wouldn't be seen too well, and the two men got out and made their way down the rocky slope toward the ravine, taking their time in the heat of the open sky, not talking unless they had to because in the dry air a man's voice would carry a mile. The request from Commander Hellman had been urgent but not explicit: it was suggested that all possible caution be taken when making any approach to the location where Judge Stevens was assumed or known to be held.

The smell of gasoline was a help in leading them to the wreck among the thorn trees, and they stood looking at it for a while, not talking. A front wheel had been wrenched clean off at the stub axle and wasn't anywhere around; the vinyl top had been torn and lay in shreds across the rocks; the hood had burst open and was slung some distance away.

"Nobody woulda got out of that with their skin on," Vorhees said, his black eyes narrowed against the glare.

"Maybe there was nobody in it, Frank."

"Huh?"

"They could've pulled him out first, put him in their auto,

then sent this one down here in the hope nobody'd see it for a while."

Vorhees worked on this for a couple of seconds, squinting thoughtfully at the Cadillac.

"Mean they didn't intend goin' far with him?"

"Sure."

"Uh-huh. Desert Winds ain't far, y'mean that?"

"It could tie in, Frank. Two and two."

They took a look inside, then covered the terrain, turning over a stone or two, one time sending a rattler sliding to new cover among the rocks.

"Well, we know it's his auto," Vorhees said. "JKS ain't a very common set of initials."

"At least, we're getting closer to a certainty," Hobart said, and his deputy grunted out a laugh from his barrel chest, because it was a phrase made famous by repetition in the captain's unit.

"Frank," he said a couple of minutes later. There wasn't any answer, so he looked around. Vorhees was fifty yards away across the sandy level ground below the rocks. He called out louder and Vorhees turned his head. "Where're you heading, Frank?"

The deputy pointed, calling something about "flashing," then turned away again, going on across the sand. He was twice the distance when Hobart saw him next, crouching on the ground looking at something. The captain would have called to him but the ravine was so quiet in the afternoon heat, so he went on down across the rocks and started over the sand, the way his deputy had gone.

Vorhees was still crouched there, and turned his head, squinting against the sun.

"Saw this bit of glass flashing, Skipper."

"What was making it move?"

"It wasn't moving. It just flashed in the distance, when I was pokin' around up there, caught it outa the corner of my eye."

Hobart crouched alongside of him and looked at the big triangle of tinted safety glass with the blood smears on it. After a time he said, "It could have been thrown this far when the auto hit those rocks."

"It could've," Vorhees said. "But it's a darn long way."

"Have you seen anything else?"

"Well, I dunno. I don't see any kinda specific objects around, but look at the sand, right here. Been turned over, all around this rectangle."

Hobart stood up and took a few paces back, looking at the terrain again, seeing Vorhees was right. Apart from the different lie of the surface, one or two seedling chollas had been uprooted, the sap still in them.

"Figure we could dig around a little, Frank." He joined his deputy again, crouching. "No, don't use that. We better use our hands."

CHAPTER FIFTEEN

CHARLIE BERLATSKY SWUNG THE CHEVY around the entrance ramp for Interstate 15 and rolled up the driver's window, speeding up and slotting into the northbound traffic and passing below the sign saying Morales.

There wasn't any problem, like he'd told Rose, but it had shaken him up badly when Mrs. Stevens had said she hadn't got the money, and he'd remembered something from way back, flashed into his mind, the time when he'd been just a kid not long out of his crib, and chasing a yellow butterfly. He'd never seen anything so wonderful, the way it danced in the air, bright yellow against the blue sky, and suddenly he'd wanted it all for himself, and he'd snatched at it and there it was in his small fat hand, yellow and wonderful and all his own now, but not moving anymore. So he threw it in the air to make it dance again, but it just floated down in a spiral onto the grass and stayed still.

It was crazy the things he thought about when he wasn't expecting to, but he knew it happened the same way with other people, he wasn't a head-case or anything.

As soon as he got to the airport he went into the bar and sat with a double rye, watching the clock and trying to cool down, saying it over and over, there wasn't any problem, everything was okay now because he'd been there with them at the phone in the lobby, the swinging door to the café shut while they talked. The Judge hadn't said anything out of turn, told the lawyer, Brenner, it was urgent he did what he was instructed, said it would be too late to do anything after midday tomorrow. Brenner had only asked two questions: Was Mrs. Stevens all right, and did they need any immediate medical attention? The whole of the call hadn't taken more than a minute and the Judge said it would be okay this time.

It'd better be, for Christ sake; he'd got the bastard off the hook and he wanted his pay and if they didn't keep their word this time he'd bust them all, smash them. He could do that.

His hands still weren't steady because there'd been Rose, too, making him think for a minute she'd changed her mind. That had been terrible and he'd stood there wondering what was happening to him, with the things he wanted most being taken away from him. Rose was almost a part of him now and he thought about her a lot of the time, seeing her walking there by the white walls of their little place on the coast, lying in the shade under the trees, laughing the way she did, calling him Charlie, like she never got tired of saying his name. It'd never happened this way with a woman before, not even with Dolores, never so fast as this. He'd always had to do all the running.

"Is that clock right?" he asked the bartender.

"Has to be. People miss their plane and we'd get the flak."

Charlie went out of the bar and stood where he could see the passengers, and at 5:45 on the big digital clock they began coming through from the American Airways Flight 487 from Los Angeles and he started looking for Brenner. The Judge had told Brenner to wear a carnation and he'd given Charlie a full description so they couldn't possibly miss each other. He was standing where he could also see anyone else who might hang around after the last passenger was through, like he'd done when Mrs. Stevens had arrived, but he didn't think they'd try anything stupid because what was the point: he'd told them plenty of times, if anybody made a wrong move then the Judge got busted.

The cop at the Desert Winds didn't worry him. Mrs. Stevens had started an inquiry about a possible accident and it was still going on, that was all, they were checking every motel in the area, it was what they'd do. Okay, it wasn't the regular CHP and he'd taken the registration cards, but they'd never heard of his name before and they wouldn't find it in criminal records. It just wasn't going to help them any, and even if it did, he'd be on the Mexican Airways flight he'd fixed for tomorrow and there wasn't anything they could do about that.

There was a guy in a tan suit coming through but he wasn't wearing a carnation and he went right on across to the baggage claim. Charlie moved a bit to one side so he could see right to the door where they were coming in, but there weren't many more people and he didn't see anyone like Brenner yet.

But he'd come. By Christ he'd get here, or the Judge was going to get smashed and they knew that.

Passengers for Las Vegas please proceed to Gate Number 4, a lot of other crap about boarding cards, five more people coming off the American Airways plane now, two kids and a youth and a married couple, retirees, nobody else, just the five. Brenner wasn't there.

Struck a match and lit up, a little shaky but no point getting uptight, looking around, nobody by the Airwest check-in where Brenner had been instructed to wait.

"Hey, miss!"

"Yes sir?"

"That was the Los Angeles flight just got in, wasn't it?"

"Flight 487, sir, that's right."

Dragging the smoke in deep, Jesus, dear Jesus, it was beginning to be like a dream, a nightmare, nothing going right, getting his hand within an inch of something and then seeing it wasn't there. Maybe he was going nuts, *you really imagine some guy's going to walk in this place and hand you a briefcase with a hundred thousand bucks in it so you can take the next plane to Mexico?*

They'd shut the door to the field now and a man was locking it and there wasn't anybody standing around in the hall, nobody in a tan suit with a carnation. He felt sick to his stomach, couldn't seem to get things to go right, those bastards were trying to rip him off. Okay, then he'd smash that goddamn judge wide open if that was the way they wanted to play it.

"Make it a double again, rye."

Sit and think and maybe come up with something. Suppose Brenner had missed the plane, broke down in his auto on his way to the airport—anything could happen—so what would he do? He'd call the airline and have a message put on the board for Mr. Rackman, or he'd call the Desert Winds, have to check it out.

"Hey, sir!" The bartender was just putting his drink down.

"Never mind."

The message board was across the hall by the telephone but there wasn't anything for Rackman so he got a dime and took the bit of paper out and dialed the number and stood waiting, knowing she'd say no, nobody had called, knowing he was just standing here trying to kid himself along, the sweat creeping on his skin and the rage coming. That bastard Stevens had waited till he'd started out for the airport and then he'd called Brenner. *Okay, then I'll bust you, you bunch of shits, so you'll wish to Christ*—the ringing tone beginning but it wasn't any use, the whole thing was like a bad dream, everything coming apart and falling away, because if you're a two-bit traveling salesman peddling junk you don't have what it takes to stick up a judge for the jackpot and go live in a dream house the rest of your sweet life, who d'you think you're kidding?

"Desert Winds Motel," she said.

For a minute he couldn't say anything, had to calm down.

"Hello?" she said.

"Rose?"

He heard her catch her breath.

"Is that you, Charlie?"

"Listen, is there a message for me, did anybody call me?"

"Yes."

After a couple of seconds he said:

"What?"

"I said yes."

He stood with his eyes shut, his head throbbing. Nobody else would call him. Nobody but Brenner.

"Charlie? Are you all right?"

"Sure. Who was it, Rose? Who–"

"It was a man asking for Mr. Rackman. He says for you to call him. D'you have a pencil?"

"Hold on." The bastard was still in Los Angeles, trying to rip him off, a fucking shyster, he should've known. "What number is it, Rose?"

"It's 2986-3871."

"What's the area code?"

"It isn't long-distance, Charlie. It's the Hotel Sombrero, in Morales."

"Where?"

"Morales."

He didn't think he could take it anymore, everything was coming at him like his nerves were being hit first one way and then the other.

"Okay. Okay, Rose. I have to hang up now."

She said quickly, "I love you."

And the way she said it, everything changed, just for a couple of seconds, and he felt he was kind of looking in on another world, a smaller one where things were simple and where he ought to be.

"I love you too," he said.

Then he hung up and it all seemed to change back and he felt for another dime and there wasn't one in his pocket or a quarter either, so he had to go across to the coffee shop and change a five, coming back to the phones. The guy must have been waiting right there in the hotel lobby because he came on the line the minute they paged him.

"This is Clive Brenner. Are you Mr. Rackman?"

His voice was smooth and educated.

"Yes."

"Are we able to talk?"

The kind of guy who thought of everything.

"Sure. Go ahead."

"I realize how very important it is to keep our meeting private, Mr. Rackman. Unfortunately that wasn't possible, so I took a slightly earlier flight, hoping the situation would improve. It didn't. I wasn't alone when I arrived at Morales airport. Do you follow?"

Charlie felt for his pack of Kents and pulled one out and stuck it in his lips. Christ, he didn't like the sound of all this. He got a match and lit up.

"Listen," he said, "how the hell did they—"

"Mr. Rackman, we won't waste time at this stage. Let me just assure you that if you meet me in the Sundeck Bar of the Hotel Sombrero as soon as possible, we shall be private—providing of course that you yourself are presently unaccompanied."

Sounded so smooth, so goddamn smooth, didn't like this bastard. He was a lawyer, it was their job to twist everything around till you were hog-tied; have to watch him, everything he said, he was a shyster.

"Mr. Rackman?"

"You better meet me here, like we said."

"I would strongly advise against it. We—"

"Listen, Brenner," the rage coming back, "you meet me here, understand? I told Stevens the instructions and you'd better do what he said," the rage back inside him quick as a fire, sparks shooting behind his eyes because everything depended on this smooth sly bastard and he was trying to put it across him and it was difficult to think clearly, think fast enough. "I'll be waiting for you here so for Christ sake don't make any more mistakes or I'll see the Judge gets it," shaking all over and the sweat pricking his skin and the cigarette tasting like shit in his mouth. He wasn't used to handling this kind of situation and he wasn't used to handling shysters like Brenner.

But there wasn't anything they could do to him. They couldn't talk back. He had the ace.

"Mr. Rackman, I know you to be a man of intelligence and enterprise, so that I know you'll see my point of view. My concern is solely for my clients, and I'm therefore most anxious for you to receive these goods as soon as possible, so that our obligations to you are *fully* discharged. I have to avoid, with every effort, the risk of your being arrested, because once that happens my clients will be compromised. You follow?"

Talked like a goddamn book, the bastard, have him in knots if he didn't watch out. But it was true enough: If the cops got him he'd see the Judge was finished, he'd take him all the way into court.

"Keep talking, Brenner."

"Thank you. My point is that since we both want to avoid the risk of your being arrested we must keep away from the airport. I assume that is where you are now."

"Yes."

"I urgently advise you to leave there at once and meet me here at the hotel."

"Listen, Brenner, they don't know me. You can–"

"But they know me, you see. They passed through there a half hour ago and they know I came from Los Angeles and they know I'll return there because that's where I live and work. The moment I show up at Morales Airport they'll be on to me, though that doesn't matter. But if we meet there, they'll be on to you too: and that does."

Trap, mashing the cigarette out, sounded like a trap, he wouldn't listen, they earned their money these shysters, con the birds off the trees but he wouldn't fall for it, that guy over there, though, the one cooling his heels by the flower shop, looking up from his paper when people went past, and the other one, oh Jesus, catching a shoeshine near the main doors, watching the passengers coming through from the baggage check, or were they just–

"In fact, Mr. Rackman, I advise your leaving the airport as soon as you possibly can, because–"

"*Shuddup.*"

Have to think or they'd get him, they'd pull something on him. The guy getting the shoeshine was just looking around, didn't even have a paper, looking at everybody. But goddammit he could be anyone, he didn't have to be a cop, it was just this smart-ass on the phone making him think *oh my God I don't know what to think anymore is he trying to trap me or is this a trap I'm in right now and is it too late I can't tell so help me, oh help me.*

Christ sake cool it or you'll blow your head. There isn't any problem, they don't know your face, but you need to think a little and it's only because you're panicking you can't get it right, so get in control now, Berlatsky, or you'll blow the whole goddamn thing just when you're all set to win.

"Brenner?"

Out of breath like you've been running, what'll he think, he'll think you're not in control.

"Yes, Mr. Rackman?"

Smooth as oil. Try and sound like him.

"Listen, I don't want to meet at the hotel, but we don't have to meet here either."

"Where do you suggest?"

It threw him for a minute because he didn't expect that kind of an answer: he expected the bastard to go on trying to sell him the idea of meeting at the hotel. When he'd had time to think about it he knew there was only one safe place. The judge wasn't trying anything fancy because he knew the score, he knew what'd happen if he did. If this shyster was out to trap him there was only one man who could stop him and that was the judge.

"Mr. Rackman?"

"Okay, listen. You better meet me at Indian Rock. You got a pencil?"

"Yes."

"Before you write down this address I'm going to tell you something, Brenner. If your concern is for your clients, like you said, you better play it straight down the line. You try just one little trick and you'll be throwing a live bomb at John K. Stevens, understand?"

"Perfectly."

"Okay. Address is the Desert Winds Motel, Indian Rock." He waited for the man to get it down. "Take Interstate 15 south out of Morales and get off at Exit 89. It's thirty miles."

There was a kind of hollow feeling in his guts because he'd told a very sharp lawyer where to find Stevens and he didn't have the money yet and it looked dangerous as hell. But he'd get there before Brenner because he knew the way, and if that shyster tried to pull anything at the motel the judge could straighten him out and give him the score: hands off Berlatsky or they all got the knife.

"When shall we meet, Mr. Rackman?"

"Start now."

At 6:15 P.M. a gray unmarked sedan with a radio communications antenna was standing at the curbside a block away and across the street from the Hotel Sombrero. It was a towaway zone but the car had been there for longer than twenty-five minutes and the man behind the wheel was reading a copy of the Morales evening paper. His name was Lucas.

At 6:18 P.M. a man in a light summer suit came down the steps of the hotel and crossed the street at the intersection, and Lucas lowered the newspaper half an inch and then raised it again, having seen all he needed. The man reached the sidewalk and came along it till he was abreast of the sedan, then stopped and got in. His name was Miller.

"He's renting an Avis."

"Which one?"

"The Buick."

Lucas nodded, folding his paper. He'd seen the crimson hardtop arrive outside the hotel about five minutes back, and a guy go in. He started the motor and checked the mirror and pulled away, crossing the signals at amber and making an illegal U-turn halfway down the next block, coming back on the other side and tucking in behind the pickup unloading liquor. He didn't cut the motor.

"This fucking antenna," said Miller, and unwrapped some gum, wadding the silver foil into a ball and flicking it away. "We might as well've borrowed a marked number with the sheriff's name written all over the side."

"This is strictly hicksville," Lucas said, and lit up a cigarette because he couldn't stand the smell of chewing gum anymore than Miller could stand the smell of tobacco smoke. "We had to take what there was." He kept his eyeline along the side of the pickup, watching the edge of crimson that was the trunk and rear quarter of the Avis Buick. That bastard had been trying to give them the runaround ever since they'd first latched onto him in L.A. "Did you call Savana?"

"You bet."

Lucas didn't like to think about what Savana did with people who flunked a tail. Gas from their own exhaust was drifting around the sedan so he shut the window and turned on the air conditioning. If they had to breathe the stuff, they might as well have it on the rocks.

"You should've stuck with him, Al."

"He'll show." Miller rolled the gum around his mouth. "It's this damned antenna we got on the roof, he'll—"

"Listen, it doesn't mean we have to lose him. He'll just know we're there."

"That'll be great. If he knows we're there, he won't lead us to Judge Stevens."

"He will. Because we'll let him lose us, like we did before. Then we'll pick him up again, like we're doing now. Boy, that gum really stinks."

"At least it isn't a carcinogen."

"They've started doing tests, you know that?"

"Sure, on mice. You callin' me a mouse?"

They both felt a little better now. They'd been getting edgy with each other since they thought that bastard had slipped them at the airport, and whenever they got edgy with each other they went into the routine.

The motor throbbed and the air duct pushed out chilled carbon monoxide into their faces and Al Miller watched the steps of the hotel and Luke watched the crimson edge of the Buick and nothing happened yet. They'd been on the tail for five hours and it was a tough one, a lawyer who was wise to them. And it was hot.

"Yes, yes," said Miller softly and Lucas checked his mirror and shifted the stick and held the wheel against the tension of the assist belt, waiting, and when the Buick had pulled out and gone two blocks he swung out of cover and crossed the first signals at the edge of the red.

After the freeway there was almost no traffic because all there was at Indian Rock was a ghost town and a beat-up motel and a lot of heat and dust and dereliction, and people didn't ever go there except when the wind blew them.

"Okay, Beauty, the road's all yours."

He was feeling in better shape now and his mind had got kind of quiet and he didn't want to think anymore, because he'd almost gone nuts at the airport, trying to think what to do. He could see now it had been quite simple but at the time he'd panicked and this whole thing had suddenly scared the shit out of him, it had got to look so big. But it wasn't so big. A couple of guys had made a deal and the payoff had been a little difficult to arrange, that was all. Now it was okay, no problem.

This was the curve where the road turned south and it was just about here, last evening, that he'd picked up the two red lights ahead of him, glowing through the clouds of yellow sand. That was just twenty-four hours ago and he couldn't believe it and had to think back, but it was right. Twenty-four hours ago he hadn't even heard of John K. Stevens and it frightened him to think that this time last evening he'd never had a chance in hell of getting out of the rat race and buying a little place in Mexico and taking it easy for the rest of his life with a girl like Rose.

Jesus, he would've missed it, a chance of a lifetime, if he'd been a few minutes later or a few minutes earlier: even, almost, if he'd just blinked! He could remember thinking he wished he *had* blinked when that auto had run off the road, so he wouldn't have to go down and help whoever it was in the wreck. It frightened him to think how he could've blinked away a whole new life, and he didn't want to think about it.

The tall green saguaros were coming up, almost black in this light, and he thought of her just for a couple of seconds, not expecting to and not wanting to, sprawled there face-down with one shoe across her neck. No way to go even for a hooker, a lousy way to go, still screaming under the sand. If there'd been a headstone for Theodora Creaturo, what could you have put on it? She was a loser.

The last of the daylight was on the motel as he came around the curve and saw it there with its few lights yellow in the dusk, a truck gassing up at the pump, the guy helping himself, one of the regulars.

There were three autos in the parking lot, Pa's crumpled blue Olds, a pickup (that was Bob Dawson's, another regular), and a five-year-old Plymouth he hadn't seen before. He slotted the Chevy between it and the pickup, turning first and backing in, cutting the motor and sliding low on the seat, watching the truck driver go into the building, walking slow and counting money from his wallet. He ought to be feeling excited but he wasn't, and it bothered him. Brenner was on his way, had to be, and he'd be here in ten, maybe fifteen minutes, pulling in here and stopping and getting out, looking around. Then Charlie would climb out of the Chevy and go across and say who he was and take the case or the bag or whatever it was, and they'd go into the motel and while Brenner talked to the Judge he'd go in his own room with the bag and open it and count the stuff and it'd all be there, this time. Nothing could stop it happening, and he ought to be feeling excited but he just felt kind of queasy, like he'd eaten something too acid.

Maybe it was normal. They said you produced a whole lot of adrenaline when you got worked up over something, and then you didn't get rid of it for a while, so it went sour on you, maybe it was that. Too, he'd been losing a lot of sleep and he'd been riding on his nerves for the past twenty-four hours and hitting the peaks where he didn't actually know if he was still of sound mind or going nuts. Those kids had to do it with grass and glue and stuff, they should just try doing it cold like this and they'd know what it was all about.

Three autos went past inside of ten minutes, and now a truck went rumbling south with its square dark shape blotting out the stars along the horizon, its lights sending a backwash of reflections across the auto court, silvering the gas pump and leaving it dull again. Some music came from inside the motel and he imagined Bob Dawson or some other guy had hit that goddamn jukebox into action at last. Twenty minutes by his watch and he pulled another Kent from the pack and pressed its end to the glow of the last one, drawing the smoke in deep and watching the road, the dark road, and listening to the silence out here where the music seemed far away.

The fifth auto went by and he checked the time again and felt the sweat beginning to gather like he had a fever coming on, his eyes sore with watching the dark and the taste of the cigarette turning bitter on his tongue. You better get here, Brenner, couldn't have missed the way, his fingers tapping on the rim of the wheel, couldn't stop them, a vague feeling he ought to stop them but couldn't. Some of the rage again suddenly, what he'd do to them, *smash them*, then it was gone again because they couldn't pull anything, he had the ace. But you better be here, Brenner, oh Christ you better be here, lights sliding past and the gas pump flickering.

Then just the feeling that it was too much to handle, a kind of tiredness taking over so he couldn't think clearly, just in images, a tan suit and a carnation he'd never seen, and a yellow butterfly, the Judge saying yes, it would be all right this time, a shoe across her neck, and finally the feeling that he didn't care if Brenner came or didn't come, somebody, God or somebody, was fixing things so every time he got close it went away again, till he didn't want it anymore, didn't care what anybody did, so long as he could sleep. Lights going past and not stopping, a long rushing flicker and then the dark, and the music far away and the sound he was making in his chest, like a small night animal, while the tears began irritating his face and he wondered what they were, not knowing, in any conscious way, of his misery.

CHAPTER SIXTEEN

"Who are you?"

"Sheriff's Lieutenant Vorhees."

"I'm Savana."

"From Los Angeles?"

"Right."

"Glad to know you, Captain."

"Sure. How the hell d'you get these things out?"

"Not like that. Lemme do it."

"Thanks."

Vorhees got his knife and bent down and cut away the cholla ball from the captain's leg. "These things kinda jump at you when you get inside of a mile of 'em."

"They poisonous?"

"Might blister a bit."

Two young sheriff's officers were coming past, making hard going across the sand, the stretcher rocking between them.

"Hold it," Savana said, and lifted the cloth. It looked like the head had been trying to part company with the body and they'd had to turn it sideways so it would fit onto the stretcher. There was sand still sticking to the eyes, and the mouth was still wide open, sand in that too.

"You take pix?"

"Sure did," Vorhees said.

The two boys stood patiently like mules, glad of the rest. The one at the head of the stretcher, Donavon, had his eyes almost shut and was white in the face because this was the first corpse he'd seen. The one at the foot, Stekler, was eyeing the man who'd just arrived on the scene, quite a little awed and trying not to show it. He knew this must be Captain Savana, the man everyone said was coming. Young Stekler had joined the Morales police force for one reason, though he couldn't admit to it because he didn't even know it himself. From age ten or eleven he had dreamed of one day swinging along the street with a gun on his hip, the way Officer Marriot did when he passed by the house every day; and by the time Stekler was eighteen he'd realized there was only one way he could do it, legally: the way Officer Marriot had done it. Twelve months after his entry as a cadet in the sheriff's department he had shot his way through to top scores on the firing range and took home the Marksmanship Shield; and he was still unpopular in his unit for not even trying to make it look difficult.

Staring at the rather ordinary-looking man in plain clothes, Stekler wondered what it must be like to be a captain of the Special Investigation Section, Los Angeles, with a flat blue Smith and Wesson under his coat and the experience to know exactly when he must shoot to kill. That must be something. That must really be something.

Savana dropped the cloth and turned away.

"Okay," Vorhees told them. "And go easy up those rocks. Hey Donavon, you okay?"

The boy in front managed a nod, and they got going again, their load swinging between them, their shadows long and darkening as the sun touched the ridge to the northwest. There were some more flashes from the wrecked Cadillac and Savana looked again at Vorhees.

"Who are those photographers?"

"Homicide."

"Came in here fast."

"Guess we all did, Cap'n." He studied Savana a couple of

seconds and then said, "We all used unmarked cars, on strict orders."

"Very good."

Vorhees got ready to put a question and looked at Savana and changed his mind because the captain looked like he was trying to think something through. He kept his mouth shut and followed him back to the wreckage in the thorn trees, watching to see he didn't go barging into any chollas.

"Did your helicopter see the grave?"

"Nope, it just saw the car. Then when we–"

"Was it on routine patrol?"

"Well yes, it was on routine patrol but we already had your APB on a possible accident to a dark blue Caddy in this area, so they were lookin' as hard at the desert ravines as they were at the traffic. Me an' Cap'n Hobart came right along when we picked up the air message. If you ask–"

"How did you find the grave?"

"Saw somethin' flashin' over there, catchin' the sun. It was a piece o' glass, outa this wreck, by the–"

"Who is she?"

"Huh? It sounded like a Spanish name, or maybe Italian. We found a handbag in the car, and–"

"Where did she live?"

"She's from Vegas."

"Had a lot of style."

"Oh sure, yeah, been a looker, you could still tell, uh?"

Savana took the toothpick from his bright white teeth and snapped it in two and flicked the bits away. He didn't see the connection yet between a Los Angeles Superior Court judge being kidnapped and a young woman with a Spanish name being found in a grave not far from the wreckage of his car, and he didn't particularly want to see it because this whole thing could begin to look political and right now there was enough political muckraking going on to outstink every skunk in the state.

"Who called Homicide in?"

"Hobart. He said it wasn't often people who got thrown outa wrecked autos went an' dug themselves a grave an' laid down in it."

Savana nodded and looked around, surprised how fast the light had begun fading. The sun was down behind the ridge and a purple dusk was falling over the desert, the big saguaros turning gradually black against the sky. There wasn't anything more he needed to look at in the ravine here.

"Which is the quickest route to your office, Vorhees?"

"Same way as you got here. Take the third exit north on the Interstate, that's Ninety-second Street, an' look for the flag."

Savana climbed the rocks, avoiding the clumps of silver-yellow chollas in the lowering light. When he reached the top of the ravine he saw a Morales ambulance turning across the road and heading back north, leaving the two young sheriff's officers taking a breather by their radio car. One of them had been watching him all the time since he came into view from below, a flat-faced and serious-looking boy with his hand resting idly on his gun. The other was sitting on the ground with his back to the fender of the car, his head lowered and his eyes shut.

"He okay?" Savana asked the one standing up.

"He's feeling kinda sick, sir." He became suddenly active, wanting to impress, nudging the kid with his boot.

"Let him alone," Savana said. "Tell him to breathe deep."

Clive Brenner saw the building show up as his headlights swung around a curve, and he began slowing, his spine tingling unpleasantly to a nerve spasm as he saw how derelict the motel looked, a sign hanging crooked and the paint peeling, the sort of place you'd see on the front page of a newspaper, the scene of a tragedy. But lights burned in some of the windows and there were several cars in the auto court, giving the impression the place was still open for business. Headlights from behind him fanned across the building as he swung in past the single gas pump, parking against a grimy window full of desert bric-a-brac. Cutting the motor, he sat perfectly still for a moment, steeling himself. His experience with violent crime was in most part academic, and though he had often come close to its protagonists in the courtroom he'd never had to face them on the scene of their operations, until this moment.

Music sounded from inside the motel, and voices; but out here there was silence, unnerving him. But this last step of his journey had to be taken, and when he felt he was ready he got out and leaned into the rear of the Buick, taking the heavy briefcase and looping its handle around his wrist, slamming the door and starting across the auto court. The sound of the door seemed to echo, and he looked up, realizing that someone had climbed out of another car and was coming toward him quickly in the faint light. He stopped, waiting, his spine tingling again in the heat of the night.

"Brenner?"

"Yes."

It was a thin man in a straw hat, his left hand wrapped in a bandage. Brenner recognized the quick apprehensive tone he had heard on the telephone.

"Are you Mr. Rackman?"

"My name's Berlatsky."

The man's thin hand reached out to take the briefcase and Brenner swung it behind him.

"Before anything else, I have to see my clients."

This was the moment when he was certain the man would draw his gun and take the case by force, but he felt it was worthwhile showing a token resistance. The result was unexpected: To his surprise Berlatsky drew his hand back.

"Okay. But is it all there, this time?"

"The sum you demanded."

"Okay."

Watching the man closely in the light from the windows, Brenner saw his face change. It wasn't exactly a smile, but it looked like that, because all the tension went suddenly out of him and his taut expression relaxed. Leading the way to the entrance of the motel he said to Brenner:

"Did you have a nice flight?"

Brenner glanced at the thin man's face that now actually had a smile flickering across it, and wondered for an instant if Berlatsky was quite normal. He seemed slightly ashamed of having tried to take the briefcase without preamble, and anxious to behave like a gentleman—possibly Berlatsky's own phrase would be "to act like a gent," Brenner thought.

"Thank you, I did. Except of course for the—"

"Did you shake them off?" a thin-boned hand locking suddenly round Brenner's arm, the voice scared and its tone raised high.

"Yes."

"You sure?"

"Quite sure."

Berlatsky stared into his face another moment and then gave a quick nod, relaxing again. "Okay. Okay."

Brenner followed him, perplexed, into the lobby of the motel, the jukebox music loud against their ears. A quick glance showed him a number of persons visible through the doorway to the café: a group of men eating at a table, a waitress serving them, an elderly man behind the kitchen hatchway. If the men holding John and Evelyn were putting on a show here in case a police patrol came in, they were doing it extremely well.

"Brenner."

"Yes?"

"It's this way."

He followed the man along the passage, waiting beside him as he tapped on the door of Room 7.

"Yes?"

John's voice, but toneless. At least he was alive.

The thin man opened the door and motioned him to go in. As he obeyed it occurred to him that the door had not been locked and that the only people in this room were John and Evelyn, with no sign of a guard anywhere. But there wasn't the opportunity to think about this: he wanted first to look quietly at these two people and absorb the fact that they were alive, seemed quite well, and were in obvious control of themselves. There had been moments during his flight from Los Angeles when his imagination had become overcolored, because of late there had been a newly emerging feature to these kidnapping cases: an increasing attitude of arrogance and recklessness on the part of the criminals. There were also some recent cases where they had been so high on drugs that they had wantonly killed their victim before any ransom had been delivered.

"Clive," Stevens said. "It was good of you to come."

He was sitting on the bed with his legs up, propped against the raised pillow, a bathrobe over his slacks. There was the smell of liniment in the stuffy room and John was holding his neck stiffly as he looked across at Brenner.

Before he could reply, Evelyn moved to him quickly and he put his arms around her, the heavy briefcase swinging from his wrist.

"Thank God," she said, and for a moment leaned her head against his shoulder.

"Are you both all right?"

"Perfectly," John told him, but then he would say that, whatever was happening. His face looked terribly drawn, as if he'd suffered a lot of pain.

Evelyn lifted her head from Brenner's shoulder and he released her, slightly embarrassed. They were old friends but he wasn't a demonstrative person.

"I'm sorry," she said low, and got her handkerchief. He saw she'd been crying recently, perhaps as an expression of shock. But there were things in her attitude, and in John's that he didn't understand, wasn't able to interpret. Again he found there was no time to think about it: he was here to deliver the ransom and take them to a safe place, and immediately.

"I have the full amount," he said to John, swinging the briefcase. "Do I hand it to Mr. Berlatsky?"

"Yes," almost impatiently, as if he had forgotten the matter of the ransom. "If you will, Clive."

Brenner looked around for somewhere to put the bills, where Berlatsky could count them. John was occupying the bed, but the dressing table had nothing on it but an ashtray. He looked inquiringly at the thin man.

"In my room," Berlatsky said. He seemed a little defiant, as if this money was his due, though he'd prefer not to be seen counting it.

"You may take the case," Brenner told him. "I should like it back before we leave here." He turned to John. "D'you feel able to come in my car, or shall I call a private ambulance?"

"I–"

"No ambulance," Berlatsky told him from the doorway. "You don't leave here till I say, any of you. Okay?"

Brenner turned back to him quickly–"But our obligations to you are now fulfilled, Berlatsky, and I intend taking my clients away from here. Judge Stevens needs medical care, and–"

"Nobody leaves till I say so." He jerked his head toward John. "The Judge'll tell you the score." He went out, shutting the door.

Brenner felt annoyed at his own lack of grasp, though he knew the situation here was in some way radically different from what he'd assumed.

"Where are the others?" he asked John.

"Others?"

"The rest of Berlatsky's gang."

"There aren't any. It isn't like that, Clive."

Evelyn moved suddenly, snapping her bag shut and coming across to the door. "I'm going to ask them for a room," she said, not looking at either of them, "where I can lie down for a little while. Then you can talk alone."

There were four reports to hand when Captain Savana reached the county sheriff's office at Indian Rock, and a message from Lucas asking him to call him up on the radio. He went into the communications room and told the deputy there, and he switched the set open.

"*Base to Car 3—Car 3.*"

"*Come in.*"

Savana took over and identified himself.

"*Lucas, sir. Brenner's gone to ground in the Desert Winds Motel at Indian Rock, south from the Interstate on Indian Rock Highway, about Milepost 18. He didn't smell us.*"

Savana was looking at the map on the wall. MP 18 was just a mile south of the ravine where the Stevens Cadillac had gone down.

"*How long ago, Lucas?*"

"*Ten minutes.*"

"*Where are you right now?*"

"*Standing by under cover, sir.*"

"*Miller with you?*"

"*Yes sir.*"

"*All right, keep station and report. Base out.*"

He cut the switch and went closer to the map, making sure of his bearings on the motel in relation to the crash site.

"Where's Captain Hobart?"

"Mobile, sir. I call him up?"

"Right."

"*Base to Car 1—Car 1.*"

There were other signals making a heavy background and the deputy had to call again, tuning out the squelch when the captain came in.

"*Hobart.*"

Savana took over the signal.

"*This is Savana here.*"

"Oh, say! I guess we just missed each other down in that ravine! Did Vorhees give you what you needed?"

"Yes, he showed me the—"

"That's just a hell of a mess down there, isn't it?"

"Can I have a couple of roadblocks readied, Hobart, soonest?"

"Why, anythin' you say. A couple of what was that?"

There was a lot of static, which the deputy said was due to magnetic rocks, but finally Savana got it across to Hobart that he needed a block north and a block south of the Desert Winds Motel, manned but not operative until and unless the orders came to start checking drivers of vehicles.

"Say, you think they're holdin' Judge Stevens at that place?"

"I'm assuming they are."

"Okay, I'm headin' back to Base right away. Soon as you're off the air I'm goin' to call up Morales and get those blocks set up."

Savana thanked him and signaled out and cut the switch and looked at the four reports that had come in, reading them twice and making a note and then picking up a phone and dialing Los Angeles.

Commander Hellman came on the line direct.

"Savana."

"Well?"

"There are some new dimensions to this thing."

"You mean the woman?"

"Yes." Hobart must have flashed him on that. "Who was she, boss?"

There was one of Bill Hellman's silences, then he noticed the man sounded weary when he answered.

"She was a hooker from Vegas."

Savana took the toothpick out of his mouth and said, "Oh my Christ." Then he shut up and knew he was going to be very careful about what he said, as of now, because suddenly his feelings down there in that ravine were being proved right on the line: it was beginning to look as if that desert grave was going to be the epicenter of the next political earthquake in California. And more: Hellman was a friend of the John K. Stevenses' and that was why his voice sounded like it did. Not weary, but worried sick.

"What's the local situation?" he asked Savana.

"Brenner's holed up in a motel at Indian Rock and I'm assuming the Stevenses are being held there. It's about thirty miles south of Morales and about one mile from the ravine where he put his Caddy in."

"Hold it a minute, Nick."

Savana heard other voices on the line, and Hellman talking to somebody in Communications against radio squelch. He looked at the array of trophies around the office: challenge cups, medallions, championship shields, you name it, they really went out to show they could win, these county boys. Picture of the bold Captain Hobart in a stetson and boots getting himself flung off a mustang, picture of a deputy among a lot of rocks and cactus and stuff, holding up a dead rattlesnake as tall as himself, an official poster on treating black widow bites; it'd be real nice, Savana thought, to be back in the health-giving smog of downtown L.A. and maybe even find a drugstore with something for these blisters.

"Well?" Hellman said.

"I split at the airport here with Lucas and Miller, and left them to tail Brenner. Hobart flashed me on the wrecked Caddy so I went right on down there to look."

"This motel. Are they watching it?"

"Yes sir. And Hobart's setting up roadblocks in case we can use them."

There was another silence, a longer one than usual.

"So far as you know, the Stevenses and now Brenner are being held in that motel?"

"Yes."

"And you assume that when the money is paid they'll be allowed to leave?"

"That's pure conjecture. I haven't any real info to go on."

"How many men are holding them there?"

"I don't know. I haven't seen even one of them."

"Did Lucas and—who's your other—"

"Miller—"

"Did they see any contact made?"

"No, or they would have told me. They were wheeling a long-distance tail and Brenner's been very sensitive, so they would've gone right on past the Desert Winds and—"

"The what?"

"The motel, the Desert Winds—"

"Right, gone past and peeled back?"

"Yes. The contact was probably inside anyway."

After a bit Hellman said heavily, "What are the chances, Nick, if you go on in?"

Savana had to think what he meant: semantically Hellman was being very vague. "The risk of a shoot-out?"

"Yes."

"That's impossible to say."

During the next silence Savana did some more thinking, because it sounded as if Hellman had something else on his mind all the time: he wasn't leading with his questions, *rat-tat-tat*, as he normally did. His voice was audible again in the background, saying something about Senator Carlberg, and there was a woman's voice answering: that would be Liz Brown still on duty. And the implication of these voices and the senator's name in relation to that grave in the desert finally got through to Savana and he began understanding so many of the things that had puzzled him before. The desert grave *was* liable to be the epicenter of the next Californian earthquake, and Hellman was already one of those trying to keep it inert.

His voice came back full volume. "Where were we?"

With great care Savana said, "I'd like to know something. Is this still a kidnap case we have on our hands?"

A long silence but this time no background voices.

"Yes."

And Savana knew he was lying. He'd worked with Bill Hellman for longer than he could remember, and he knew the guy and he knew that for all his faults he didn't ever need to lie. Unless it was to save a man's face. Or his skin.

Savana took a deep breath and thought okay, if his chief said it was a kidnap case then it was a kidnap case and he'd play it according to the appropriate rules. It didn't change the local situation: the people who were ripping off Judge Stevens for a hundred grand were the kind of people who'd react violently if provoked and they were almost certainly into drugs, and you couldn't ever tell what would happen when you went into a thing like this: you could call them on the horn and talk them down and walk in cold and they could change their minds or panic and it'd be all you could do—if you could do it—to get out alive, let alone save anybody else. There'd been a bad one just a few months ago in San Francisco: five dead, three of them cops, one of them an ex-con and one of them a vice-president of the Kruger-Armor Bank.

"Do you have any information at all," Hellman was asking, "about that place?"

"The motel?"

"Right."

"Nothing we can work on." He looked at one of the reports he'd been reading. "A reserve CHP in this area checked the place out with a photograph of Judge Stevens and said one of the staff reacted 'apprehensively' as if she were 'concealing information.' But that just seems to confirm the fact they're in there. There's a Chevy sedan with Vegas plates that's standing around the auto court a lot of the time as if one or more of the guests are staying on, and we're checking with the Vegas DMV right now because it isn't the sort of place anyone'd want to stay for more than a night stop. I guess that's all we have, this end. The only other reports coming in since I called you last were about the crash site and the dead woman."

He could hear other faint voices on the line again, and some radio static, Hellman telling somebody to do it again and get it right this time, not the way he normally talked on an open network. Then he came back and said tonelessly:

"Nick, there's a night flight out of L.A. that'll get me into Morales soon after midnight. Have somebody meet me."

"Sure thing."

"Meantime what are you going to do?"

"Send a man in to case the joint. That way I can keep down the risk of any possible bloodshed when we finally—"

"Savana."

"Yes sir?"

"There is no question of bloodshed at any time. Hear me: no question at all. Your first task is to safeguard Judge Stevens and Mrs. Stevens."

"Understood."

"Also when you send your man in, he is not to carry arms. If you can't get anybody to do it that way, forget it. It's entirely their option. Anything you have to report, I'll be here."

The Communications background began again and then the line went dead and Savana hung up and crossed slowly to the window and slid his hands flat in his back pockets and stretched his arms behind him, watching the headlights go streaming along Interstate 15 and thinking this was about the closest he'd got to being involved, in the line of duty, in a big political scandal. And frankly he wasn't pleased about it, because you could somehow understand a guy shooting his bride for whoring around, or a nut setting a hotel afire because he was a nut, or a bunch of guys busting into a bank because they thought the world owed them a living—they were just ball-less or nuts or thieves and they didn't try to make out they were anything else, better or worse. But these people in high places who set themselves above their fellowmen and persuaded John Q. Public to trust them with his welfare should really try to keep their noses clean or get out of office and run a legitimate crap game in Vegas or somewhere. He didn't have any time for them.

"Cap'n Savana?"

"Uh?"

The young deputy was looking at him through the hatch of the radio room.

"Just got your DMV query." He slid the sheet across the hatch counter and Savana picked it up.

Owner of Chevrolet sedan ALU-27578 is Charles Melville Berlatsky of 302 E Block Dunes Vista Apartments on 74th St. Las Vegas Nevada.

Savana turned the sheet around on the counter.

"Put it into Ident."

The computer came back with it inside two minutes.

"I have a negative, sir, on Berlatsky."

"Big help. All right, call up my men again."

"*Base to Car 3, come in please.*"

"*Lucas.*"

Savana took the mike. "*Situation?*"

"*No change, sir.*"

"*Okay. I need one of you to go in there with a cover.*"

"*I'm ready.*"

"*You have to go in unarmed.*"

Lucas didn't respond immediately and Savana waited. A Los Angeles cop knew that when he got into trouble with his gun on him he stood a chance, just a chance. At this moment Lucas was sitting there cursing his luck: it could have been Miller who picked up this call.

"*Okay, sir, if that's the way it is.*"

CHAPTER SEVENTEEN

THE SMELL OF THE LINIMENT in the stuffy room was getting to Brenner's stomach, reminding him fleetingly that he'd had no time to eat any lunch today. He stood at the window, looking out across the auto court at the sand-blasted gas pump isolated in a pool of light. He had been standing here for almost fifteen minutes without moving, as John K. Stevens informed him, sometimes haltingly, of what had taken place. Now it was finished but Brenner still didn't move.

He had the feeling that this was a nightmare he'd walked into, a shift of reality into a different dimension. He had come here to release his friend and client and escort him to safety, the innocent victim of outrage. Instead he found himself involved in a crisis in which his friend and client would probably find himself destroyed.

Watching him from the bed, Stevens waited, his eyes half closed under their heavy lids, thinking how out of place Clive Brenner looked in this shabby place. Well groomed, tanned and elegantly tailored, he seemed like a traveler lost on some benighted railroad station. The wan light from the bathroom glowed on the gold of his wafer-thin wristwatch and the rims of his tinted glasses as he turned at last and took a pace into the room, looking at the floor, his hands clasped behind him.

"Rather a bombshell for you," Stevens said. "I'm sorry."

"Yes it is."

Brenner couldn't remember any event in the whole of his career that had so shaken him, and he was unpleasantly surprised to find he wasn't taking it too well.

"I would understand perfectly, Clive, if you preferred that I found someone else to represent me, as of this time."

"No, that's all right, I'd like the chance of seeing you through this. Unless of course you'd rather have Billings, or Hartman and Schneider—we don't specialize in very high-level political fields, as you—"

"No, Clive. If you're prepared to go on, I know I'll be most ably represented."

His voice sounded tired to death and Brenner glanced at him. Until now he'd been avoiding John's eyes, out of kindness to him. In his present condition, in pain and with his clothes rumpled, lying on the bed of a run-down motel room, he wouldn't thank anyone to look too long at him. His eyes were closed now, and Brenner felt compassion for him, an emotion so rare that he wasn't quite sure what it was. It was mixed with a certain distaste: it was hard to understand how a mind so good and so sensitive had come to inhabit so gross a vessel; hard, too, to believe that a mere restless sexuality could bring him so low, to the point where he was virtually destroyed.

It had happened, God only knew, to men greater than John K. Stevens, but that was no consolation to Brenner: he hadn't had the job of representing them. This one was his pigeon, and he was privately worried that he might have taken on something too big. On the other hand he knew perfectly well that Daniel Weinstock would want the firm to stay in, on the slim chance of somehow shielding John and even enabling him to top the polls in the race for governorship. A gubernatorial victory would achieve a position for the firm of Weinstock, Simon and Brenner that would take them ten years to reach in the normal course of events.

"I've told you everything, Clive. Now I'd like your opinion."

"On what we're to do?"

"Yes."

Brenner took an initialed handkerchief and patted it over his face, moving restlessly around the room.

"I suppose I should advise you to take the obvious chance and withdraw your gubernatorial nomination and resign from office on the plausible grounds of ill health consequent to the accident. But you wouldn't have let matters go this far —with Berlatsky—if you hadn't thought there was a hope of coming through. Knowing you as I do, I'm not prepared to suggest you give up the fight at this early stage—and if I did, you'd get another lawyer. So we have to deal with Berlatsky, and—" He broke off, for a moment helpless. "I frankly don't find it credible to envisage the powers of the state governorship being vulnerable at all times to the whim of one undistinguished citizen."

"You think he'll make further demands?"

"Are you serious? The man's stumbled into a goldmine!"

"I thought that, Clive. But in all this time I've had a chance of coming to know him."

Brenner didn't dismiss the thought. For the past twenty-four hours Berlatsky had been critically judged in everything he'd said.

"So?"

"He has honor, of a kind. And he sees this situation as one in which he's rendered me his services for a fee commensurate with their value. In fact, as you can imagine, I would have paid him considerably more. He—"

"But he didn't know that."

"True—"

"He would have asked for double if he thought he'd get it."

"Possibly."

"Certainly."

"No, Clive. He lives to a certain code, for one thing, that

lets him peddle merchandise that must be nine parts rubbish, but that wouldn't let him steal."

"It turned a bit of a blind eye when he demanded money with menaces."

"It wasn't a demand for *money,* Clive. It was a demand for money *quickly.*"

Brenner stopped pacing, wiping his face again.

"What does that mean, John?"

"I'd agreed, tacitly, to pay him. He could have gone with me to Los Angeles, put up at a first-class hotel, and waited for a few days while the cash was withdrawn, without hazarding his position in the slightest. But he didn't have the experience in these things: he's a small man, and to him the sum was so dazzling that he was afraid of missing it if there were any delay."

"It's certainly true that his nerves are about shot. On the phone to him I thought at one time I was handling a nut case."

"His code," Stevens said gently, "is still intact. Evelyn" —he paused, thinking of her, for an instant desolate—"Evelyn brought three thousand dollars with her, and we offered it to Berlatsky, on account. He walked away from it. You see what I mean?"

"Possibly," Brenner said, "he's not quite stable. I mean to protest his integrity and at the same time play the extortionist."

"He doesn't see it like that, Clive. He felt he couldn't trust me to pay up, so he forced the pace."

"That's fine. For how many years is he going to force the pace when he's short of a hundred thousand dollars?"

Stevens shifted his position on the bed, thinking perhaps he could get up and walk around a little; but pain shot through his nerves and he kept still, clenching his hands, until Brenner came over, looking down at him.

"John, I've got to take you out of here. You need treatment, just as soon—"

"Yes." It was a whisper and Brenner waited, embarrassed, as always, by suffering. "Give me a moment, Clive."

Brenner turned away, deciding to call Evelyn back. He was on his way to the door when Stevens spoke again.

"Clive, listen. Berlatsky is a small man. He couldn't think beyond the sum he asked. Also he has pride, and feels outclassed by people like ourselves, so he doesn't trust us. He—" but a spasm came and he kept still as the pain flared up and burned in his head. It was a minute before he could go on, in hurried and jerky whispers, wanting Clive to know this because everything depended on it. "I think he has too much pride to go—to go on asking for money, or privileges. He considers himself paid now, and I don't think we would hear from—from him again. In my judgment, we don't have to fear him, provided he remains free." There was a long pause and then Brenner heard a note of irony in his voice. "In the moment of my undoing, I met an honest man."

Brenner turned away, needing desperately to think. Using one of Daniel Weinstock's axioms—"Think of the worst that could happen first, and work back"—he decided that if for some reason the body of the woman were found, or if Berlatsky were arrested and questioned, there was a strong case to be made in behalf of John Stevens: an eminent man, of acknowledged worth to his community, had for a moment succumbed to temptation, had suffered an accident, and by further ill chance had become exposed to the ruthless machinations of an opportunist. Whatever John had just said to his credit, Berlatsky was the kind of man one could easily shoot to ribbons in the witness stand, since he lost control on the slightest provocation.

Result: John would withdraw his nomination, resign from office and retire from public life. He would at least be able to keep his head up among most of his friends, but it was hard to see a man of his impressive abilities being put out to grass at the height of his powers. Conceivably it could kill him. Brenner felt sudden aversion to Daniel's little axiom: in this case the "worst" was pretty black. But in the scales against it there was a featherweight chance of getting through. If the body were never found, and if Berlatsky could keep out of the hands of the police, there would be hope for the future. Of course they'd never know, from one day to the next, that the past wouldn't come up and knock everything away; but John had clearly thought of that and was ready to live with it.

"Clive."

He turned back to the bed.

"Berlatsky has—some aspirin for me. I wonder if—you'd mind asking—"

"I'm going to see him anyway. Hold on."

Stevens heard him go to the door, and light struck through from the passage, hurting his eyes. The strain of confessing to Evelyn had left him weak, and he began drifting into a state of twilight consciousness, sometimes hearing the sounds of water pipes, once seeming to hear a soft far voice, *Kenny, what happened,* sleeping and waking fitfully until the bright light struck again and water gushed in the bathroom and Clive was standing over him, small things rattling in a bottle, *aspirin,* Clive was saying, and then, *he won't let us leave here till the morning, he's adamant.*

Charlie Berlatsky lay on the bed looking at the ceiling. The place had been quiet for a long time, and there weren't any more cars going past. The phone had rung once, some time ago, and someone had answered it, Rose he supposed. He thought of her.

He thought of Rose, and the blue sea there, and the purple creeper hanging over whitewashed walls, and there was a kind of softness in him, all over his body, like he'd just had a woman.

It felt like both his hands were bandaged but he knew what it was. He hadn't meant to sleep: he'd meant to go and see Rose. It had just crept over him. He'd come in here with the heavy bag, shutting the door and going across to the bed, putting it down, then he'd counted the money, taking his time, with the room very quiet, putting the bundles in rows, neatly, not just thrown down, feeling how crisp they were, seeing how bright the new green printing looked against the white paper. Even the elastic bands were new, smelling faintly of rubber in the hot room, and they'd given a kind of dull music when he'd rolled them across the bills. Sometimes he'd had to stop counting because his hands were aching, not being used to this kind of work, sweet Jesus, that was true enough, then he got to the end and they were all there, fifty bundles in five rows of ten, with twenty hundreds in each, there on the bed for him to look at, and touch, and riffle through, sliding his hand among them and turning them over, with nobody who could stop him, because they were his own.

Then Brenner had come and he'd kept him in the doorway so he wouldn't see what he'd been doing, it'd look kind of vulgar, counting money out on the bed. Brenner had asked for aspirin for the Judge, and said they wanted to leave, arguing about it till Charlie had said they couldn't leave till he went to catch his plane. There were police looking for Brenner, he'd said so himself, and they might see him and ask him things, and he'd give things away. They could go in the morning, he'd said.

Charlie hadn't been unsympathetic about it—the Judge was an ex-associate of his and he didn't want him to suffer —but he couldn't risk any trouble now.

Lying with his face to the ceiling, he thought he couldn't be unsympathetic to anybody ever again. It was all over now, the worry day after day that he wasn't going to make it, that life was going by and he didn't have any more now than he did ten years ago, that something was wrong and he couldn't seem ever to get it right. It was all over and he'd made it, still quite young and with a whole lot of life still ahead of him. Too, he'd be able to help people now, like that poor bastard picking up garbage at the airport, and people like Rose, slinging hash all day and getting her ass pinched by those bums in there; he could show people the real world, the way it really could be.

Thinking again of Rose he looked at his watch, straining his eyes to see it in the faint light from the lamp over the gas pump outside. There didn't seem to be more than one hand on his watch, then he saw they were both together because it was midnight. He sat up, untying the knot he'd made when he'd put his necktie through the handle of the bag, the other end around his wrist, so nobody could come in here and take it. There was the whole of his future in this bag, his and Rose's, and he wouldn't ever let it out of his reach.

Everything seemed different when he got up and went into the bathroom to splash his face. He was moving sort of slower, like he had all the time he wanted, and the floor felt kind of solid under his feet. The things he touched, like the tap and the towel, felt more real, like he was noticing them for the first time, and appreciating them. He had to stand still for a minute to think about it, wondering if it was because all the tension had gone, if it was because there'd never been time to see the things around him, and feel them, because life had been behind him and kicking him in the ass so he couldn't ever stop to see where he was at.

The bag was on the edge of the basin, he'd brought it in here, and the light from the twenty-five-watt bulb in its cracked shade was shining down on it, and he thought he'd never seen anything so beautiful in his life, with the leather kind of glowing, and the letters standing out in gold, C.S.B., solid and warm and rich-looking, the kind of bag a man like him would buy, you could tell by the way he dressed. He must remember to send it back to him from Mexico after he'd put the money into a bank: Brenner had made a point of asking for it.

When he'd washed he used his shaver and spruced up a

little, noticing how steady his eyes looked in the mirror. There was something about his face he'd never seen before, kind of confident, everybody's friend. Putting on a clean shirt he thought he'd better do a little shopping at the airport in Morales, on his way out, a few shirts, some good quality ones, not like these, and some gold cuff links like the ones Brenner wore, and some new white calfskin shoes. He'd have to get used to looking the kind of man he was, somebody of substance.

He opened the polished leather bag and broke one of the bundles, putting ten C-notes in his pocket, zipping the bag shut and looping the handle around his wrist, going to the door.

In the lobby there was the smell of stale coffee and burned potatoes, and somewhere he could hear a cricket chirping, maybe got into the kitchen and couldn't get out again. He went down to the door marked *Private* and knocked on it gently. He had to do it louder before she heard.

"Who is it?"

"Charlie."

He kept his voice quiet because he didn't want to wake any of the others up, along the passage, this had been a shocking time for all of them.

Her voice came again, nearer, just the other side of the door.

"Charlie?"

"Yes. It's me, Rose."

He heard the bolt being pulled back, then the door opened and he saw her in the glow from some kind of a night-light, her gold hair across her smooth white shoulder, one of her eyes shining, the other one in shadow. He could smell her warm body as she stood there close to him, bent down a little in the doorway with her arm across her breasts, and he said, "Rose, oh Rose," going in as she moved back for him, her blue eyes very big and staring at him in the dim light, wondering about him.

"Charlie," she whispered, "what's in there?"

"It's for us," he said, and put the bag on the floor, wedging it between her dressing table and the wall. The shotgun was lying across the rumpled bedclothes and he saw it as he turned and straightened up.

"Rose! What's that for?"

She swung it and pushed it under the bed, crouching on her haunches to do it, trying to cover herself because she was naked.

"I wasn't sure it was you," she said, a little soft laugh exploding on her breath as she dived back into bed, pulling the sheet up around her knees. "Sometimes a guy gets ideas and comes knocking on my door, you know, somebody staying here." She sat with her chin on her knees, looking up at him. "Gee, I missed you, Charlie."

"Oh, Rose," he said again, her name soft in his mind, part of all the softness that had come into him since he'd counted the money, "Rose," looking down at her as he pulled off his clothes, a lace snapping in one of his shoes, the bandage tugging at the inside of his sleeve because he'd got it wet again, washing. She jumped off the bed and began helping him.

"Charlie, is everything all right?"

"Like what?"

The soft warm smell of her was so close, the light on her long hair shining against his eyes.

"Well, I–I mean everything. Charlie?"

She sounded worried, but that was because he hadn't come to her room earlier, and she hadn't known why.

"Everything's perfect, Rose."

"Is it?"

"Don't worry. Everything's perfect."

"All right," she whispered, wanting to believe him. Later he'd tell her, not everything, because it was sad about the girl, just tell her he and the Judge had done some business together. She didn't say any more but went on helping him with her quick warm fingers, folding his coat and putting it over the chair near the bed where her panties were, and then they were together on the bed where her warmth still was and she was holding him, her legs wide for him and her breath shaking out against his face as he found her and thrust inward and knew that this was the first day of his life and nothing could go wrong ever again.

CHAPTER EIGHTEEN

THE HEADLIGHTS of the approaching car picked out the unmarked sedan that stood among the trees, then it slowed and swung off the roadway, parking alongside, its lights going out. The motor was cut off and a door opened, the sound sharp in the silence.

Hellman got out and looked around him in the moonlight.

"Captain Savana here?"

"Yes sir."

Savana came out of the shadows.

"Who's this?"

"Sergeant Hockley."

"Who's the other man?"

"Miller."

"Where's Lucas?"

"Sleeping. They're working shifts now."

"He tired or something?"

"He was on thirteen hours."

Hellman didn't comment. He'd so far been on sixteen hours, since eight o'clock this morning, and he wasn't stopping yet.

"Did you come here straight from the airport, sir?"

"Yes. Why?"

"Couple of reports you may have missed." Savana recounted them, noticing that Hellman was leaning against the sedan, his head down as he listened, not the regular Hellman stance.

"How long was Lucas in there for?"

"More than an hour."

"Didn't see Brenner, even?"

"No."

"Brenner's car still outside?"

"Yes."

"Because I called the motel myself," Hellman told him, "from Los Angeles, soon after I had your message about it. I asked to talk to Mr. Brenner but the woman said she didn't know anyone of that name. So he hasn't registered."

Savana didn't answer, partly because Hellman normally became lost in thought immediately he'd said something, partly because there didn't seem to be any answer required. Hellman had taken a risk, though. The people holding Stevens hadn't known the police were already on to the place, because Lucas and Miller had made sure their tail was clean. Anyone calling Brenner at the Desert Winds just had to be the police, unless he'd left the number with someone and that was unlikely.

"This woman he questioned. Would she be the one who seemed apprehensive?"

"Yes, the descriptions tally."

"You check out the other people in the café?"

"Yes. The area CHP knows them all personally—he eats there himself sometimes."

Headlights brightened from the dark, silvering the leaves of the thorn trees and gilding the ruts of sand lying along the shoulders of the roadway. They turned their backs until it went past.

"Who's on the motel?"

"Four of the sheriff's reserves."

"Radio?"

"Yes. We can throw the roadblocks across inside twenty seconds—we timed it."

"Have you got a helicopter standing by?"

"Yes."

"Where?"

"There's a pad alongside the Indian Rock office."

Hellman was silent for a while, leaning against the police car, hands in his coat pockets, head down. Savana didn't say anything more because with Bill Hellman in this mood whatever he said would be the wrong thing anyway.

"You find anything fresh on that man—what was his name?"

"With the Chevy? Charles M. Berlatsky. No, nothing fresh."

"That's all we've got on him? That his car's in the auto court most of the time?"

"Yes."

"By God, it's not much, is it?"

Savana didn't say anything.

"He could be our man, or there could be a dozen others there with a submachine gun trained on the doors, how can we tell? Lucas didn't go into any of the rooms." He slipped the mug shot into his wallet.

"However many there are in there," Savana said, "we've got them in a bottle with the cork in."

Hellman thought about that for a bit and suddenly went across to the radio car and spoke to the driver. "I want a message put through. General alert to all U.S.-Mexican frontier checkpoints, special vetting of U.S. nationals crossing or trying to cross the border today, nineteenth." He waited until Indian Rock had repeated. "Priority check and immediate notification on white Caucasian named Charles M. Berlatsky." He gave a description and stood listening until the deputy had finished sending; then he walked a little way toward the road and stood looking northward to where the Desert Winds Motel made a patch of light in the distance.

"I don't see any problem, Nick. It looks as though Brenner had the money on him and it must have changed hands by now. So why don't they release their captives?"

"It could happen," Savana said, "any minute."

Hellman nodded. "Are you staying here?"

"Till they make a move."

Hellman dug his hands into his coat pockets again and stood looking at his feet. After a time he said, "I'll be at the Indian Rock office."

He went across to the car and the motor started up and Savana stood watching as it turned onto the roadway and gathered speed, becoming smaller, its moving patch of light passing close to the glow in the distance. Then he went over to the sedan and unclipped the mike and called up Base, asking someone to lend him their private car and send it down here to the checkpoint at MP 19 some time before dawn, with not more than one gallon of gas in the tank.

Then he signaled out and slid lower in the seat and shut his eyes and told Sergeant Hockley to wake him if anything happened.

There was an alarm clock near the bed, with a loud tinny tick, and it had kept Charlie awake most of the time. It had luminous hands and he saw it was a quarter till six. He could hear water running somewhere, maybe her pa getting up for his morning trip to Morales. He liked her pa, a nice old guy, all Holy Christ and hash blacks and the hell with you, not many of them left now. What would he do without Rose here?

She moved beside him but didn't wake. He must get up in another ten minutes because the plane for Mexico left at 7:40 and he didn't want to rush. The quiet feeling was still with him, the sense of having reached a place in time where everything would always go well, where there was only goodness, and peace. A while ago she'd awakened, yawning and suddenly jerking in surprise to find him here in her bed, then laughing softly and nuzzling into him and stroking him, and they'd made love again, and it had been as good as the last time, and the first time when they'd spilled all the colored stones across the dirt floor. But the feeling that was inside of him now, inside and all over him, wasn't to do with that.

He could see the outline of the briefcase against the wall, a patch of moonlight showing it up. He'd left it there, wedged between the wall and her dressing table, because the door had a lock and a bolt and nobody could get in without waking him up, and there was the shotgun under the bed. In the faint light he could make out the pattern of the photographs she had all over the walls, and let himself believe he could see one of them that wasn't actually there, with them standing together against their white Cadillac convertible outside the pretty little Mexican-style house with its arches and shaded patio and palm trees, a film star's discreet and very private hideaway, though actually the property of Mr. and Mrs. Charles M. Berlatsky.

Thinking of it, he wanted to laugh, like he'd done before, but had to stop himself because she wouldn't understand, she'd think he was nuts. When he looked at the clock again he saw it was past twenty to seven, so he got out of the bed as quietly as he could and put his pants on, finding his shoes.

"Charlie?"

Her voice was sleepy and he loved her more than he'd ever loved anyone in the world, because of the way her voice was sleepy, and because she said his name in the way she always did.

"I'm coming back, Rose," he whispered. She hadn't opened her eyes, or he would have seen them in the faint light the moon was sending through the window, the moon or the first of the daylight, he couldn't tell. "I'll be back," he whispered.

He found everything except one sock, but he could leave it for now. The bag made a sliding noise when he pulled it out of the space where he'd left it wedged, but she didn't say anything, even when he had to pull the big bolt back. He thought she was awake now, but just not talking. Then there was the smell of stale coffee again in the lobby, and the bleak gray-green light she always left burning all night in the café. He didn't make any noise passing Room 7 but there was a crack of light showing under the door already, and he thought he could hear the deep voice of the Judge, talking very quietly to someone.

In the middle of shaving he heard Pa go out and the Olds starting up in the auto court, and now the light was getting stronger every minute in the window and he could see the sky was clear and growing blue. When he'd finished in the bathroom he got a clean pair of socks out of his case and put them on, making a ball of the dirty one and stuffing it in the bottom left-hand corner where he always put things to be washed. The last thing he did when he left his room after an overnight stop was of course to take the twelve black cases from wherever he'd put them, disarming the burglar alarm he always put on top. He went to do it now, and stopped, remembering, and stood there a minute looking at them and thinking of all that junk they had inside, wondering how he'd ever kept on going, day after day, talking people into buying this stuff, mostly people who couldn't really afford it—he ought to have been ashamed of himself. It'd be stupid to take it along, but he found it hard just to leave it there because it had fed him, and given him a roof, so in a kind of way it had value for him and he remembered how he'd sold half the stock in one of the cases, the Bermuda Reef Collection (pearls and gold coins and that kind of stuff, like out of a pirate's galleon) when he'd busted into a wedding party in Palm Springs.

He just couldn't walk out of the room, leaving the stuff there, even though he'd got it for peanuts, so he tore a sheet out of his order book and wrote the name of the little chicana on it, Pepita, the kid with bright eyes and fat legs who did the cleaning here:

Pepita—These are all for you, and you will look pretty wearing them. They are what the stars wear. Good luck —he began putting *Ch* and crossed it out and put—*Mr. Charles M. Berlatsky.*

He took the alarm off the top and brought the cases down, stacking them in the bathroom where she'd go and clean, so nobody would poke their head in the door from the passage and see them there and rip them off before Pepita came.

Rose was out of bed when he went back to her room, and standing by the window with a towel around her and her arms folded, just looking out across the backyard to where the desert began.

"Rose," he said, "you look beautiful. Like an Arabian princess."

She came to him quickly, laughing softly, kind of relieved, he thought, and wanted to stay in his arms, her head against him, till he had to kiss her and push her gently away.

"Rose," he said, "I've got to go."

She nodded, not saying anything, and he pulled the wad of bills out of his pocket, holding them for her to take. "Here's a thousand dollars, Rose, for your ticket to Acapulco and a few things you'll want to get yourself, a few clothes, get the best ones, and don't worry about the price," watching her eyes growing big as she looked at the wad of new bills and then up into his face, worried about something.

"But Charlie . . ."

He didn't know what she meant.

"It's for you, Rose."

She took the money, like she didn't want to look ungrateful.

"Charlie, I—don't want to take anything from you. Not till we—we're—"

"It's just for the air fare, see, and a few things—"

"I know. Charlie, do you know anyone called Brenner?"

"Who?"

He'd heard the name all right but he needed time to think because he hadn't expected her to say it, talking about Brenner when they were really talking about the money for her to spend.

"Mr. Brenner."

"Why?"

"A man called last night, that's all, asking for him."

Nobody could have called him. Not here.

"On this phone?"

"Yes."

Nobody knew Brenner was here. It was a mistake.

"What did you tell him?"

"I just said there wasn't anyone here called that."

"Sure. You didn't know."

"Did I say the wrong–"

"No. It doesn't make any difference to anything."

But she looked so worried, standing watching him with the towel round her and the money in her hand. She didn't have to be worried about anything.

"Then I thought it must be his car out there," she said, "the red one."

"Yes."

Her eyes were stone-blue, gray-blue, in the early morning light coming through the window. She watched him steadily.

"What's wrong, Rose?"

"Nothing." She looked down at the money. "I just didn't know who Mr. Brenner was. We have to register people and–"

"Sure. He's just an associate of mine."

"Is he?"

"Sure."

"There was another guy, Charlie, last night."

He wasn't quite listening to her, because he was trying to think how anyone could have known Brenner was here at the motel. But it wouldn't make any difference, he'd be on the plane inside of an hour and there wouldn't be anything anybody could do.

"There was what?"

"A man in the café. An insurance man, he said."

"What was his name?"

"He didn't say."

"Well, what did he do? I don't understand what you're—"

"Oh Charlie," she said, and came close again and leaned her forehead on his shoulder. "He asked me a lot of questions. I think he was a cop."

The wad of crisp new bills made a sound, its edge brushing his sleeve as she stood against him, waiting for him to say something. It was a rhythmic sound the bills were making, a soft beating in the quiet of the room, the beat of her heart transferred to her hand where it rested against his arm. He listened to it, as if it was important. It was all he wanted to think about, but he couldn't leave her worrying.

"What kind of questions?"

"Oh, talking a lot, you know, saying it must be tough, running a busy motel, and we must get some odd people looking for rooms, and what did we do when they acted up and gave trouble, things like that. I can't remember all of them, but he wanted to know who the Chevy belonged to, out there, because he was looking for just that model to buy. I think he meant yours, so I said I didn't know, but he wanted to go on talking, so I put Mabel to serve him and went to help Pa in the kitchen, but he threw me out," and she began shaking against him, laughing quietly. "Pa's like that, he can't stand for women to get in his kitchen when he's, oh I don't know," shaking against him, and it wasn't laughing, he could tell now, laughing and crying were so much alike, it was hard to tell the difference. "Oh Christ, I got so I didn't know what to do, Charlie, don't you see? I thought I should tell you about him before, then I thought I was maybe just imagining he was a cop, I mean people ask about cars they're looking for, and—then when you came in here you said everything was perfect, and you looked so —so happy, and I knew I'd been imagining things and I didn't want to spoil it by telling you about the man. There wasn't any point."

He held on to her, feeling her shivering, wanting her to stop.

"Everything's okay, Rose."

She didn't answer for a minute, and he listened to the clock ticking noisily by her bed, knowing he had to go, but not feeling ready.

"But all this money, Charlie," she said against him, "it scares me, and people coming here I don't know anything about," lifting her head and looking at him with her eyes red, "I thought it'd be easy, not caring what was happening here so long as it was more exciting than slinging hash to a bunch of truckers, you know? But now it isn't easy anymore. Charlie, are you in trouble?"

"Of course not," he said, letting go of her and picking up the bag, Brenner's bag, not thinking of where he was going or what he had to do. Everything was going to be all right, he knew that, but there were things he'd have to take care about. "Everything's okay, Rose," he said, and smiled to let her see it was true.

Then he was opening the door, carrying the bag, saying something else to her, something about not worrying, but he was walking quite fast along the passage and couldn't hear if she answered, his thoughts kind of floating around his head instead of going on inside, maybe because he knew everything was perfect today, the first day of his life, and these other things didn't fit in. When he got to Room 7 he had to put the bag down so he could open the door with his right hand because his left hand had been hurting quite a lot under the bandage, maybe it was infected. He didn't knock because there wasn't time, there was something kind of pushing him in here, bursting the door open.

"*Brenner!*" he was shouting.

They looked like dummies, all facing him with their mouths open, the Judge on the bed and Mrs. Stevens sitting near him and Brenner standing in the middle of the room like he'd been walking about, the place stinking of liniment. They didn't move, they just stared at him, and he stood in the doorway shaking all over like he had a fever, couldn't get his breath, his fingers gripping the handle of the bag because he mustn't let it go, ever let it go, it could save him from everything, it didn't matter what happened.

"Brenner," he said with his voice shaking, "did you tell anyone you were here?"

The man looked at him through his gold-rimmed glasses, couldn't see all of his eyes because of the light on them.

"No," he said.

"Then how did they know? *How did they know, for Christ sake, you lying–*"

"How did who know?"

Brenner's voice cut across him, very cool, and he tried to stop the shaking, get a grip on himself, making an exhibition, they wouldn't ever panic this way, not these people, they had class.

"Some guy–somebody phoned here, asking for you."

The light shifted across Brenner's glasses as he moved his head an inch.

"For me?"

"Yes."

"By name?"

"Yes. Who was it?"

Brenner thought for a minute.

"It could only have been the police."

CHAPTER NINETEEN

At the south checkpoint the three men stood in the clearing among the thorn trees, feeling the first warmth of the sun on their faces. The morning was desert-quiet, and no one spoke.

Savana leaned against the trunk of the patrol car, pink-eyed from three hours' fitful sleep in the front seat, and he couldn't seem to stop yawning. Sheriff's Sergeant Hockley was standing nearer the trees, a radio pack on his back, watching a lizard that had come from a cleft in the rocks and frozen into immobility, aware of the men. Miller was unwrapping a new stick of gum, screwing the silver foil into a pellet and flicking it away, causing the lizard's head to turn a fraction and become still again. About an hour ago one of the Indian Rock deputies had brought his private Mustang down here and a patrol had run him back. "I won't break it," Savana had told him.

A couple of hundred yards distant from the group, across the road and down among the sandstone rocks, young Sheriff's Officer Stekler was standing to face the north. Knowing that Captain Savana was one of those manning the south checkpoint, he had volunteered to work the midnight-to-eight tour of duty, and felt proud and excited to be part of the group headed by the Special Investigation Section officer from Los Angeles. On Stekler's back was a radio pack tuned to the one Sergeant Hockley carried, because from this point the boy could see the front of the Desert Winds Motel in the far distance. A pair of field glasses rested on the rock beside him, and he lifted them at precise intervals of one minute, centering on the gas pump and seeing clearly the red blob of the lawyer's Buick standing in the auto court.

At the north checkpoint Sheriff's Lieutenant Vorhees was in charge of three men: Sheriff's Officer Donavon, Sheriff's Officer Martin and Detective Lucas from Los Angeles.

Young Donavon was leaning against the barrier they had ready, watching the sun ballooning distantly to one diameter above the desert horizon. He was now recovered from his malaise of last evening and had volunteered to work this tour because Stekler had already done so, and whatever Stekler did, Donavon usually did the same. He admired the rather serious boy from the Midwest, and tried his best to follow his example.

Lieutenant Vorhees was listening to the intermittent croaking of voices on the network, sitting in the front of his patrol car with the radio on. Apart from a trailer truck jackknifing on Interstate 15 just north of the state line, there wasn't any real action going on in Hobart's unit. Occasionally the lieutenant glanced across to where Sheriff's Officer Martin was sitting on a rock with a pair of field glasses raised to watch the road south. Detective Lucas was lighting another cigarette and wondering if they'd had a clean tail on Brenner after all, or if he'd seen them and told the gang in there. It seemed to be one of the few reasons why Stevens hadn't been released yet: they could be preparing for a siege.

A few minutes after six o'clock a walkie-talkie message came through from the reserve unit observing the motel: the veteran blue Oldsmobile was leaving the auto court. A couple of minutes later it came past them with an old-timer at the wheel who didn't even notice them. Lucas watched him drive by, seeing it was the old guy they called Pa who did the cooking, if that was what you could call it. Pa had burned Lucas' steak to a cinder for him last night.

Watching the Oldsmobile go rattling past them they couldn't see if there was anyone lying on the floor in the back, out of sight, or riding in the trunk. The area CHP had informed the special unit of Pa's daily schedule and if Commander Hellman had wanted the checkpoints to stop the car and search it he would have said so.

The sound of its rattling died slowly away, and the morning stillness returned.

In the stuffy motel room nobody spoke.

Charlie hadn't moved from the doorway. None of them had moved. Brenner was still standing in the middle of the room staring at him through his gold-rimmed glasses, but Charlie could see he wasn't really looking at him, but thinking about what he'd just said. Then Brenner looked at the Judge.

"This is quite serious."

"Yes."

"I thought I'd managed to slip the police before I got to the hotel. If they—"

"*Brenner.*"

Charlie didn't shout this time because he didn't have the breath, he was shaking and felt empty, like he'd had nothing to eat for a long time, and he felt cold too, he felt cold.

"Brenner," his voice shaking, talking through his teeth, "you brought those bastards here after me, you told them where to—"

"Mr. Berlatsky." The man was close to him suddenly. "The last thing we want is for you to be arrested. Our own safety depends entirely upon—"

"I don't trust you, you bastard! You're all trying to—"

"Don't you see," Brenner was saying, "if they arrest you and interrogate you, there won't be any hope for any of us —you'll find yourself obliged to admit—"

"*I'd smash you!*"

It was a shout and Brenner looked shocked and turned away and Charlie didn't say any more because he didn't know what to believe, they were too clever for him, they knew all the tricks, oh Christ it was hot in here and he wanted to go but he didn't know where. The cops might still be at the airport but then they didn't know him, he mustn't forget things like that, it was dangerous, he mustn't forget they hadn't ever seen him.

"They don't know me," he said, but nobody was listening and he watched them, not knowing anymore what to do because he wasn't clever like these bastards, Brenner standing over the Judge and talking to him. It made him scared because they might be setting a trap for him, stop him getting that plane.

"Mr. Berlatsky."

"Yes?"

Brenner came close to him again. "I am going to call the police. If possible I shall—"

"*Jesus Christ, you wanna get busted?*"

"Please listen. Your only chance of getting away is in letting me call the police and dictate our terms to them. It is now apparent they followed me here and I'm quite certain this motel is under observation. I shall say that Judge and Mrs. Stevens and I are in danger of our lives unless the police withdraw and call off their attempts to rescue us."

"You're trying to trap me!"

He heard his own voice a long way off and put his face in his hands and tried to think what to do. This bastard was cunning and he knew they mustn't let him get caught or they'd be finished, his face buried in his hands and the sweat pouring down his sides under his shirt, couldn't keep still, couldn't stop shaking, it was just his nerves, that was the trouble, he'd thought everything was going to be all right today but now there was this and he wasn't ready for it.

"Berlatsky, think about what I'm saying, and you'll see it's logical. It's the only chance I can see for you. I'll persuade the police we're being held at gunpoint under threat of immediate death if they attempt to stop anyone leaving this building. We shall become your hostages, in effect, and—"

"Wait a minute." He was backing away from the man. "Wait a minute will you Brenner?" He stared at the lawyer, his brain clearing suddenly like there was something inside of him that knew he'd have to take notice of what was happening or they'd get him into a trap. Brenner was looking at him blank-faced like he didn't understand and the rage was coming back into Charlie because listen if this fucking shyster didn't understand then he had to be told—they all of them had to be told.

"Okay Brenner, you know who that guy is? That guy there on the bed? He's a judge! He judges people! He has so much goddamn money and so much goddamn power they call him a paragon and he goes around telling the rest of us what we've done wrong. And he tells us how we have to pay for it, you know that? Five years, ten years, life—a life sentence. Because he says so! Because *he* says so, that crooked phony two-faced shit over there!" He wasn't shaking anymore and he wasn't scared anymore, there was just the rage inside of him as he turned away from the lawyer and went across to the bed and looked down at John K. Stevens. "You know something, Judge? I thought you had class. I thought you were a better man than me, can you imagine that? But you're shit. You're shit, Stevens, not because you're any worse than most of us, but because you make out you're better."

The Judge wasn't looking at him. He sat propped up with his massive head lying against the pillow and his hooded eyes closed, looking like one of those statues you see in the museums, a noble Roman nose and a face like a priest, and so goddamn superior to the rest of the world they finally died of it.

"Okay Judge, you didn't do anything so bad, picked up a Vegas whore, that isn't my business though frankly I don't ever do it because I like keeping clean, but what the hell.

Then you went off the road and I helped you, thinking you were just another human being, I mean not realizing you were some kind of a paragon, is that the word? Then we made a deal, didn't we? You wanted to cover the whole thing up, right?" He swung round and saw Brenner still standing there in the middle of the room, watching him. "Concealment of a death, is that the legal phrase for it Brenner? You know the fancy phrases, I don't. Me, I'd call it running out on his responsibilities, but like I say, what the hell." He looked back to the man on the bed. "You got me to do the job for you and I did it. You said you'd pay me and finally you did that, though I had to push you till you couldn't stand the strain."

The bag was heavy and he put it on the end of the bed, resting it, keeping his hand on it, looking at the woman now, beginning to feel there wasn't any point trying to tell them because they weren't anything to him. The heat in here was like a clamp on him, pressing down from the ceiling, out of the walls, and he wanted to go. But he'd have to go in his own way, not the way they wanted him, into a trap.

"You said you had the money," he told the woman, "and I took your word for it, I didn't even ask you to show me the stuff at the airport—okay, I was crazy, thought you were someone I could trust." She was watching him steadily, not shutting her eyes like the Judge, she had more guts. "What the hell," he said, looking away, looking at Brenner. "But just what are you talking about, Brenner? Calling the cops and telling them that? Just what the hell are you trying to make out of me—some kind of a dangerous criminal?" He went up close to the guy, wanting to smash his fist into this smooth suntanned face with its fancy gold-rimmed glasses. "You know something? I never took a cent off anybody in my whole life, that I didn't earn. And I never picked up a gun in my whole life either, so what's this thing about me taking you as hostages, for Christ sake? Who are you trying to frame?"

"It's for your own—"

"Why don't you call the cops and tell them you've got *me* at gunpoint?" He'd begun shouting again and heard it and turned away, hefting the bag off the bed, looking again at the lawyer and not seeing him too well, there was sweat stinging his eyes, saying quietly, "Because you have, Brenner, that's about the way things are," the sweat getting into his eyes and making them sting, the heat pressing down on him like he was being squeezed in a clamp, his hand throbbing under the bandage, a bell somewhere, ringing somewhere, the gas-pump bell, his nerves on his skin and crawling. But they didn't know him, they hadn't ever seen him, so they couldn't recognize him—he'd take his chance at the airport, they couldn't stop everybody who wanted to get on a plane, the whole system would break down.

Brenner saying something to the Judge, no answer. Someone going through the lobby to the entrance, maybe it was Rose, pulling the door back, a voice again somewhere, in here with him, Brenner's, something like *at least a chance* and the Judge answering, but he wasn't going to listen to them or he'd miss the plane, the heavy bag swinging as he walked out to the passage, a sharp pain like a knife across his knuckles as he hit the edge of the door because the bag was—

"Berlatsky!"

He shouted back at them saying he didn't trust them and went on down the passage to the lobby with the bag hitting things and then the phone began ringing and it shot through his nerves and someone was coming behind him, Brenner or someone, the bell ringing and ringing.

The Mustang rolled to a stop alongside the gas pump and Savana switched off the motor so he could hear things better, sitting with his head turned to watch the building. There was a pneumatic strip and he'd heard the bell sound from inside, but nobody was coming yet.

The Chevrolet sedan was here, ALU-27578, and the lawyer's rented Buick. He thought he could hear somebody shouting inside the motel, then it was quiet again until the door came open and he dropped a hand to rest it on the flat checkered butt, watching the door. It was a girl coming out, long hair and jeans and a T-shirt, looking as though she'd just gotten dressed, stopping to tie the lace of one of her sneakers. It could be a signal, and he left his hand where it was, casing her as she came up, the T-shirt and jeans so tight she couldn't be concealing even a toothpick.

She didn't look at him or say anything as she went to the pump. He got out and let the door swing shut and stood facing the motel across the top of the Mustang.

"Fill her up, will you?"

"Sure."

She looked like she'd been crying.

The phone was ringing in there, then somebody answered it. He could see a thin guy standing in the doorway, his back to the door, looking inward. Nobody seemed very interested in him or the Mustang. It was just another nice sunny morning and the world was waking up and it looked safe enough to go into that building without a gun, but he was going to leave it just where it was. It was against Hellman's orders to go in there with a gun but he was beginning to add a few things together in his mind and he was beginning to think he was good and ready to go and screw the orders.

He looked at the girl again.

"Can I get a coffee in there?"

"Sure." She stuck the nozzle into the tank orifice. "Café's on the left, help yourself."

"Okay."

He took a breath and walked around the car into the open and began making his way across to the building.

Brenner took the receiver in the phonebooth.

"Yes?"

"Do you have a Mr. Clive Brenner staying with you?"

He thought the voice was familiar but he couldn't place it. Berlatsky was watching him with his eyes flickering and the sweat bright on his face. He was holding the briefcase against his chest as if he thought somebody might take it from him.

"Who is this?" Brenner asked.

"This is Mr. Brenner's office. We have an urgent problem with one of his clients. Is he with you at the motel?"

He thought he recognized the voice now.

"This is Clive Brenner."

There was silence for a second.

"Are we liable to be overheard?"

"I shall be careful."

Another brief silence.

"This is Hellman, Los Angeles Police. You came to see me today."

"Oh yes." He waited.

"Can you tell me the situation right now at the motel?"

Brenner hesitated and then decided. Later he could say, if necessary, that what he had said on this telephone had been said under instructions and duress.

"Yes. The situation here is dangerous in the extreme." He paused, to give the impression he was speaking from dictation. "For the safety of John K. Stevens and his wife I must ask you to call off any operation you may have mounted in the hope of saving them from harm or disarming their captors. Can you hear me clearly?"

"Yes."

"Anyone leaving this building must be given absolute freedom to go where he pleases. There is to be no interference and no surveillance." Another pause. "These are the explicit terms by which there is a faint hope of saving the lives of my clients, and incidentally my own. Do you want me to repeat them?"

A brief silence.

"No."

He was signaling to Berlatsky, trying to make him wait until he'd finished talking, but the man looked feverish, staring at him and listening as if he didn't believe any of this.

"I must warn you, Mr. Hellman, that you will be held fully responsible if by any kind of police action or provocation any of these lives are lost."

Berlatsky suddenly turned and went out, the heavy briefcase swinging and hitting the edge of the doorway. There was nothing Brenner could do about it. He listened for Hellman's answer.

"Understood."

Brenner hung up at once to avoid questions.

Captain Savana came in from the auto court and recognized him from the description currently circulated.

"Is your name Clive Brenner?"

"Yes."

Savana looked quickly along the passage to his right, then through the doorway of the café on his left, one hand held near the opening of his coat. A car started up outside and he swung around to look and then turned back, showing Brenner his credentials.

"Savana, Los Angeles Police. Are you in any danger here?"

"Not now," Brenner said carefully.

"Is Judge Stevens here?"

"Yes."

"Is he in any danger?"

"No."

Savana heard the sedan rolling and looked out to see which way it was heading and turned back and went across the lobby to the telephone and as he put a dime into the slot and began dialing Brenner saw it all go, everything go, a life's work in jurisprudence, a state governorship, and a good man's name.

"Sir!"

"Well?"

"Phone—urgent."

"Right." Hellman took it.

"Yes?"

"Savana. Berlatsky's just left the motel heading north, got a bag with him, he looks like our man."

"It's no good," Hellman said. "They've got Stevens as a hostage there. We can't make a move."

"I'm at the motel," Savana told him. "They—"

"You're *where?*"

"I've just talked to Brenner—there's no danger here."

Hellman took three seconds and made his decision.

"Right." He dropped the receiver and called to the radio operator—"Set up those blocks!"

Charlie swung the Chevy onto the road and went too wide, pulling the wheel and straightening up and giving her the gas, going north and heading for Interstate 15 and the airport. There'd been a man going into the motel and he thought he'd seen Rose near the gas pump but he hadn't stopped, even for Rose, because he had to get the plane.

He still didn't know, he still didn't know if Brenner had framed him or if it was really someone else he was talking to, not the police, just trying to scare him, setting up some kind of a trap, he should've grabbed that phone to find out who it was, should've stopped that bastard, *should've smashed him* but he wasn't sure, he didn't know what they were doing to him, he just had to get away.

"Oh, Beauty," he said; "oh, Beauty," but it didn't sound like his own voice, it was a shaky kind of whisper and he could feel there was something wrong because this was the first day of his life and everything was going to be all right, but he couldn't seem to stop shaking and there was sweat in his eyes and he felt kind of dizzy and couldn't think properly. Everything was rushing past and the shimmy was starting in the wheel the same as it always did when he went too fast; the man at the garage had told him it was a wheel-balance job but that cost money, everything rushing past and then there was the barrier across the road, right across the road with red and white signs, *Stop* and *Police,* and he was doing things without thinking about them and the Chevy was sloping forward as he hit the brakes and the bag slid off the seat and then he was spinning slowly with a burned-rubber smell in the air and sand going up from the roadside and a can rattling and then he was facing the other direction with the sun on his left side now and the motor coughing as he hit the throttle and then roaring as the gas went in. The smell of burned rubber was making him feel sick, it was a horrible smell.

He'd just better go on driving and he saw the motel on his left and the wind rushed against his face and he knew he was going very fast now and didn't see the barrier this time till he was almost on it because there was a curve in the road and the sun was in his eyes and he heard himself shout something as he swung the wheel hard over and the front of the Chevy hit one end of the barrier and a man was jumping to get clear and then everything tilted and he saw the rocks coming up at him, sailing up through the air like they didn't weigh anything then it all exploded, metal ripping along the rocks and a tree snapping and white bark and everything going over, sand coming in like water, in a wave, till it all stopped and he saw what to do, crawling out through the smashed glass and going a little way on his hands and knees with the blood coming into his mouth, remembering and crawling back and finding the bag and bringing it clear and getting up and trying to walk, trying to run. *Stop,* someone was shouting but he went on, the heavy bag weighing him down on one side, salt in his mouth, and thickness, going on because they didn't know him, they hadn't ever seen him, the pain getting worse in his chest and a kind of whimpering sound and he tried to stop it because it wouldn't do any good. The boy in uniform shouted again, quite close now, but he mustn't stop, ever, the first day of his life and the yellow butterfly dancing in front of him, somewhere in front of him all the time and out of his reach.

Sheriff's Officer Stekler called again and the running man seemed to trip, a rock catching his foot and turning him. The thing he was carrying swung round quickly, black against the dazzling sun, and Stekler went down low to protect himself as he fired six slow shots.

	DATE DUE		